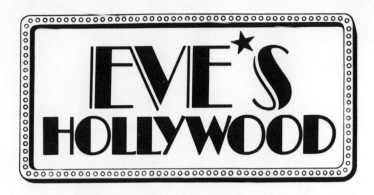

EVE'S HOLLYWOOD

BY EVE BABITZ

DELACORTE PRESS/SEYMOUR LAWRENCE

Several of these chapters first appeared in
Rolling Stone and *The Los Angeles Flyer*.

Library of Congress Cataloging in Publication Data

Babitz, Eve.
Eve's Hollywood.

I.   Title.
PZ4.B1154Ev [PS3552.A244]   813'.5'4   73-17458

ISBN 0-440-02339-4

DEAR READER

I want to tell you a little about myself. I am really an artist, not a writer. So, I like the way Arabic numbers look un-written out on a page. When I say someone is 15 years old, I like the way 15 looks. I like the way 9 million looks and I hate the way nine million looks. 9 seems like more of a number to me.

Also, I believe that places should be capitalized. North, South, East and West are all places as far as I'm concerned I don't care what anyone else thinks. When I think of North, it's capitalized. West, especially, is a serious place that should ALWAYS be capitalized. It also sounds more adventurous to go West than to go west.

★ v ★

Since this is my book and since the advent of James Joyce, why don't we let me have my way? It's such a small thing, and just think, I could be James Joyce writing in latin all the time and stuff.

DEDICATION

To Mae and Sol Babitz, mainly.

But also to Mirandi and Laurie living next to the sea.

And Diane Gardiner without whom fewer strange arrangements might pass uninstigated.

And to Earl McGrath to whom I admit I owe Everything.

And to the record company president of my choice, Ahmet Ertegun.

Plus any other Atlantic Record Executive who's ever taken me out to dinner, will again or has said, "Here, you do this album cover."

And to Annie Leibovitz and her trusty companion, Citizen Wenner, gathering moss to the North. And to Grover Lewis who dispels gloom with blue eyes in a blue town with blue rugs, Texanly. And Sara and Charlie and the girl with the coke.

And to Brian G. Hutton, always the Prince but not Mr. Right, thank heavens.

And to Carol Grannison-Killorhan, hostess of sanctuaries and goose cook.

And to the Hollywood bouncy agent of my choice, Mike Hamilburg, green eyes. And to the Boston publisher of my choice, Seymour Lawrence, a tough customer.

And to Ginny Ganahl, if you have to ask you'll never know.

And to the Beverly Hills Hotel.

And to Robert L. Marchese, my partner in Lawrence of Arabia exchanges. (A handsome devil.)

And to Marva, the best hair cutter on earth and, besides, she makes you look beautiful.

And to Rainier Ale.

And to Andy Warhol and Paul Morrisey who I'd do anything for if only they'd pay.

And to the Didion-Dunnes for having to be who I'm not.

And to Ned Doheney, postcards from hot Hollywood peacocks.

And to all the handsome devil artists especially Ron Cooper, the possessed, and Wudl and Larry Bell, the master of glass, and Billy Al Bengston to whom I apologize for putting a cigarette out on his white floor 10 years ago. And Kenny Price. And Ed Ruscha, a man of simple tastes but no one makes those kind of wings, so he's stuck with a white Rolls and no wings.

And to Barney.

And to Derek Taylor. Tell them, Derek, how great I

am. Like you once introduced me to a Beatle as "the best girl in America."

And to Robert and Harry Deutsch for their breathtaking dashes into the breech. And not Phyllis.

And to Marie, a friend indeed.

And to L. Rust Hills for the ice cream story and the one about taking sides and anagrams. That *Esquire* is falling apart. Mine is Babe Vizet.

And to Eggs Benedict at the Beverly Wilshire.

And to Ingolf Dahl, Clark House and other long agos.

And to Marcel Duchamps who beat me at his own game.

And to Jim Morrison running guns on Rimbaud's footsteps.

And to Stephan Stills for "Everydays" and letting me do the art part.

And to the Sandabs at Musso's, the Eggplant Florentine, the guy who makes the pancakes and my friend in the parking lot (not the one on the ground, the one who parks your car, the young one). And to the crabpuffs at Don the Beachcomber's.

And to Joseph Heller, Speed Vogel and the guy who ran off with the baby sitter. And Milo Minderbinder's inspiration.

And to Anne Marshall, the beautiful friend to us all.

And to Michelle Guilliane for calling first before bringing Kim Fowley into my house.

And to Kim Fowley for at least the $6.

And to Van Dyke Parks for anything he cares to take a bow for.

And to Simon Rodia.

And to the purple mountains' majesty above the fruited plain.

And to Linda Ronstadt for "Long, Long Time," earrings, Arizona and that voice, my God.

And to Glen Frey of the Eagles so he'll still talk to me.

And to the *New York Times* book review section and every critic in it.

And to Chuck Berry, a brown eyed handsome man who knows what he likes even if it is astroturf and 21 tvs. And to Bo for telling us about the bed.

And to Sara Harrison, Noel Harrison, Simon Harrison, Harriette Harrison, Kathy Harrison, Zoe (my friend) Harrison, Margaret Harrison and the new twins.

And to Stuart Reed in whom I believe.

And to Jackson Browne anyway.

And to Billy James who saved me.

And to Virginia Team as those who know her know.

And to Aivars Perlback.

And to Pauline Kael who we discovered on KPFA one glorious day and whose sentences don't parse either. (He told me the same thing. I was shocked.)

And to the future good will of Consumer's Liquor, the best liquor store in America and aptly named.

And to the Chateau Marmont.

And to Joseph Cornell. A Real Artist.

And to tempura.

And to Camilla McGrath.

And to Terry Melcher, for Culver City Blues Again.

And to Dickie Davis for loyalty in spite of the spill all over the floor of the Troubadour ladies' room.

And to Dr. Boyd Cooper, gynecologist extraordinaire.

And to Kate Steinitz who liked my collages before I could make them.

And to Jock, Michaela, Nini, Jocky, Brook the impos-

★ x ★

sible and deviled marrow bones, watercress and cheese pie, anything vinaigrette and decent wine.

And to Mr. Major, I'm sorry I turned out this way.

And to the land, the beach, the trees, the hills, the sky, the Bradbury Building, the Broadway Hollywood and all the flowers in spring.

And to Marc Foreman and Wilhelm Reich.

And to freeways.

And to Dan, Mrs. Alcerro and the Valentino episode.

And to Orson Welles, the light of my life.

And to time immemorial and the suspension of disbelief.

And to Connie Freiberg, her crosses to bear made of angel hair but heavy on such burnt shoulders.

And to Michael and Sheila Rainey for Roman follies, curry and mean tricks.

And to Marcel Proust.

And to Sally Stevens.

And to "LUNCH Poems."

And to Sandy & John Gibson, kicked upstairs.

And to Fred Roos, another Sheik that could cast this movie and his silent dog, Rover.

And to Alan Sororti, our dieting assemblyman.

And to tea cakes, chocolate rabbits, Pupi's, Clifton's, and fried squash blossoms à la Ron Cooper.

And to David Anderle and Michael Monroe for upping the tone.

And to Michael McClure whose secrets are safe in Jean Harlow's head.

And to Marshall Ephron for the first book and the mariachi Ubu.

And to Kuilli Anton, the most beautiful girl in Lake Arrowhead.

And to Bonnie Jean, The Fred C. Dobbs and psychedelic chili.

And to sour cream.

And to the Hawaii Theater of my youth.

And to Les Noces.

And to Terry O'Shea and his magic wands that shine
in the dark made of ivory and plastic emeralds who
never should have told anyone.

And to Joyce Haber and her Francis Albert, a L.A.
Saga.

And to Jack Smith, the wicked chronicler.

And to Claudia Martin for Ginny's life.

And to David Geffin and the lost Picasso found in
Silver Lake. I *still*, David, think that Picasso came and
took it back.

And to Colman for the wine.

And to Mrs. Bungay for the fur coat on New Year's
just like that.

And for that New Year's and Wudl, a Dill and an
Arnoldi at Berrigan's and the mole sauce. No, Arnoldi
passed.

And to Brandon's Memorabilia on 13 E 53rd St on the
3rd floor for being there when I needed them.

And to Michael Bloomfield and his hot guitar and
cool eyes, or vice versa.

And to Paul Butterfield over yonder's wall, a har-
monica lays playing and it must be greener than here,
I've always thought.

And to the Corey's.

And to the color green.

And to See's Candy, the Bordeaux being an unforgot-
ten favorite.

And to tea cakes. And white buns.

And to Leon Bing, a girl with a past.

And to Michael Elias, on strike!

And to the Fords, the Harrisons not the Henrys.

And to Dianna Gould, a woman of stormy nights and tearful days who laughs.

And to Jack Gross and the Chateau Nose.

And to mirrors. Especially the kind that can be manipulated.

And to STRAWBERRIES and ASPARAGUS, the season is upon us.

And to Champagne and Easter.

And to the way the whipped cream comes in a silver gravy dish in the Polo Lounge when you order Irish Coffee. And the way the whipped cream comes in a silver cup at the Cafe Antico Greco on the Via della Croce in Rome when you order hot chocolate con panna (panna is whipped cream in Italian).

And to the Tartuffo con panna on the via Buffalo or the Piazza Navona where you think at last you're getting enough chocolate. And you might be.

And to Saturday.

And to Nick at Custom Print.

And to David Giler who couldn't have turned out the way Mr. Major wanted either. What with Nancy Kwan and everything . . .

And to Fred Myrow and his wife, Elana, in spite of the dinner.

And to Alan King Moffitt and Frances for my teeth (the best in the entire family).

And to Sister Mary Agnes Donahue for looking like a trading card and leaving the garden for good. And to Goode.

And to MacGillivray and Nuuhiwa for the wash in the blood of the sea.

And to Guido and Adolpho.

EVE'S HOLLYWOOD

And to Art Pepper for playing SO good. And telling all.

And to Wickham and Ochs, a marriage of convenience.

And to Clair Miller.

And to Desbutol, Ritilin, Obertrol and any other speed. It wasn't that I didn't love you, it was that it was too hard.

And to Dennis Morgan, Valentines, Enrico Macias and les choses Francaises.

And to the Photomat.

And to cheap retsina.

And to telephones.

And to the observatory where I used to try to find James Dean after he died.

And to the word, brouhaha.

And to Steve Martin, the car.

And to the one whose wife would get furious if I so much as put his initials in.

And Margaret.

And for Chico with love and squalor and a hi-ho silver.

"Where are you from?"
"Hollywood."
"Born there too?"
"Yeah."
". . . What was it like?"
"Different."

CONTENTS

★ xviii ★

CONTENTS

Photo Scrapbook follows page 166

★ xix ★

DAUGHTERS
OF THE WASTELAND

My mother emigrated to Los Angeles as a young girl in the Depression. In the town in which she lived—Sour Lake, Texas—there was a Catholic priest who had been born, raised and trained in Chicago. He could perfectly understand my mother's absolute need to get out of Sour Lake and he arranged for her to travel to Hollywood with some friends of his and I think he also got her a job. The job she had at one time was as receptionist to the doctor whose wife, Mary Astor, was keeping a diary about her thing with George Kaufman, but I don't think that's the job the priest got for her.

My mother was enthralled with Los Angeles and was so overcome that she became an artist. She drew the houses because she loved them.

★ 1 ★

My father emigrated to Los Angeles when he was 16 from Brooklyn with his mother and father and two sisters. They lived in Boyle Heights which is where all the Jews lived then who lived in L.A. My father's aunt, who was the sister of my grandmother, was a movie actress. She was not a star, but she was important. She played Yiddishe mamas and made a mint. My father had studied classical violin since he was a small child and he won the gold medal as best kid violinist in New York City by the time he was 15.

In those days, to get into the studio as a contract musician was a matter of nepotism as it would be today if there were any contract musicians left. My great aunt, Vera Gordon, the movie actress, convinced her friend Harry Lubin to give my father a chance to play in Harry's orchestra which would be a good job because there was lots of money and security. My father brought a Stravinsky score to play.

"How the hell could I tell if he could play?" Harry laughs, still delighted at the joke my father solemnly acted out. "*I* couldn't even read the score to see if he was playing the right notes!"

Everyone in my family was involved in "the Arts" and so we grew up surrounded by "the Arts," my sister and me.

I don't remember how old I was when I first heard Los Angeles described as a "wasteland" or "seven suburbs in search of a city" or any of the other curious remarks uttered by people.

It was never like that for us growing up here.

For one thing, there was always so much going on, so many different people, and my mother's constant soirees and dinners.

★ 2 ★

"Wasteland" is a word I don't understand anyway because physically, surely, they couldn't have thought it was a wasteland—it has all these citrus trees and flowers growing everywhere.

I know they meant "culturally." But it wasn't.

Culturally, L.A. has always been a humid jungle alive with seething L.A. projects that I guess people from other places just can't see. It takes a certain kind of innocence to like L.A., anyway. It requires a certain plain happiness inside to be happy in L.A., to choose it and be happy here. When people are not happy, they fight against L.A. and say it's a "wasteland" and other helpful descriptions.

Vera Stravinsky once told me that in 1937 she went on a picnic, in a few limousines, that Paulette Goddard had prepared ("because she was quite a gourmet . . ." Vera said). On the Picnic was the Stravinskys, Charlie Chaplin and Paulette Goddard, Greta Garbo, Bertrand Russell and the Huxleys. They got into the cars to drive to a likely spot, but there were no likely spots and they drove and drove. There had been a drought and everything was dry, there was no grass and so finally they spotted the measly L.A. "River" and decided to spread their blanket on its ridiculous banks and make the best of it. The "L.A. River" is a trickle that only looks slightly like a river if there's been a downpour for three months but even then it doesn't look like a river. Anyway, they spread out the food, the champagne, the caviar, the pâté and everything and sat on the banks of the "river" beneath a bridge over which cars were going.

"Hey!"

They looked up and there was a motorcycle cop with his fists on his hips, looking cross.

★ 3 ★

"Yes?" Bertrand Russell stood up to inquire.

There was a sign that said that people were not allowed to picnic by the "river."

The cop pointed at the sign and looked at Russell and then said, "Can't you read?"

If the story's details are different, if it was another year and the Huxleys weren't there, still, it is an L.A. "wasteland" story. It's a story of L.A.

The cop only relented when he recognized Garbo.

My life as a child was about things and times like that. There were the Evenings on the Roof and the Ojai Festivals for concerts in our wasteland. Both of those organizations were not started by the city or anything because the city of Los Angeles has never cared about culture. It doesn't care and that's all there is to it. So the Evenings on the Roof were small concerts of chamber music performed by studio musicians (who were real musicians like my father none-the-less), and the Ojai Festivals were sponsored by the ladies of Ojai, a small community of old ladies who were seduced by John Bauer, an Englishman, who did a lot of things in Los Angeles by dint of sheer charm and energy and did them because he was mainly a child and children love L.A. A 6' 4" child.

The Luau, a tacky Polynesian restaurant, was Stravinsky's favorite restaurant. Only children like it.

My father collected Dixieland records. He has thousands of old 78s, and I grew up listening to Ledbelly sing, ". . . fly to the east, fly to the west, fly to the one that you love the best." When we got old enough, he played us dirty Bessie Smith records. And when we got really old enough, he played dope records like "If You The Viper" with Stuff Smith pretending, or perhaps

DAUGHTERS OF THE WASTELAND

not, to inhale quickly on a joint before breaking into
. . . "Dreamed about a reefer, five feet long . . . the
Mighty Mezz, but not too strong." And I knew who the
Mighty Mezz was. I was not culturally deprived.

My father used to jam with Stuff Smith and Nat King
Cole at a bar across the street from NBC on Sunset and
Vine where my father was a studio musician.

Studio musicians and musicians in general, men who
have grown up practicing minute things their whole
lives, are special. The general rules accepted by the
players are that violin players are all lovers of women
to an extravagant extent, oboe players are crazy and
French horn players are sexy. Everyone else is square
as square can be as far as I'm concerned, and if you go
to an L.A. Philharmonic rehearsal you'll see a bunch of
accountants sitting around in plaid shirts and you'll
realize that musicians are the most innocent benders to
Art there are. Imagine binding yourself into the
confines of an orchestra, under the stick of a conductor,
having to play what someone has written 200 years ago!

The only kind of musicians we usually had at our
house were either people like Stuff Smith, who was
crazy, or composers. Musicians were too square for my
father to want to spend more time than he already was
doing with them.

Opera singers are a different story. One day I walked
into the living room where my father was having a
rehearsal. He was sitting at the harpsichord explaining
in serious tones about Palestrina, and on a folding chair
with her feet in pink flats crossed neatly at the ankles
but resting on the seat of another folding chair was a
teen-ager. She had on a green plaid vest, a green plaid
pair of pants and she wore an ivy league shirt. Her red

★ 5 ★

hair was in rollers and she'd tied a scarf around it like everyone in my high school tied their scarves that year. They looked up when I came in from school. I didn't interrupt them but went on to my room. The voice that followed came from a crystal spring out of a fjord, cold, clear and careless. It nearly broke my heart, the sound. I dumped my books on my bed and rushed back into the living room. It was that teen-ager, singing.

I sat on the stairs and listened to the rest of the rehearsal. She never took her pink flat shoes off the chair in front of her and she sang in Italian, Vulgar Latin, German and French and in between talked in a kind of thin Californian which said "wader" for "water."

She was what, at Hollywood High, they'd describe as "cute."

At the end, my father said she was Marni Nixon. Marni Nixon did everything. She sang medieval songs and she sang the voices in "West Side Story," "The King and I" and she had a few children. She was one of the wasteland's inhabitants.

Marilyn Horne, the opera singer who *The New Yorker* says is called "Jackie" by her friends, *is* called Jackie by her friends, even by me. She once told me that she felt the same way about Marni Nixon as I did and not only that "but her pitch . . ." I suppose she meant that Marni was always right there with that crystal casual voice, right on top sliding by, her pitch . . .

Joseph Szigeti, the violinist who recently died, lived in Palos Verdes. I loved him and he answered my letters so he probably liked me. He lived in the most beautiful house I ever saw in my whole life and it was there that I first ate figs. Before then, I would never eat figs because I thought they were vile threats to happi-

★ 6 ★

ness but there in his house on a hillside overlooking the Pacific with his oval swimming pool surrounded by concrete urns of geraniums, his crystal glasses and white wine (even for children) and his wonderful wife, I ate figs. I was glad my father was friends with him, but then, my father was friends with all sorts of fabulous people.

There was a composer named Bennie Herrmann. Bernard Herrmann, it said on the credits as the one responsible for the music for most Alfred Hitchcock pictures and "Citizen Kane." But I didn't know anything about his past in the Mercury theater or that stuff. My sister and I just loved him and his wife and they'd invite us to swim in their pool in the summer and we'd think we'd died and gone to heaven. Lucy Herrmann, the wife, brought lemonade and we floated on rafts and drank lemonade and Lucy told us stories with her beautiful Vassar voice. In fact, to this day, it takes a real long time for me to start getting nervous around one of those Vassar voices because Lucy had one and we were just so in love with her. It's only lately, in fact, that I met a girl so terrible with her "How divine!"s thrown into the air that my memory of Lucy has been overshadowed and the natural HATE most americans feel for that snotty nasal sound just jumps to the fore.

Eugene Berman, a man who designed sets for the Metropolitan Opera and who was a wonderful painter, was married to Ona Munson (the one who ran the whore house in "Gone With the Wind"—the one Vivien Leigh was jealous of cause Clark Gable hung out there) and they lived a block from us. I never met her, just him, and he was always a prince to me until I grew up and then he treated me the way he treated most adults which was with tantrumic impatience and nasty remarks. But if you were out of town, he'd write to you and he wrote to me just before he died. He wrote from his house in Rome and told me that he was not sick, that he was perfectly fine.

The best fun we had was when Edward James came into town and told us what he'd been doing. Edward James is an Englishman with an American mother ("so we had plumbing and bathrooms for each bedroom and it was considered, at that time, obscene!" he'd laugh). Poor Edward, he once told me, "When Papa died, they'd just changed all the inheritance tax laws so that Mummy and the girls each got 10,000 quid a year and all I got were the castles and the paintings!" Edward is in a perpetual state of catastrophe. There are always things going on in his life which would put rapid-shooting to shame. For one thing, Edward collects snakes. He *likes* them and took them with him to the Prado in Mexico City where one escaped in the lobby. Edward is the first person who wasn't French to buy a Picasso ("I later traded it for 40,000 head of cattle and a state in southern Mexico"). He came to America to see his "deah friend, Lawrence" which meant D.H., but Lawrence soon died so Edward and Huxley drifted West to L.A. "I was writing a novel then," Edward explained, "and I so wanted to call it *After Many a Summer Dies the Swan,* but Aldous took that one, you see, and there was simply nothing I could do." Edward *did* write a novel called *The Gardener Who Saw God* and it's just wonderful in a fantastically English and just dandy way and he's got a part about Ottoline Morelle that is heaven but then, the whole book is heaven and I suppose it didn't do well because he was so rich, nobody believed him. In 1939 or 37, Edward designed the World's Fair Pavilion with Dali. Edward James was another example of our cultural deprivation, the wasteland desert we inhabited. Edward told me that I was as beautiful as the Marquis de Sade's great granddaughter —even more beautiful! My girl friend sitting next to me nearly died of envy and chagrin, the Marquis de Sade being her favorite person.

Kenneth Rexroth and Kenneth Patchen were both in our house for poetry readings. My mother was a fool for poetry but it bored me and my sister to distraction and we'd wind up getting someone like Lucy Herrmann to tell us stories in another room. Or go hang out in the kitchen, where my mother was not listening to the poetry but cooking instead.

Robert Craft was there as we grew up and I was always perversely and maddeningly taken with him even when I was about 10. He was so mean, how could I help it? He once made a harp player run from the stage in tears during a rehearsal. And another time, when they'd just come back from Japan, he showed me a book of Japanese architecture and he started to cry because it was so beautiful. That finished me off, there was nothing I could do. People said jealous mean things about Robert Craft, but I always thought, "Everyone hates him except Stravinsky." And now that I've read his writing, it's just scary, it's so good. Robert Craft as a young man was "adopted" by the Stravinskys, came to our house to rehearse Corelli, and it was the first time I thought that music was beautiful. And he was so mean, that harp player fleeing in tears from the stage of Royce Hall only came back when Stravinsky arrived all tiny and muffled up in plaid wool scarves.

★ 9 ★

Vera Stravinsky is the most naturally aristocratic person on earth. From the time I was able to see, during the time children see adults and find them all phony and creepy, Vera always remained outside that circle of judgment, because Vera was Vera and her brilliant innocence is something that is so charming and so sexy and so purely about life that you have to have been there, you have to have heard her laugh, you have to have seen her roomful of flowers and her purple satin capes made in Rome lined with iridescent taffeta to know that it is possible, that Anything is Possible and that a woman spun out into the finest silk makes the strongest rope. I waited until I got around her to eat caviar, otherwise, I knew I'd never get the point.

Stravinsky himself was Stravinsky.

He was tiny and happy and brilliant and drank. He used to slip glasses of scotch to me underneath the coffee table when my mother wasn't looking when I was 13. At my 16th birthday party, I wore white (very low necked white, of course) and he slipped rose petals down my top when my mother wasn't looking.

The city of Los Angeles being what it is, the L.A. Philharmonic never played anything past Brahms except once when they let Stravinsky conduct one of his own pieces and my father took me. I think I was about 3. We sat in the rafters and my mother was not there and my father said, "See that tiny man way down there?"

"Uh-huh."

"That's Stravinsky."

Since everyone in the whole place seemed to be dependent on that tiny man for their focal point, I got the idea that Stravinsky was bigger than most things even if he was tiny.

For Christmas one year my sister and I gave him an ant farm but alas, he told us, all the ants died. He collected insects in glass cases, beautiful ones.

They had Picassos all over the house.

My father met Stravinsky early in Stravinsky's American adventure and helped him with bowing and other violin/viola things that come up for a composer. My father also played the violin in *L'Histoire du Soldat,* which was the first time I ever heard music like *that* before. I was 5.

They performed the thing at the Ojai Festival and Stravinsky conducted the dress rehearsal (Edward Rebner did the actual performance). I saw both. Victor Burton who played drums with Red Nichols 5 Pennies played percussion in that. It was the first I ever heard of the devil (it's about this guy who sells his soul to the devil for the princess and money). I had nightmares for years about the devil who sprang out like a jack-in-the-box from behind the bed of the princess. He jumped up TEN FEET off the floor with horns and a black tail. My father told me that the tail was really a long tongue coming out of a mouth where the devil's ass should have been because the dress designer was droll. But that wasn't why I had nightmares. It was the TEN FEET.

L'Histoire du Soldat is still a piece that excites me Russianly and makes me think of the devil.

We were always being taken to rehearsals when we were little and it is probably because of that that I like rehearsals better than concerts. There is something about listening to a group of people try over and over to get it right and at last do that provides a tension of drama you don't get when they're all dressed up giving a concert. Conductors have different styles of getting it right. Robert Craft makes harp players cry. Others, however, like Henry Lewis, who is black and married to the opera singer Marilyn Horne (Jackie), was more subtle. He'd pick a few measures just ahead of where it wasn't working and say that *that* was the part they had to iron out, and what usually happened is that the musicians would concentrate so hard on a part they already were doing well that the part they were doing badly followed without a hitch.

How is it, one might wonder, that I did not become an accomplished musician and became instead a beach-going blonde? When I was 5 my father presented me with my "first" violin (implying there would be more as I got bigger). There was nothing I could do, I was trapped. But I was a resourceful child and have always known there was a way you could get free of torture and quite by accident it turned out that I couldn't tune the instrument. I couldn't tell when it was out of tune. I'd practice out of tune. I drove my father crazy (what he was doing to me too), so that was the end of that. I remained culturally deprived of the violin my whole life.

We knew no movie stars and we were as completely infatuated with them as everyone else. I stole *Photoplays* for pictures of Tony Curtis.

If we were growing up in a wasteland, my sister and me, it was hard for us to see then and it's hard for me to see now. Naturally, the city was a complete Kansas-run operation and the museum only showed landscapes and stuffed animals. But the people who could do things were thrown upon their own devices and had to do them without sanction because the mayor was only going to the Rose Parade. After all, there had to be *some* adversity in the middle of all that sunshine and money. And people like Stravinsky and Schoenberg and Thomas Mann and those kind of people weren't completely talking to themselves in the bathroom for lack of friends.

The people, as my sister and I grew up, were always so nice to us. Both Eugene Berman and Szigeti wrote to me still just before they died and they both really only knew me as a child. Nobody even got mad the time my sister and I got stuck together with bubble gum in the middle of the premiere of a Schoenberg piece, the high point of the Ojai Festival that year. We were taken backstage and detached with alcohol and laughed.

But probably if it hadn't been a wasteland, there wouldn't have been bubble gum there in the first place.

HOLLYWOOD AND VINE

When I was 14, I began writing a book, my memoirs, entitled *I Wouldn't Raise My Kid in Hollywood*. A few weeks earlier I had let a spectacularly handsome man drive me home from a party I wasn't allowed to go to, and when I told him I was 14, he dropped me off a block from my house and said, paternally, before he gave me an unpaternal and never-to-be-forgotten kiss, "Don't let guys pick you up like this, kid, you might get hurt." After that I never saw him again except on the front page of the papers two years later when he was found dead in Lana Turner's bathroom. He was called Johnny Stompanato, poor guy. I'd been writing that book sort of before that, but afterwards I began writing it for real. After that, I've always been writing it.

★ 14 ★

That was the same year, only later, in summer around August, when I saw a small family, tourists, standing outside the Broadway in Hollywood. The Santa Ana winds had driven everyone from sight except them. Windswept in a 105° morning as an actual tumbleweed careened into them and then flew down the middle of the street alongside of a 91 W. Bus, they were dusty and overdressed, especially the mother. She was haggard and skinny and wore navy blue with white polka dots and sighed with unnoticed despondence, ". . . Well. . . . here we are . . . Hollywood and Vine."

My father was a studio musician under contract at Fox (as we heard it casually referred to by adults). So my sister and I grew up not 10 blocks from this Hollywood and Vine that people sighed despondently about. But there was never any visible Hollywood, though by 1956 even the *in*visible Hollywood was being ground under the spurred heels of Brando's Zapata. Brando was young and there were no more Cary Grants.

My father, like so many other studio musicians, was an excellent musician who yearned to play real music instead of movie music, so once a year he contracted the orchestra for the Ojai Festivals which were three-day weekends past Ventura almost to Santa Barbara in a breath-taking place called Ojai. Affluent elderly ladies let musicians and their families stay in their houses for the three-day festival. Our lady had a wonderful semi-farm with lots of kittens, which was fortunate, for my sister and I were maniacs about kittens and they compensated for having to go to concerts which I, at least, have never been good at. The only other things Ojai had besides the festivals and the affluent ladies (third-generation Californian aristocracy) were private schools for the sons and daughters of the very rich who sent them there to keep them out of Hollywood. Cheryl Crane was sent there, Lana Turner's daughter, I read later in the paper—to the Happy Valley School in Ojai. By that time I no longer had to go. I could stay home, Hollywood, reading and writing.

Except for the Ojai Festivals and two weeks in summer when my father would expose the family to a "vacation" (perpetual carsickness for me accompanied by cranky remarks about why couldn't *I* just stay home), except for about 20 days a year I grew up and became entrenched in Los Angeles and our angel's prop halo, Hollywood. The only other place I've ever felt comfortable was Rome, and Rome is just like Hollywood to me. Rome catered to my taste for slapdashedness, affects and effects, false but gorgeous fronts, tawdry tears, people walking around inside of *"Morocco"* or *"Gone With the Wind."* I sail along and function, I am ready for the fist through the windshield or the ring thrown off the pier. I believe in afghans on snakeskin leashes. I'm a push-over for an entrance, a "darling" hurtled across a café by a fox-furred blonde of supernatural radiance ablaze with diamonds, arms gracefully outstretched to embrace the "darlinged." Rome was distilled Hollywood for me, I knew it would be from *La Dolce Vita*. Mastroianni, I remember thinking at the time, was no fun at all. I, myself, would aid and abet splash and splendor and try to be equal to flashy occasions.

I was probably 13 when I realized there was this whole, huge, unexplored and exciting expanse of guys who were mainly adventurers with talents that they were hoping to connect into the Hollywood carcass while there was still time. I remember the day it hit me,

I was standing across the street from what is now Cyrano's on the Strip when, from out of the West a white, top-down Jaguar pulled an illegal U-turn and an incredibly stylish, tousled, white-teethed, blue-eyed, sunbleached, eyelashed young man reined in his car and was silent for a moment in front of me before saying, "Oh, you're just a kid," and making another noisy U-turn before he continued on his way. I was 13, it was 1956, I was wearing my leopardskin bathing suit and eating a Will Wright's chocolate burnt-almond ice-cream cone, and I suffered a broken heart.

I dreamed about that and began to see how many others of him there were. I found that they all took acting lessons from people like Jeff Corey and Sandy Meisner in the afternoons and hung out at the Crescendo or the Luau at night. In the hot summer they'd go to State Beach after picking up their unemployment check on Santa Monica Boulevard. The Unemployment Building was a glamorous outing for me and I had, luckily, an older girl friend who'd take me sometimes.

Since it wasn't very likely that anyone was going to take me to the Luau, I figured the only sound course was to take acting lessons, though I had no interest in becoming an actress ever in my whole life. The man I took lessons from was the guy who went over the cliff in *Rebel Without a Cause* named Cory Allen (he was called Buzz in the movie) and he was trying to teach acting to a bunch of people, the youngest of whom was three years older than me. Cory was 27 or so, I imagined, and I was 14 and I fell in love with him in a hopeless kind of way as he attempted to teach us how to "act." (Someone teaching you how to "act" is really something to think about in your spare time.) I had

★ 17 ★

visions of us living happily ever after together, but all that happened was that I learned absolutely that I could not "act." No one stylish was in Cory's class and I couldn't "act," so after a while I quit.

I never had the necessary ability to suspend my own disbelief enough to act on a stage or in front of a camera with other people's words. Besides, even *I* could see that something was the matter with Hollywood, though I didn't know it was terminal. And those stylish young men in Jaguars, when I finally got old enough to attain them, would crumble upon closer view into silly names like Sean or Carlo or Phillippe and by that time it was the era of the whiners and I am unable to appreciate whiners. Is that all they could figure out to do about Montgomery Clift, James Dean and Brando? Whine?

The Fifties, as everyone points out, was a peculiarly charmless time in which to be an adolescent, but no one ever felt more bliss than I, accompanying an older girl friend to Unemployment or inventing lives for fractionally viewed, careless young men in Jaguars.

Though I have no kids and Hollywood doesn't exist, I firmly believe, however, that it *did* exist. And like Rome, we are living amidst the fallen columns and clothes-lined courtyards, in the ruins of an empire of the self-enchanted which was once, briefly, more devastating than Caesar's and still brings respectable families to a hot, windy intersection in August to sigh with unnoticed despondence, ". . . Well . . . here we are . . . Hollywood and Vine."

★
BUNKER HILL

In the beginning of Los Angeles there were the adobe
buildings and the Plaza, the architecture of the land,
organically trickling North with El Camino Real and
the Franciscans. It did not take too long, however, for
Los Angelesness to show its hand and when the American Ladies moved West and landed in L.A., they constructed for themselves living quarters which are now
almost all gone but which once were plentifully cen-
tered on Bunker Hill. My mother fell in love with those
houses at first sight. They made perfect sense to her.

She came from Texas where nothing made sense to
her. She came in the '30's to get away from Texas and
find her own life. She married my father and they lived
near downtown at first so that it was not far for her to

drive to Bunker Hill and she often took me. She brought her card table and very fine, fine pencils that had to be sharpened with sandpaper and she drew the houses on rough water-color paper which was innocent enough to hold the houses down without looking coy.

I wore a lavender and white checked dress and sat beside her in our old Mercury as we drove down Sunset and then to Bunker Hill. Her pencils were kept in a wooden cigar box with a catch. Everything smelled of fresh wood.

Bunker Hill was populated with bums and winos, gentlemen who all knew my mother and who sometimes could afford to live in the houses, now fallen into slums, that my mother drew. I would talk to them while she worked and would sit on the sidewalk beside the winos, leaning as they did against the stone fence opposite the houses while the sun beat down and our eyes sometimes ran from smog.

The houses were wooden and Victorian like they have in San Francisco only they were not so narrowly side by side and, besides, they were Baroque rather than the thin-lipped austerity that prevails up north. They were colonial in the desert/tropic valley and the shingles, carving, porches, gables and doors were all wonderfully whittled from memory while flanked by palm trees, sweet peas, wild roses and poinsettias.

The stone fence we sat leaning against was overgrown in some places with Lantana, a purple flower matching my dress and the reason I liked purple. This flower attracted little brown butterflies, monarchs, swallow tails and the white ones, cabbage butterflies. When I was done talking to the men, my mother gave me a brown paper bag which I filled with caught butterflies so that by the time we were ready to go and the sun was ready to set in that Florentinc filmy amber it gets like down there at about 6 in the summer, I had caught a lot.

I'd wait until the car was all packed and we were just driving off and then I'd open the window, tear the bag quickly and watch the silent explosion of color fly out. "I'll always remember this," I thought, "forever."

Then we'd go home and eat dinner I suppose, I don't really remember.

GRANDPA

My grandfather died and in his obituary in the *Jewish Voice* I found out who he was. I thought he was "grandpa" and that he went to meetings all the time.

"Where's grandpa?"

"At a meeting."

It never occurred to me to ask what kind of a meeting or what they did there. He presided over seders and we drank Manischewitz out of small colored shot glasses which were beautiful empty and beautiful full. Jewish food was something you only get to know when, after hating it your entire childhood and thinking everything from the horse-radish on the gefilte fish to the no desserts were without sympathy to the human condition, you find yourself alone and cold in a strange place and suddenly discover that you have to have kasha or you'll shrivel up and die. I thought his meetings must be like the seders only with all old men like him.

The photographs of him as a young man show those empty eyes of William S. Hart because they hadn't discovered how to make blue eyes visible then. My grandmother showed me a photograph of the two of them she found just lately in which they look like The Prince and The Princess.

"You know when that was taken?" she asked.

"When?"

"We were in New York. We'd just come from Toronto and gotten married and Papa had no money, we were very poor. Then he got one day's work and made $5.00. So, instead of buying food or anything, we had our picture taken. This is the picture, it cost $5.00. Weren't we beautiful?"

"Yes."

Grandpa was born in a little town in Russia and died exactly 80 years later in L.A. (The best capsule description of F. Scott Fitzgerald I ever read was a brief biography which began, "Francis Scott Fitzgerald was born in 1896 in St. Paul, Minnesota, and died 44 years later in Hollywood.")

What I learned about Abraham Babitz (pronounced Abram Babbich) besides that he'd been the editor of the *California Jewish Voice*, was that he was a "strong voice in the International Ladies' Garment Workers Union" and he met my grandmother in Toronto in 1907 in the midst of a kind of bohemia that seems to have existed there of which my movie-actress great aunt was a part. My grandfather was a labor organizer and a Zionist, it says.

But my favorite part is "During his early career

. . . Babitz earned the reputation of being an iconoclastic writer with a powerful sense of humor with which he could devastate a two-hour speaker with but one sentence . . . he was a kindly but holy terror . . ."

He was also described as "witty, droll, brilliant and a demon in the causes he espoused."

When I die, they won't have to change a thing. Anyway, I hope not.

I didn't even know my grandfather. All I know now is that he was able to spend his only $5.00 on a photograph because he was so handsome and that his best friend called him a demon in his obituary.

GRANDMA

Jewish grandchildren in L.A. call their grandfather "Zaidie" and their grandmother "Bahboo" until they realize not to. They then call them "grandma" and "grandpa" like everyone else.

My grandmother is brilliantly charming and a complete manipulator and a whiner and has a laugh that makes the birds shut up so they can learn something. She told me, one day as I was doing the only good deed I ever did in my entire life, taking her to Pasadena to the junk stores, about how she won my father's gold medal in violin playing for him when he was 15 and how she used to go to all his lessons and make sure to hear everything in case when my father got home he forgot anything. She has a beautiful voice and is always in tune and my father survived his childhood with only a few major rents in his heart and brain.

Grandma is about 75. She has eyes that sparkle like the day she was born and skin that blooms wrinkleless, like a child's. She left Russia at the age of 13 because she almost got caught carrying documents for the Revolution. She had to stash the papers down an outhouse toilet and so she came to Canada. She learned how to shoot a rifle, she told me once, in Russia for the Revolution. When she was 6 or 4 she hid in a cellar during a pogrom in the house of some un-Jewish Jewish sympathizers.

The entire family tries to bear this in mind but it doesn't seem to prevent outraged slamming down of phones and raised voices. No one ever raises his voice in our family except at Grandma. She *knows* how to do it.

Grandma recently had her house broken into when she was out and was so terrified that my mother finally elicited the reason. Grandma thought it was a pogrom.

We try to bear this in mind.

"Evie, darling," she says, "when do you get married?"

". . ." slam goes the phone.

"Who was that?" a friend asks.

"My goddam fucking grandmother . . ." I cry, livid.

"You mean the grandmother I met that night at your mother's party?"

"Yeah."

"God, she was fantastic. I wish *I* had a grandmother like that. I mean you can talk to her and everything and she's so beautiful and intelligent and so funny."

My grandmother wants me to get married like her

★ 26 ★

and have ingrates for children and grandchildren who hang up on her. When she was 6 or 4 she was in a pogrom.

We try to bear this in mind.

I have inherited her skin.

(It would be unfair of me not to mention that my grandmother is responsible for all of her children and grandchildren regarding art as the only possible occupation.)

AGNES

My mother left Sour Lake, Texas, and Agnes forever in 1930 about. Agnes lived in Sour Lake and had three children. One she named Woodrow Wilson, another she named Eugene Debs and the third she named Lily Mae. The two boys had a different father from the girl who was the oldest and whose last name was Laviolette. My mother's name before she left Sour Lake was Lily Mae Laviolette. Her name is now Mae Babitz. She only has a Texas accent when she gets mad. ("You're just a little piece of shit on a stick!" she used to threaten when we were obnoxiously young.)

Agnes ran a restaurant in Sour Lake called Agnes's, the culmination of an effort begun years before on a capital of a dollar fifty which she spent to make chili for the oil field workers. Agnes makes fantastic chili. She also never, after a lesson or two, allowed herself to become financially dependent on anyone other than herself.

Once when I testified before a Senate Committee about LSD, Bobby Kennedy asked me how many people I knew smoked marijuana. Brazenly I announced, "Everyone I know smokes marijuana except my grandmother."

"Why don't you turn your grandmother on?" the lady from the NY *Times* asked me afterwards.

"She's high already," I sailed past.

Both grandmothers got wind of it.

My Jewish grandmother sent me a photograph to run with an article in some fashionable short-lived NY publication about the "grandmother who was turned on already," and her smile shining forth did indeed look beautific.

The other grandmother's relatives in Beaumont telephoned to taunt her. Without missing a beat, Agnes said, "Evie's got another grandmother, you know." I wonder which one I meant.

CARMELITA

Ballet in Hollywood was taught to little girls at the Perry Dance Studio on Highland Avenue by a branding-iron-hot Spanish zealot named Carmelita Marachi. Trailing after her came her assistant, Peggy, who tried to salve the seared flesh left by Carmelita's acid observations.

"You're a clumsy elephant," Carmelita hissed, snapping her head back sharply like a whip, her long black hair disciplined into an immaculate bun.

Peggy followed, dispensing kindness.

What I could never put together was, what all the years and years and years of taking lessons, decades on toe shoes and ticking your feet into white chalk had to do with Margot Fonteyn down there in feather dreams dying a swan's death, limply broken. I couldn't see how we were going to get from where we were to where she was.

Carmelita once gave me the ultimate compliment of telling me and my mother I was "graceful" and should "go on." My mother was seriously pleased at this unheard-of pleasantry. But I had watched carefully through the binoculars and had seen the way Margot Fonteyn held her hands, the two second to the last fingers together, the others sweeping through the air as though it were the Loire, and I used that trick to extract "graceful" from Carmelita instead of doing pliés.

I was a sinister child, lazy and cynical.

THE CHOKE

Pop's was where the Pachucos hung out a block from Le Conte and I would sneak looks as I went by on my way home from school, irresistibly drawn by a web of thrilling daydreams awash on a shore of panic. Now and then I could convince myself that Pop's was "just a hotdog stand" but it didn't last and sometimes I left without my change, my heart beating like thumps. All the rest of the way home I burned with intimidation until my cat would run to greet me and together we'd go lie out in the back yard where I'd recover my junior-high balance.

I yearned to be invisible so I could go to Pop's and watch while they led their wild, exciting lives—their real lives as opposed to my 13-year-old aimless one where all I ever did was wish someone would abduct me into white slavery and carry me off to Pago Pago or *some*thing instead of just lying there with my cat listening to the thumps subside. They had real lives, they'd been expelled from schools for carrying knives, they stole cars, fought, and their style of dance, the Choke, was so abandoned in elegance it made you limp with envy. They were called Pachucos, the ones who had real lives. And no matter how much I practiced the one thing they did that wouldn't get you busted, I was never intrinsically Pachuco enough for the Choke.

Perhaps, I thought as I quieted down in the cool grass staring into my cat's eyes, if I had a Pachuco partner . . . But that was impossible because they were too austere to dilute themselves with us.

As the days passed indistinguishably with hot spells in "winter" and cool days in July, we went from grade to grade and each semester we got new lockers. So when it rained it sent a flash of exhiliration through the spinal column of our school like an electric ribbon.

When it rained, they used to let us spend our Phys Ed class "social dancing" in the gym. Instead of having to get dressed in hated gym clothes and go outside to play hated volleyball, we kept our regular clothes on and danced to the records that were kept there for School Dances. The ones they danced to at night were ones like "Sincerely" and "In the Still of the Night." But those were too slow for girls to dance together so we'd always choose Chuck Berry and Little Richard since they were as fast as you could get and a song by the El Dorados called "Crazy Little Mama" that I always thought was terrific. We threw ourselves into those dances with rainy-day recklessness and 13-year-old hys-

teria from being cooped up in steamy classes all day.
Sometimes we even dropped our poses of nonchalance
to forget it all and do the polka, which was like stock-car
races or destruction derbies where we all landed in a
heap in the middle of the floor, hilarious . . . But only
if it rained.

Of course, gym teachers being what they are, they
couldn't just let us alone, they had to tell us what to do
so they used to have "dance contests" with processes of
elimination and envy and all that other stuff they have.
The idea was to applaud who you thought was best—
judgment by your peers, it's called—and the ones who
got the loudest applause won. Only the gym teachers
decided which applause was loudest and it was never
for the Pachuco couple no matter how obvious it was.
Because how could kids who weren't white and who'd
been sent to Le Conte because they'd been expelled
from other schools win? So the runner-up always
won.

Everyone knew exactly what was happening but it
didn't make any difference. It kept on happening.

The runners-up were always two plain wholesome
energetic girls who gave their all to the Bop so that
their quilted cotton circle skirts were perpendicular to
their waists and their stupid crinolines showed underneath and their arms swung like hammocks in their
abundant good spirits. They usually wore braces and
had stringy mousey ponytails and their cotton blouses
came out from their belts in their exuberance. They
were *so* white. Brother Malcolm when he described the
Bop could never have known what it would come to
3000 miles away in our Junior High. And if anyone tried

★ 34 ★

to give the Bop some joie de vivre it was immediately intercepted and was secretly known as the "dirty boogie."

So if you wanted to do anything, it looked like they'd nailed you from every angle. They had rules for everything, but they didn't imagine the Choke, and when the Pachucos came that's what they brought and the Choke was not dirty. The Choke was enraged anarchy posed in mythical classicism as a dance. So far as I know, they never figured out how to whiten it up.

The Choke was a Pachuco invention. The Pachucos were what we called kids who spoke with Mexican accents whether they were Mexican or not and who lived real lives. The Choke looked like a completely Apache, deadly version of the jitterbug only you never thought of the jitterbug when you watched kids doing the Choke. There was no swing in the Choke, it was stacatto. It was Pachuco, police-record, L.A. flamenco dancing.

It was all done on the heels.

And the knees, unlike in the dirty boogie, were irretreivably glued together. The arms, instead of being swung were just, when not being used for some split-second-clue maneuver, forgotten about. So the arms fell where they might, as though they belonged to a dead person. The shoulders were hunched up and never relaxed once during the dance so the contrast between the dead arms and the hunched shoulders was kind of sinister like the villain in the movie smiling with a knife in his hand.

But it wasn't just the dance that made the Pachucos such a thrill in our Presbyterian cream-of-wheat days.

(They didn't even say "Presbyterian Church"—they called it "the First Pres," that's how the texture of even as innocuous as watered-down Protestantism was watered down.) It was everything, but especially the clothes.

Maybe in their bleached immaculate hearts those girls like Judy and Susan actually imagined that they danced better than C.C. and Nina. Maybe their unblemished records of AEEs (the E's stood for Excellence in behavior and attitude) should automatically make them better than the ones who got DUU (the U's stood for Unsatisfactory, which they were). Maybe they thought all that cotton and the skirts they made in Homemaking were more right than the coral sweaters of the dancers who danced a real dance with deadly authority from a real world where icy, serious things happened. But I never believed it. No one with an ounce of human sympathy for style or even a passing appreciation for design could ever have preferred those never-to-be-sexy, washed-out girls to the explosive danger of the Pachucos.

C.C. hit three other schools before they finally got her as far away from Temple Street as they could and put her into Le Conte. Temple Street and Alpine were the two opposing gangs and C.C. was in the ladies'-auxiliary division of the Temple Street one. The last school she'd been expelled from was Virgil and Virgil was the toughest school we'd ever heard of. It had a reputation for sex and violence and luscious, mouth-watering, comic-book-type stories about girls in razor fights after school underneath the freeway stripping down to black slips. (Black Slips!)

C.C.'d actually been expelled from Virgil. There was

no place for her to go except Betsy Ross, the delin-quent-girls place—or Americana. They tried Americana.

C.C. dressed to precision-edge as a Pachuco. Even in gym clothes, she came through and not just because of the tattoo on her hands that said:

that they all wore. You could tell all the way across the baseball field that she was tough because she stacked her hair. The way you stacked your hair was that there was a long V point that hung straight in the back like an arrow toward your ass and the longer the better. The rest of your hair was cut about 5 or 6 inches around your face and curled real tight and then tempted upward so that it added about 3 inches to your height which, if you were a short Mexican, was desirable. Curls were all around your face and looked adorable and it was only from the back that you saw the deadly straight V and wondered if the rumors were true that in that tangle of curls on top, they hid wrapped razors for their boy friends to kill other guys after school.

Her ears were pierced—theirs all were—and she wore little dangly rhinestones or gold hoops.

The kind of writing used in the tattoo for the c/s is the same kind of Pachuco writing they still deface buildings with all over L.A. only now instead of using paintbrushes, they use spray cans. I could kill them for

★ 37 ★

some of the places they choose to deface and that spray is nearly impossible to get off, but I don't know . . . when I'm away sometimes for too long, I think about it and think, I wouldn't mind seeing that damn Pachuco writing even if it is on cliffs in Malibu, just so I could be back in L.A.

So even in gym clothes, C.C.'s individuality was not, by any means, stamped out. Maybe that's why sailors get tattoos.

I dressed next to her in gym (on my other side was this nice girl named Cathy whose only flaw was that she was kind of gullible and that kept me from being too shocked when I saw her in *Life* magazine crouched under a rock as one of the "Manson Family" and called Gypsy). C.C. dressed with another Pachuco, a quiet girl named Amy who was Oriental but also spoke with that same clipped, contemptuous English-Mexican that all the Pachucos did.

So I got to watch her dress up close every day for a whole semester and she had so many clothes that it was then that I learned what the word "kype" meant. It meant going to the Broadway and leaving without paying. But all her clothes had been altered so that they suited the particular style to which C.C. aspired.

She was only about 5 feet tall and she was 14 years old. She wore a size 32 DD bra, had a tiny Mexican waist and flat broad hips. Her legs were short and adorable and her arms were dimpled and if she'd been in Mexico, she'd have been married and on her way out by then, but she was in L.A. and she was tough and she wanted furniture and a paddy husband. Paddy means white in Pachuco. I found this out from Amy, who took a kind of patronizing interest in me when she learned that I read Little Lulu comics and could quote whole passages by heart. Amy and I stayed strange friends long after she was transferred to Betsy Ross and up until she married a Paddy and it depressed me so much that beautiful Amy would marry white trash that I gave up on the entire deal, it was too culturally unbridgeable in spite of the Little Lulu. (Our favorite line was when Tubby knocks on Lulu's door one day and says, "Hello, obnoxious," turns around, and leaves.) C.C. and Amy dressed one over from me and sometimes when it rained and we only had to put on our gym shoes, we'd get so electrified, we'd actually race to the dance floor to be first at the records (if the white girls got there, who'd tell what they'd play—"Mr. Sandman" was one of their favorites and that was shit as shit could be).

So even in gym clothes, C.C. with her glittering ears and Amy with her Japanese disdain and almost natural sneer were not Presbyterians, and though they wore heavy gold crosses, they weren't regular Catholics either.

Their voices, when they spoke to authority, loomed with cynicism and mockery as they overdid the conso-nants and spoke their vowels in some special version of their own. On the records put out by people in L.A. around that time, even the blacks talked with some-what a Pachuco accent. The most obvious Pachuco was Little Julian Herrera (probably still in jail for statutory rape—how come the Beatles never got busted for statu-tory rape—because they're white?). And the Medal-lions and the Five Satins all talked like that too—it's like a Mexican Nat King Cole. They say "lahve" for "love" and whole phrases like "Aiiii give miiii lahve toe yow." I tried to talk like that, but just couldn't. You had to do it all, if you were going to do any of it, and I was afraid of the tire irons and getting sent to juvenile hall and stealing hubcaps, so I just watched and wished I were invisible.

C.C.'s regular school clothes carried with them the same spirit as Monroe in "Niagara" combined with a whore of Batista's Havana. She wore skirts so tight (altered from the Broadway) that the semester after she was expelled, the new rule on the code of Dress said something about there having to be at least four inches' leeway between your knees in skirts. C.C. had about an inch. Try walking like that and you'll see how Monroe had the same charm as the Chinese women with bound feet—they can't get away, it's sexy if you go for that kind of thing, chains and that . . . Usually C.C.'s skirts were pastel and huge plaids with matching cardigans buttoned down the back (so the front would be tighter) and matching woolly socks as some sort of vestigial tribute to something East Coast and "school-girly."

Her shoes, though, were the best. When she came to Le Conte, she wore, on her first day and for the next week, the kind of shoes known as Bunnies. They were white soft shoes that were higher up the foot than loafers and had two little ears pointing at the top and two just in back of your heel. You could slip your size 7 foot into a Bunny and look like you wore a size 4. By the end of the week, half the girls in the school had them and the other half were tiding themselves over by calling the first half cheap.

There were all sorts, we learned, of shoes that made your feet look like eraser stubs and C.C. had them all and she already wore a size 4, so her little feet looked like they were nubs. A double threat with the knees

THE CHOKE

already sewn together, if you like that sort of thing
(which most everyone does). There were ladder shoes
—round-toed shoes with two straps, there were tear
drops—round-toed with buckles and designs like tear-
drops cut in the leather, and there were Mary Janes like
little girls' shoes. They were all like little girls' shoes
except for Bunnies, which were new. I ran through
about 5 pairs of Bunnies in my Junior-High career. All
the shoes were white and they were also subversive.

One of the main bones of Contention in the Code of
Dress was that none of the girls could stand bucks or
saddle shoes. They wanted to wear flats. Like ballet
slippers. Flats look pretty and the administration didn't
want anyone to look pretty so they said that if you
wanted to wear flats, you had to wear socks with them.
Flats with socks look like a 3-year-old. So everyone was
stuck either staying after school as a penalty for wearing flats without socks, or wearing saddle shoes. When
Bunnies came in, the whole thing was that they looked
more deliciously Lolita with socks. They were sexy.
And so within C.C.'s first week, half the girls had them.

Now, standing back to take a look at C.C., the general
impression was this. Here was this short, adorable, dimpled, stubby-toed, stacked, cuddly, gold-crossed girl
with sparkling earrings and a hostility that shone like a
nimbus for all to see and there was no way they could
get her. And she had this tattoo.

And there was us, in all that stupid cotton, trying to
figure out how to look decent in Pat Boone bucks, dying
to be rescued. Some girls were so tantalized, they went
completely to her side without a backward glance. But
I was afraid to turn myself over completely to anything
so all of a piece. Amy, who was more eclectic than most

★ 41 ★

of them, and I had a bond of friendship that survived a long time and huge distances (because she lived way downtown and it was an hour for either of us on the bus), but I still, though, wished I could forget and just do it, just be them.

Especially when C.C. would do the Choke on rainy days. Or when I'd pass her and this guy named Mario after school at Pop's. To think of a guy for a partner, especially one like Mario, who was so blandly opaque, was like I said enough to freeze me awash on a shore of panic. And I was afraid to do anything more than just watch them for a second, sneak a look, as I walked by, whereas in gym, you were supposed to judge the dancers so you could look all you wanted.

C.C.'s partner was a tall girl who also wound up in Betsy Ross called Nina, and Nina was the man.

Nina danced invisibly like a champion yo-yo expert who never moves though the yo-yo goes everywhere and does everything and though she never moved, it all came back to her since she must have set the spinning-heeled C.C. into orbit. C.C.'s tight shoulders and bullet heels (we wore taps on our heels, real loud) were like a controlled avalanche that went in a circle of complicated orbits around the man, hurtled out and whipped back, spun on a string that was invisible, toes contracted like Balinese fingernails away from the floor and toward her shins.

Clues are transmitted in Pachuco Braille that sent C.C. rolling up in the circle of Nina's arms, heels on, and in between each beat for one paralyzed trap before she's cued out, spinning around Nina's back as they touch for the more fractional point in time and are off again, "goin' tell Aunt Mary 'bout Uncle . . . he says she's got the misery but he's . . ." Without thought she's taken the cue to spin out into infinity, blindly she twirls, clicking, when somehow Nina moves an arm and touches C.C.'s hand with one languid finger that sends C.C. back into the folds of the orbit and not into comethood to wander through the universe forever alone. Nina, the man, stands as straight and implacably as Manolete at his last corrida, bringing bull in, cape throw by cape throw into narrower arched passes, wetting his suit of lights with streaks of both their death's blood.

The girl, C.C.'s eyes never leave the floor, she is modest, her shoulder muscles have been disabled by the picadors and she must hunch them and hold her gold cross so that it does not fly out, a weapon, during the dance. Her right arm is rigidly expecting temporal clues from Nina and is close to her body. All is strict except her left arm that falls dead in gravity.

The man is so rigid with his arms close to his sides and his shoulders hunched, hard and austere, his knees cemented together as though he were cold—freezing. All that must move, then, is his right hand, but you never see it, you only see C.C. spinning in and out, touching his back with hers, and the clatter of heels. He does not see her, his eyes are fixed on some point beyond this time, long past the dance, aloof into the horizon of some purely masculine, deadly domain.

Sparks seem thrown off—too much in too small an orbit too carefully controlled and accomplished too scornfully by one who is not even participating, who doesn't move, whose eyes see far, far into the distance where the gym teacher can never go and the Presbyterians can't allow.

Thoughts aroused on this rainy day are vainly

squashed by calling others the "winners" as though everyone hadn't heard the applause. But unfurled flags from unknown lands, once glimpsed, cannot be washed like the dust on the asphalt from the rain.

I was in Rome at a party, in an embassy where they'd let movie people in, so that's how I got to go to such a swanky event. I headed straight for the hors d'oeuvres and was on my second caviar when I felt someone's hands on either side of my waist lifting me up and putting me down so that I faced a man who was strikingly in my heart but there was no name for the handsome face.

"Hi!" he said, delighted in recognition.

It was an American "hi," a Californian "hi," not an Italian one, though he looked so Italian in his vented suit and his pin stripes and his dark hair and lashy eyes and he held out his hand to shake mine in the European and Italian fashion.

I looked down at his hand, stalling for time in confusion which only got worse when I saw the white scars left by the machine that takes away tattoos and once, carefully removed and now a ghost, had been a cross and c/s on the skin between his thumb and index finger just like C.C.

"Ummm," I said, trying to think.

"You went to Le Conte, didn't you?" he asked.

"Yeah, but . . ."

"I'm Mario," he said. "I used to see you . . ." He was effervescent and happy and he told me how he'd become a Pachuco because it seemed the only sensible thing to do. His family had been deposed from their Central American government and were in exile in

THE CHOKE

L.A. and since he spoke Spanish anyway and everything else looked so abysmal, he decided to bide his
time where the fun was. But then, he went on, the new
Central American government had been overthrown
and so now, he, Mario, was the ambassador to Italy! He
lived in a huge apartment in Vigna Clara, and he was
so happy to see anyone from California that I must
come see him, I must appreciate his new Mercedes
which he'd had painted candy-apple red for sentimental reasons, I simply must!

"My god!" I said.

We were drinking champagne now, out on the ter-
race beyond the waxed inlaid wooden floor from which
the rug had been removed for the party. They'd been
playing Umberto Bini songs all night, those heavenly
mushy Italian things where you slip along with chiffon
drifting over your shoulder. Le Twist was now the rage,
as well as the Mashed Potato, and since a few of the
statelier older people had gone, the host put on music
for the twisters and played "Runaround Sue." ". . . here
is my story, sad but true . . ."

It's not Little Richard, but it is faster than anything
the Italians ever allowed themselves and Mario and I
went in to dance Le Twist.

I don't remember how many seconds it took me to
recognize the tightness that could only be familiar
there to me in Mario's shoulders, the curious hunched
torso and the ridged unnatural arms, things that aren't
Le Twist. Without even looking up, because by this
time my eyes were on the floor and my left hand held
my pearls so that they would not fly out, I slid my right
hand into his and as thoughtlessly, only remembered
through his body, he clued me as he must have done

★ 45 ★

C.C. into the Choke. Into his arms and click, I was off, around and in back for a fraction with double beats of my tapless heels, my eyes never leaving the floor though my dress was brocaded satin and my hair was straight with bangs. The Romans stopped Le Twist and watched us because the precision was obvious and inbred in the dance and yet it had never been seen. I could not resist it, for a tenth of a second, I looked up at Mario, up past his immovable feet and his knees together and his ridged body to his opaque, bland face that had, on the patio, been so animated and urbane.

His eyes had long ago gone out the window, past the Campotellini, past Gibraltar and the Midwestern United States, perhaps back to Pop's where I watched him in the afternoons with C.C.—the ordinary smoggy afternoons, when I yearned to be invisible and he led a real life.

RICHARD GREENE, THE VIOLIN PLAYER

Richard Greene, the bluegrass breakneck violin player sounds the way The Girl in the convertible looks when she runs her fingers underneath her honey tresses at a light to free her hair for a moment from its own weight.

Sometimes a violin sounds spooky and you wonder why anyone could play it. When Richard Greene begins to play, you remember. The Walls of Jericho could easily have been seduced down by the sound of the bow on Richard Greene's strings, the tone.

The light has changed, The Girl is no longer anywhere and you are stranded back in mortality as Richard Greene retreats from the mike, his solo over.

FROZEN LOOKS

The past is entered through creaking iron gates laced with fog and the sheer sigh of Joan Fontaine's memory as she begins, ". . . sometimes I think of Mandalay." So the movie *Rebecca* commences. Hitchcock's lesson always is that nothing is as it seems, the past too teaches that—and the trick is to unravel with one hand and rearrange with the other so that the complicated mechanics of certain stretches of time have their rhythms evened out. But even Hitchcock doesn't tell everything, and at the end of the movie you don't really know if Rebecca was murdered by her husband or if she used him in her own suicide. Hitchcock knows you can't ever know it all, because time keeps shifting the combinations, time releases details at later dates, time can't be bucked by life except for trapped moments in frozen looks.

The gates to my past aren't rusty, creaking, laced with fog. They're the unceremonious whoosh that the sound of the rear door of a bus made as down I stepped, impatient to drown in the hot, open days of my 14th summer. Barefooted on the rough rubber steps, I'd jump from the bus and hurry past the old people on the Palisades, scramble down the cool cement steps to the bridge over the Pacific Coast Highway and turn delirious at the sight of the day of heat cooled only by moments frozen into the summer, isolated like prickly cactus standing in the dawn.

In the mornings of that summer I would awaken seriously at 7:30 already afraid that it might be 7:45 or a tragic 8—but it wasn't. My bathing suit lay on the sandy floor right where I'd taken it off the night before and that and my father's old Mexican shirt, 66¢ for the bus, a dime for a snow cone and a nickel for a frozen Look Bar were securely in my purse as out I went. Sometimes my mother would thrust an orange my way before I was halfway down the block, or a fried egg sandwich, but I wasn't hungry much in those days except to hurry up and get to the beach.

The beach from that summer was called Roadside. It was 1958 and a lot of kids from West L.A. went there —tough kids with knives, razors, tire irons and lowered cars. No kids from my school or any of the schools nearby went to Roadside, they went to Sorrento where there were never any fights and where most of the kids from Hollywood High, Fairfax and Beverly spent their summers listening to "Venus" on the radio or playing volleyball. If I had only known about Sorrento, I never would have gone to the beach so passionately, since Sorrento was a dispassionate beach involved mainly in the junior high and high school ramifications of polite society, sororities, *Seventeen* magazine, football players and not getting your hair wet.

I found out about Roadside from the cousin of a friend of mine about a week before school let out for summer. Her name was Carol and she wasn't like anyone I'd ever met, though she seemed perfectly suitable as a playmate for 14-year-old virgins, us, and she was a few months younger than us too. She could have been one of those perky types with the ponytail and the rolled-up jeans and called "adorable" because she was small and had large blue eyes. But there was something luxuriously corrupt about her even that first day at my friend's house where we were swimming. She complained of pools as she reclined voluptuously on the canvas mattress, making no attempt to hide her total immersion in the sensuality of being alive and wet under a hot sun. She spoke slowly, she drawled in a nasal, rich-girl nonchalance that pools were all right she supposed but the real thing was the ocean, the waves. "What beach do you go to?" my ordinary school friend asked her Beverly Hills cousin.

"Roadside," Carol drawled. "The surf's always better there."

My friend was shocked and amazed by this blatant confession to cheapness (girls only went to Roadside if they were "cheap"). But Carol's decadence was much more elaborate than mere cheapness and it wasn't until a couple of years later that I learned from another friend, Joy, that Carol, that summer when I knew her, was having simultaneous affairs with a concert pianist friend of her parents, a burglar she'd caught in the living room one Saturday and Joy's brother who later hung himself in Chicago and whom Carol could never entrap, his death being his final adieu.

But even I could see that Carol's ponytail had something to do with her sense of humor which was obscure, jaded and waltzing to a different drummer. And that shocking her cousin with tales of Roadside was giving Carol the same subtle pleasure that some people get behind the wheel of any functioning car. I listened attentively and later made plans to meet her down there when school let out.

Ever since I was little I'd always spent hours in the ocean when I got near it but the best I could do with a wave was dive through or under it before it crashed and got me. Carol taught me to ride the waves in to shore, to await huge fraught-with-peril breakers with giddy dominance so that I could turn my instinctive fear against itself and foam to shore, a beached, elated body ready to pit myself against the waves again and again until I never got crashed to the bottom of the ocean with my chin in the sand from a wave, not knowing which way was up, until I even lost my giddiness and slid out to sea to await the waves enslaved by hypnotic rhythms. I became a gliding sea-mammal. Fierce, arbitrary waves of green tons escaped out the other side of the complicated mechanics of things not being what they seemed so that finally even my instincts altered and what had before been certain death became a toy, greeted calmly with a relaxed look over the top for perhaps a bigger one. Those were the hot open days of summer I awoke desiring so passionately each morning an hour and a half away by bus.

Few kids from Beverly went to Roadside, and the ones that did, like Carol, went for their own reasons and not to hang around with other kids from Beverly, so Carol and I became accomplices at sea and put our towels next to each other on land where we rarely spoke. (Was she recovering from her lovers by befriending fresh me whose only depravity lay in a consuming determination to master the ocean? Did she find my apprenticeship diverting? I never wondered about that then, though questioning motives is a lesson I've finally had to bone up on.)

The real hoods, the serious ones who'd been up the night before fighting with churchkeys and tireirons or knocking up "cheap" girls, spent the days dozing fully clothed or with only their shirts off on blankets adjacent to the wall that encircled the bathrooms. The rest of us, including Carol and me, lay much nearer the water next to the lifeguard stand and wore bathing suits. But there was no set rule, and there was a loose trade around of people who "went in" and people who "hung on the wall."

The "wall" was autographed with the names of most of the hoods who hung on it and the biggest name, five feet across in giant red print, staggered out unevenly spelling PREACHER.

From the first time I went to Roadside the minute school let out, not a day went by that Preacher wasn't mentioned. Rumor had it that he would be getting "out" in July sometime and then, *then* . . . well, you wouldn't have these penny-ante poker games, these halfassed brawls, these opaque silences when plainclothesmen ventured out onto the beach. When Preacher got out things were gonna really get bitchin' . . . "Did you ever hear about the time the Preacher dumped a naked girl into the lifeguard station when the chief was there? . . ."

Carol had only heard about him, which put her in the same boat as me, and she'd listen to the stories spun out extravagantly in his absence with her wide-open blue eyes and her deceitful ponytail drying in the sun.

The day Preacher got there the texture of the beach changed, emanating from the wall with impulses of dangerous craziness. Three lifeguards instead of the usual one were there with frequent visits from the jeeps that patrolled the shore. Is it because lifeguards don't have guns that they needed three? I scooted past the wall trying to be invisible but anxiously fascinated and heard, "Hey, pass that bottle to the Preacher." It was 9:15 a.m.

Carol was lying on her stomach when I got down to our part and I fell on my towel, thrown next to her trying to get back to the relaxed hot and open from the dizzy tight and foolhardy of the wall. The sun bleached my bones into driftwood and burnt all from my thoughts but white, and by ten it blazed overhead so unchecked that Carol and I got up simultaneously without speaking and headed West. Great green Pacific gave way to hours of splendid murderous waves for us to emasculate and adapt fiercely to our foaming trails. And then back out for another . . . the wave and us, to try another combination.

We went to the hot-dog stand at noon and both got our daily rations of snowcones (mine, pineapple—hers, cherry) and frozen Look bars which we shattered against the counter in their wrappers and ate the splintered pieces which were heaven—nougat so sweet and reluctant and coated with chocolate. Heaven.

On our way back, just as we got to the wall a fight

broke out, noisy and violent with people leaping to their feet in order not to be fallen upon or hit accidentally. A young hood was running and right behind him was the Preacher, who chased him half a block in the hot sand under the scorching sun until he felled him and dropped on top of him purple with rage. The bystanders clotted to the fight, blocking our view, so I asked someone why and they said the guy had accused Preacher of cheating at cards, which he did, but you're not supposed to say anything about it, everyone knew that. A ghastly slash of pain rose from the center of the mob, from the fight, a high groan of surprise and horror it was, followed by an echoing murmur of disbelief from the crowd. It filtered back to us that Preacher had bitten the guy's ear off, which made my frozen Look suddenly inedible.

The thing was over, the guy was helped to an emergency hospital by some other hoods, Preacher led an awe-struck parade back to the wall with blood on his face and someone said the ear was in his pocket. Carol and I, in the crowd farther back, stood with some others unable to move when the arbitrary force cruised by and suddenly stopped, stared at Carol from twenty feet away with the eyes of a mad Dutchman and then began lurching toward her, stopping only to pick up a fistful of money from the deserted poker game. People began backing away from Carol, so singled out, but I got closer, I think it was to see.

"Hey, you snotty Beverly Hills bitch," he snarled, hitting the nail on the head and looking much older than I thought he'd be, and weatherbeaten—someone told me he was 20, but he looked a ragged 30. I thought he might try to tear her bathing suit off, but he shook the money at her impassive, demurely lowered eyes and said, "You rich bitches is all whores of Babylon but you ain't gittin' my money, you can bet your sweet baby ass on that." He waited, gathering strength, deadly and crazy.

From her warmly tanned face she languidly opened her expensive blue eyes wide before narrowing them, transforming them into the eyes of an aristocratic animal whose defense lay in some rapid, paralyzing venom which hissed from the pupils and stopped him in his tracks. She stirred her snowcone while she took her time assessing him from his bloody face to his sandy feet to his blood-soaked pocket and then she lowered her eyes, shrugged, and strolled through the space the crowd had opened for her with me floating in back of her, having no wish to stay on after witnessing that crisis of frozen looks.

Years and years later I heard that Preacher was killed —shot in the stomach five times by an irate husband and that his last words had been, "Go ahead, shoot me." So the gates to my past are the unceremonious whoosh of the bus doors letting me out into the open summer when I began to learn about the complicated mechanics of things not being what they seem so that later I had the feeling that Preacher, like Rebecca, may have committed suicide and that Carol could somehow see past what things seemed into what things were.

But what, then, must Carol have been, that 14-year-old creature riding waves, silkenly prone in the sun on hot open days, introducing novices like me to the practice of ignoring instinct, of going beyond giddiness, until I could treat certain death like a toy and calmly look over the top for perhaps a bigger one. She seduced me

that summer to trails of corrupt and luxurious enter-
tainments of the moment, to Mandalay . . . At least,
that's the way it *seems*, especially after the way she
presented her would-be killer with his own death in the
heat of the day when everything stopped in a frozen
look.

ANGELS FLIGHT

It cost a nickel to go on Angels Flight, the world's shortest railroad, located once in downtown L.A. and now gone. The car went up and down the steep side of Bunker Hill all day so people with groceries wouldn't have to walk up endless steps, which were parallel. It was a luxury railroad.

There was a man at the top only who collected the nickel from the people coming up and took the nickel before you could go down. He dispensed tickets from a little booth and also ran the cable car/railroad.

My mother would take me and she would buy a two-way ticket for us both, round trip. I asked the man once, "Didn't it ever just . . . crash?"

We directed our gazes to the store across the street at the bottom which lay ready for a direct hit.

"Oh, once," he said, "the cable broke."

"Oh."

THE POLAR PALACE

My hair went straight even though I used an entire bottle of Tweed Hair Spray (89 cents) on it every Friday night when Sue and I would go ice skating at the Polar Palace. It went straight though I set it in pin curls and didn't take it out until we were there in the ladies' room putting on our skates. It went straight and limp, while Sue's got naturally curlier as the white fog lifted off the white ice.

The worst thing about the Polar Palace though wasn't that my hair went straight in the midst of fog and Tweed, it was that I didn't like it. The reason I went was because Sue always went and, besides, the fierceness of the previous angry summer at Roadside was so irreconcilable with Le Conte Jr. High that I gave up. Perhaps it was the musty Americana trapped in Southern California and muffling Le Conte that finally got me, but whatever it was, I gave up. It no longer mattered to me that Le Conte's smiling self-assurance was lumbering obliviously away from real life toward the precipice of extinction. I joined them and my straight hair went limp. I had a terrible time, all smelling of Tweed.

The Polar Palace was an old place used by the Ice Capades for practicing and for tryouts. It was an enormous indoor rink with dry wooden bleachers all around that went up to the rafters where no one but kids necking had sat in my lifetime. It was between Paramount Studios and the old Jewish cemetery on Santa Monica where sometimes kids would sneak into and make out on the graves beneath the standard palm trees which flourish even in cemeteries here. There were no palm trees, however, in front of the Polar Palace. Inside it smelled like dry timber and skates and sounded in the hallways like an army dressing for battle. Once you left the hallways and pushed the swinging doors to the main-rink part, all you heard was the imagined propulsion of frozen circlings and the records of "Winter Wonderland" and other bygone music we didn't like. Once each night they'd play one for the fast skaters, "Rock Around the Clock," usually. Then the ones who wore racers became glazed and charged as they slammed around the rink like centrifugal ball bearings sent by the devils of the present, made visible finally as the lady trios and organ music was mowed down by Bill Haley and the Comets for a little longer than two minutes. The ones who played the records and gave us the Polar Palace must have had their hands up to their elbows in the sluggish backwardness of Le Conte. It all went together.

There were murals of cozy show scenes all around the ceiling of the frozen cavern and there were other bear murals in the café where Sue and I sat with our hot chocolates and mustardy hot dogs before Sue, who liked anything to do with physical motion, would dash once more into the whiteness on her black racers and I would gingerly and reluctantly step out once more to sail around, ankles straight, on my figure skates. Straight ankles was all I was ever able to manage in that essentially empty dream on ice. The wide green waves of July beaches where we stood in our own black shadows had now ingloriously fallen before those straight ankles atop rented steel blades.

Every Friday I went with Sue and I didn't like it.

There was nothing going on in the whole world, nothing. The best thing anyone could think of to fascinate themselves with at school was a constant reappraisal of who was popular and who was the most popular. The word "popular" guided our lives and spirits to the exclusion of real stuff. In fact, real stuff was banned as inappropriate and faintly smelly. Nice people didn't have anything to do with it. God, it was awful.

In the scheme of things, I was in the second circle of popularity, which wasn't as bad as being nothing at all but was certainly not as good as being anything at the center. In my more lucid though occasional moments, the ones that passed like tear drops evaporating under the summer sun across my thoughts, in those moments I knew that this whole thing had nothing inside of it. In my rare conversations with the most popular girl, one named Julie, I was stirred into confusion by what appeared to be a bunch of petals not stuck onto the flower.

Squashed into acquiescence by the weight of Le Conte, I tried to behave like you were supposed to and to keep from peering around for real life or clear focus, though I must have secretly prayed for the fire that would come from somewhere and burn off the prairies of dreary pastiche, burn them naked. Roadside was like a hole in my past.

I met Gary at the Polar Palace. He was one of the most popular of the popular. He was popular with the clubby handful of guys who lived inside the center and he'd gone steady with Julie twice. He began coming to the Polar Palace right when I started to and on the second Friday he asked me to skate Couples Only. I could have passed more easily through the eye of a camel than have believed that wondrous thing could happen and later we went to the dark upper bleachers and necked. My diary was filled with conjecture that weekend afterward and Monday I dressed and curled with every consideration on earth.

Gary never acknowledged my existence, except for an occasional "hi."

But each Friday the same thing would happen and end in the rafters and the terrible part was, I didn't like that either.

If it hadn't been for my hair and its tenacious inability to stay curled, I'd probably be pulling down my girdle in Covina playing bridge and losing. It was a close call.

If it hadn't been for Aces Butler, I'd be settling for what they try to give you even though I know that what they give you has always been just more smothered Le Conte, and Le Conte was a place where the devils of the present were invisible and unheard (as they hollered under my skin for sunlight). I narrowly escaped.

Aces Butler was real.

The disruption implied each time he glanced across

a room at a teacher and touched his mouth with his thumb was real. The scorn behind his straw-colored eyes was sabotage plain and simple. His existence was scorching the hallways and traditions as he shrugged and glanced at the floor that first day he lowered himself into the last row in Algebra.

He could only be described in Le Conte's limited official vocabulary by the words "poor attitude." What an anxious and innocent word to try to pin on Aces, "attitude"! He was an enemy inside their walls. It was too late and there was no way to get him out of there because he was only 15 and the law says that 16 is the earliest you can get anything like him permanently expelled.

"Attitude" was the word they used for someone who knew what they liked. They didn't want anyone to find out what they liked until it was too late.

The second day of Algebra I pulled out my habitual Tweed to try to save my hair from the walk through the overcast morning. The mornings were usually overcast and dewy on our way to school, so every day was a battle. And the Tweed flowed like widow's tears.

"Shit, what the fuck's that?" he asked, screwing up his face.

"My hair's always going straight," I said, trying to decide whether I should recoil at his swearing and pretend I cared. For some roadside reason, I didn't. "It just won't stay curly."

"I can't stand curly hair," he said. "I bet you look much better with it straight anyway. Curly hair's too . . . too cute."

During the entire time I'd gone to Le Conte no one had, until that day, ever said what they meant if it meant something beyond the confines of the past. For me, the lucid moment expanded like a blow, stunning my real life open. But then he was gone and I was left with nothing. I didn't believe in Le Conte any more and the clarity was gone once Aces had left the room.

They transferred him out of Algebra the next day. In fact, one by one all the lady teachers had devised reasons about why they couldn't have Aces in their classroom. After only three weeks he had the unprecedented and illegal (as far as the school system in L.A. was concerned) curriculum of 5 shops and gym. When you thought about it, you knew who'd won.

It wasn't just the way his yellow eyes stripped the plaster off the walls that threw the school open for grabs. And it wasn't his black hair that fell to his chin in the front in criminal defiance. It was that the girls went along with him at once, all the whole school did. Who could resist the way he threw back his head and slapped his thigh in unheard-of abandon, in our starved colony? He dressed in black, black motorcycle jacket, black shirts, black Levis and black boots with his black eyelashes framing his acetylene eyes that flickered out in pure hate at the concepts of anything being "for your own good" or anyone "who knew best."

His ears had points on the tops like a Martian. For all we knew, he could have come from another galaxy and been made out of something else. He certainly wasn't made out of anything we'd ever seen before.

He was about 6 feet tall with broad shoulders and serious-looking arms and he moved so fast that no one toyed with the idea of challenging him. And besides, he looked out at us with resigned tolerance at our childhoods we seemed unable to shake, and when he wasn't being sharply funny, he was disinterestedly pleasant.

In the counselor's office where I worked each day, I stole a look at his Cume Card once when no one was looking. Where it said I.Q. someone had written 178. That was the highest I.Q. I'd ever seen. 140 was supposed to be genius in those days, though now it turns out it's a question of privilege more than brains. I wonder at Aces' privileges, then. Another moment of transparency shook me as I saw how it must have killed them, being beaten at their own game by his absolute refusal to join them when they had given him such qualifications. The words "Poor Attitude" were written helplessly across the top of his card in red pencil.

He didn't join anything we had. He didn't even enter into that masculine camaraderie of the inner circle where they tried to welcome him. His only friend was a little tough kid he'd drawn from the invisible lower third, a kid named Louie, who shadowed him as though he'd always been there.

Walking around the cafeteria in a loose oval was the whole focus of the popular hopelessness. At the Polar Palace you could only go one way, clockwise. But during lunch you could either walk clockwise or counterclockwise around the cafeteria unless you decided to sit on the steps of the cafeteria's south wall, watching. It was during this that Gary never said hi to me.

Julie was the most popular girl in school and she traveled each noon in invariable circles on the asphalt with her friends. Julie gazed out with wide-open powder-blue eyes which went with her powder-blue sweaters and her powder-blue socks. She had black curly hair shiny down her back and she had a Sweetheart Pink lipstick mouth so cute that all you could think of when you were talking to her was cupcakes (it was only afterwards that you wondered at all those unattached petals). Julie's posture was pronounced. She had a sway-back and it made her already darling ass even more adorable and we all stood that way though no one could get it to go as good as hers. Years later a friend asked me if I was standing that way because I had to go to the bathroom, so I finally gave it up. She stood with her arms tightly at her sides, squishing her breasts together in front with her hauntingly obvious rear end sticking out in back. She was the grand finale of what it meant to be darling, adorable and cute.

When Aces showed up that first week, the drama ran high. Julie smiled like sugar icing over her shoulder in welcome and he smiled at her charmingly, like he smiled at everyone. No one had ever been disinterest-edly polite to her, or something, because I was combing my hair in the basement girls' room when a noisy com-motion on the top of the stairs made us all turn and watch. Julie was in tears in the arms of her three best friends, her mouth pink and tragic and her little white collar with the eyelet around it was coming undone. We learned, as did the entire school, that the reason for her tears was Aces. She had, we learned, asked him if he were going to the dance the next night and he'd said something that made her cry. I hoped it wasn't just swearing, since that hadn't made me do anything at all, but I was afraid it could have been. We never found out.

"I don't think I'll set my hair tonight," I told my mother, who was concerned over the amount of money I spent on hair spray, which took almost my whole allowance. She was careful to say nothing and just went on washing the dishes.

My father said, "I thought those curls looked like Shirley Temple which . . . You're too tall to look like Shirley Temple."

I was 5' 7", which I regarded as a tragic flaw. Julie was 5' 2" (eyes of blue).

The days of Roadside rolled back on me that night and the next morning I saw myself as belonging to them and my hair as meaning something about the ocean and those days that had a lot more than met the eye tied up in it.

It was the first time since I'd given up that I did something that I could understand.

I walked out of Algebra that day right into Aces' amber-eyed glow.

"See!" he said. "I told you your hair would be much better like that." He stood back squinting and tilting his head. "You know, you look really beautiful. I was really getting sick of looking at all those teensy dolls with falsies propped up in this dump. Shit."

"Oh."

We walked across the space between the cafeteria and the math building, his easy hand on my shoulder leading me to the steps on the cafeteria's South wall where we sat, through divine intervention, down.

He took my algebra book and opened it. Then he asked, "What do you think you're going to learn out of this?"

"Algebra?" I hoped that was right.

". . . What else?"

"What?" I couldn't function from the daze.

"What do you expect to really learn?"

I tried to think of the right answer and it took so long that he began to laugh with mystifying abandon, hitting his thigh with the side of his hand, his primary eyes glinting out at the confusion he'd thrown me into so simply. Finally, I got it.

"You schmuck!" I cried then.

He abruptly stopped and asked closely, "Schmuck?"

"Oh . . . never mind." I prayed to retreat into blushes, only I can't blush.

"Come on." He was impatient. "What's it mean? I want to know. Now. Tell me."

". . .Well . . . It's Yiddish for prick."

"Yiddish, huh?" he pondered. "You Jewish?"

"My father is . . ." I said. "My mother's from Louisiana —Cajun."

"Oh, like Evangeline," he said. "I've never met anyone like you before." He tilted his head. "What's it like?"

"I don't know . . ." I thought. I was still trying to think of right answers. One of them was "boring," which I said.

"Boring?" He looked at me.

It wasn't boring at that moment.

"What are you doing after school?" he asked.

"Walking home . . ." I said.

"I'll walk you," he said.

"Oh."

The murky gumminess I had tried to join was now thrown into open chaos and splendid days. How could I have avoided everything that I had known all along? Aces' starkness tripped me into real life so much that I would have forgotten to eat except that Louie brought us candy. The shadows in the rafters of the Polar Palace were knocked out by the noonday sun, which fell around us like a moat. When the bell rang for fifth period, going away from him seemed awful. He said to meet him at Pop's after school, that he'd be busy until then. So I went to fifth period, and for reasons having to do with Aces, it didn't seem likely that he would be busy with Le Conte.

Everyone in the entire school said hi to me on the way to my class, including Gary, who actually approached me and asked, as Julie had the day before to Aces, if I were going to the dance that night.

"No," I said, my eyes narrowing. So it turned out that power was the quality of knowing what you liked. An odd thing for power to be.

Aces and I fought it out for a couple of weeks until he finally shrugged and decided that my fast notion that I was a virgin and would be forever was too much trouble for him to wrench me out of. When he wasn't tangling me up in passionate kisses and blowing in my ear, he kept me enraptured with an almost professional elegance through which he recounted his stories.

He told me he'd lived in Birmingham, Alabama, right before coming to Southern California. His mother's family and his mother lived there and he would still be there if it hadn't been for the school and the principal. The principal had accused him of stealing something and had tried to hit him, which was standard procedure, only Aces grabbed a chair and broke three of the principal's ribs and then set the office on fire. The principal escaped just in time. They thought he might need a man's guidance, so they sent him back to live with his father, an actor, in Hollywood.

It had been his father, he told me, who'd given him the ridiculous name of Rhett with the already waiting Butler like "Gone With the Wind." Aces had had aces tattooed on his arms when he was "over in Liverpool" with his father on tour and since then that had been his name. Not Rhett. His father had been in troupes of touring actors since Aces was little, they'd been together a long time. So Aces was sent to Hollywood to live again with his father.

★ 69 ★

Only he didn't live with his father at all. Aces lived in the Hollywood Stables, which was in the same hill the Hollywood sign is on. They rent horses there for tourists and people who like to ride around the foothill brush (where no holly grows) and play that they're cowboys. Aces lived in with the horses in the hay. Sometimes it still stuck in his black Levis. I could hardly believe it, but it was true.

"He shovels horseshit," Louie told me, city-stunned. "He says he *likes* the smell."

"I *love* the smell up there in the morning," he told me. "It smells like hay, fresh."

One night he came when my parents weren't there in a stolen car which he was determined to take me for a ride in. I knew he stole cars—he told me he did—but actually riding in one turned me fear-livid.

"Uh . . . what about the police?"

"Oh, come on," he pleaded. "Just around the block."

The jerky ride around the block was the most difficult journey of my life before or since and broke my love apart. When we got back, I told him I didn't like it. It was too much and I guessed I'd have to give him up. It broke my heart.

He didn't come to school the next day or call and neither did Louie. In fact, they both vanished until about 10 days later Louie was up at Pop's (where I looked every day for Aces), drinking Coke, waiting empty for me.

"Where is he?" I asked.

"Busted."

"For the car?" He didn't answer. "Grand Theft Auto?"

"No. . . ." He stared vacantly before him. "Grand Theft Yacht."

"A yacht!"

"Yeah, we were down in Balboa and he thought he'd like to hot-wire one of those yachts and take it over to Tahiti. Only the Coast Guard caught us before we were even out of the harbor."

"How come you're not busted?"

"He told them . . ."

"What?"

"He told them I was just a kid and didn't know what I was doing." He stuck his straw into his Coke ice so hard he bent the straw irrevocably.

"Oh."

Passion and high skies were scattered before the remaining Le Conte days and after a while I stopped hoping for him and prepared to graduate with the rest. The smell of Tweed, though, still reminds me of the time when I didn't make sense and a dropped panic of thankfulness glints golden through the scent in gratitude for Aces' laughter that afternoon with straight hair.

I can't remember when I heard that the Polar Palace had burned to the ground, but no scrap of sweet longing flutters even momentarily for those Friday nights of white. I hadn't liked it with it's damn silly music and rented skates.

And you know, I'd much rather go to Tahiti.

SECRET AMBITION

My friend Tina and I were talking again last night. Sometimes we only call for one minute but wind up for an hour comparing notes. Our lives are unexpected and we have pretty much lost any bitterness we may once have thought necessary because things didn't turn out like it says. Tina is not married with children and a station wagon. Instead she's a kind of enormously paid companion to a fabulous, handsome, wealthy, talented young man whom she loves but cannot make love to because she "can't see any future in it." He loves her, too, but goes places with starlets and takes drugs and only calls to tell her, at 6 a.m. not to "let me get too crazy."

"Just go to bed," she says, "and things will be all right."

"Why do I hate all the women I fuck?" he asked her lately.

"Why do you fuck the women you hate?" she replied, just as his girl friend returned to the table.

"I just can't be Katharine Hepburn," Tina told me.

"Yes, you can," I said. "You're doing it."

"But it's too hard," she said.

"Yeah, I know," I said.

"It's just impossible," she went on. We've stopped using the word "rough," that was last year.

Last year we took a drive one morning, the first morning we seriously became friends or unseriously. It was a beautiful Sunday, windy, and we drove up the coast to Ojai, which is inland and just South of Santa Barbara. I hadn't been to Ojai since I was about 9 and had been at the mercy of my parents who went and participated in the Ojai Music Festival each year. Each year we visited an old lady; she let us stay in her house. Her house was made of stone and she had a goat and everlastings and orange trees and a dirt road. In her study was a knife brought back from the Orient by her brother in 1903 or something and it had a carved red ruby handle which I coveted each year until finally I stole it. I was so overwhelmed by what I had done that I buried the knife in our back yard when I got home and never looked at it again. But the way she lived, her house, the old bungalow graciousness and tiled bathrooms with enormous bathtubs and yellow curtains, the kitchen and pantry and the place they folded sheets— it stayed with me. Tina and I drove up there, but I didn't tell her about that house, I just said that Ojai was beautiful.

I hoped it still was beautiful because it was a long drive and Tina was driving. But it was even more beautiful than I'd remembered and there was a lake now added and these gigantic haciendas that I hadn't remembered for sale. "Gee," Tina said. "I'd like to just get some land up here and sleep on the ground."

"Not me." I couldn't see it.

"I don't know," I said, on the phone now to Tina, thinking about her handsome boss, who would always get into trouble and break fragile things.

"You know," I said, "it's always been my secret ambition to get one of those stone houses up in Ojai."

"Really?" She sounded a trace lightened. "God, it's beautiful up there."

"Yeah, well, what I wanted to do was have this house and all these cats and orange trees and even a goat. A stone house with a dirt road."

"Oh, that sounds fantastic," she said. She could see it clear as day.

"And the thing was, my secret ambition has always been to be a spinster."

"Yours too?"

"And then we'd have this house and every now and then we'd be visited by M. and other flashy people but then they'd go away and we'd have this house and the sun would set and you'd be able to smell orange blossoms and we'd never die."

"Gee, that sounds terrific. Let's do it."

"O.K.," I agreed.

So that's what we're going to do if we can ever get out of Hollywood. And we both felt so much better, we met for a drink at Musso's and ran into some friends.

SCARLET FEVER

We had a governess once who had been a practical nurse, so when I suddenly developed a fever of 105° and a red rash on my stomach, she knew it was Scarlet Fever.

Luckily, penicillin had just been perfected, so I lay on my back for six weeks and listened to soap operas with a black-and-blue ass.

The house was quarantined. They actually came and put a quarantine sign on the door like the plague while I lay upstairs smugly listening to "Our Gal Sunday" and eating cupcakes.

Before I had Scarlet Fever I had been unable to spell, and it was only through dint of writing a word hundreds of times that I could even come close to getting it right on a test. It just didn't make sense to me, and there was no relation between what a word sounded like and how it was spelled and don't tell me there is. I can spell in Italian, so I know. But once I "fell behind" in spelling, that was the end of it.

It's strange to hear my friends' astonishment the first time they receive a letter from me and find the word *sacriledgess*—but how *is* it spelled?

By the time I graduated from Hollywood High, I dreaded people's discovery about my spelling and wondered if I was going to have to be a house maid because of it. When I got to L.A.C.C. and took history, the teacher said, "Your papers are very good, but your spelling, I'm afraid . . ."

". . . makes me look stupid?" I finished, noticing her fluster over how she could say it nicely.

"Yes." She looked relieved.

"I had Scarlet Fever," I told her.

THE SHEIK

Remember Rudolph Valentino? His most famous role was in "The Sheik," a movie in which he lunged, nostrils flaring, into the lives and dreams of the world. The Sheik is Hollywood High's mascot. Valentino died of a burst appendix because he refused to go to the hospital (too brave), and like the Jim Morrison phrase which occurs to me whenever I think about some foolhardy, glamorous, and fatal adventure, he was "trapped in a prison of his own devise." In fact, Hollywood herself was always trapped in a prison of her own devise, but don't think about that (because if you do you'll start wondering what devises are, anyway, if not prisons, and if you're going to have to be trapped in one, it might as well be a Hollywood devise).

Today is one of those cold Hollywood winter days—it's not supposed to get hotter than 60 degrees, and the sky is gray. It will rain for sure tomorrow, the weatherman says, and the longing for a real rain is a Los Angeles undercurrent. When the weather gets like this and sometimes when I smell rain, the past appears in all its confusion and doubt and pleasure, and my high school days surface. They come dancing in like a well-rehearsed chorus line and, unlike most people my age who claim to recall Elvis when they think of high school or think of high school when they hear Elvis, I can only see faces, clothes, and hear the laughter of the girls who went to my school, and the feelings—the aches and pirouettes and joys come not from music, books, fear of finals, hatred or love of teachers—but from the people who sat next to me or who I saw in the halls during the years I spent in Hollywood High.

At the Troubadour bar, a smart music business bar with hardly any Mafia, people sit around sometimes and recall their high school days. I go there, too, and listen but never attempt to describe my high school days, which had nothing to do with music and nothing to do with hot rods, nor acne, greasy hair, flunking, or being ugly. Strange thoughts sometimes enter my head when I listen, though, slightly drunk—because sometimes people sit and try to top each other on how much more ugly and forsaken and dependent upon music for any interest whatsoever in their lives they were than the other. The implication is that they can talk about it now since they are past all that, having achieved the security and positively unshakable position of where they are now. Like Einstein joking about flunking math. Only with these guys, their position now depends on who their friends are—and their friends, sitting across the table from them—are telling them how ugly and stupid *they* used to be before they sat down at this table in the Troubadour. The thing about prisons of your own devise is that most of them are designed for traveling and can be taken anywhere, even from small towns in Michigan where you were ugly, all the way to glamorous rock shows where you have to have a pass to get backstage.

In my high school, I was pretty and smart and scornful and impatient. I scorned American history, which I thought was capitalist propaganda; I despised art class because it had nothing to do with adventure; I hated gym because I hated lines. I was usually triumphant and had fun being wide-eyed and sarcastic in class.

But nothing that was really going on in my high school happened because of classes of the administration's arrangements. The *people* were what was going on. And *The People* were the girls.

The girls at our school, and I'm sure the girls who attend Hollywood High to this day, were extraordinarily beautiful. And there were about 20 of them who separately would cause you to let go of reason. Together—and they stayed pretty much together—they were the downfall of any serious attempt at school in the accepted sense, and everyone knew it. They were too beautiful for a high school—they were too romantic, too fiery, too interested in designs—and the school was in constant chaos with whispers of their love affairs, their refusals to go along with anything that interrupted their games, scandals, tears, laughter—peals of it in empty corridors while everyone else sat in class, their condescension so brutal as to be unmistakable to authority. Beauty so matter-of-fact that school

★ 79 ★

monitors and disciplinary teachers aided the girls in their intrigues instead of trying to impose order.

A blonde girl with Estonian slanting green eyes and high, wide cheekbones made an English teacher apologize in front of an entire class for telling her to be quiet during a test—her pout was devastating and tragic and universally personal. As a measure against this constant disobedience and as, I suppose, an American effort to prove that "all men are created equal" and therefore should equally obey the laws, the administration decided to disband these 20; it said the sororities these girls were in were undemocratic and they would have to stop. An assembly was called in the auditorium, not by the administration and not even by the girls themselves—it was a spontaneous uprising by the rest of us who were not going to have this fantastic show dismantled and taken away from us. The girls' principal publicly changed her mind.

In most high schools, you learn social things along with the rest of it. In mine, I learned irrevocably that beauty is power and the usual bastions of power are powerless when confronted by beauty. Most of us, even though we were ignored by these girls, were on the girls' side and wanted them to succeed. To have one of them in a class made life much more interesting, since they never became quite tame, and a teacher trying to explain that success depended on practice, diligence, sincerity, and going to bed early was flagrantly and silently contradicted by the girl sitting in the third row, second seat, who would be staring out the window or at the clock. There were 20 of them who were unquestionably staggering and another 50 or so who were cause for alarm, or would have been in a more diluted atmosphere.

These were the daughters of people who were beautiful, brave, and foolhardy, who had left their homes and traveled to movie dreams. In the Depression, when most of them came here, people with brains went to New York and people with faces came West. After being born of parents who believed in physical beauty as a fact of power, and being born beautiful themselves, these girls were then raised in California, where statistically the children grow taller, have better teeth and are stronger than anywhere else in the country. When they reach the age of 15 and their beauty arrives, it's very exciting—like coming into an inheritance and, as with inheritances, it's fun to be around when they first come into the money and watch how they spend it and on what.

The guys who went to our school weren't their equals and were for the most part as in awe of them as everyone else. Two weren't. There were these two guys who were immune. These two guys thought the whole thing was pretty funny. The girls adored them. There were other guys, somewhat like them, but they were not immune to all of them—there was always at least one they took seriously. But the two guys never were attracted to that prison which others found so delicious. They seemed to be on a different track, to care about something, but what it was was a mystery to most of us —they weren't interested in *school*, that was obvious. They seemed to care about the sea and were usually there in convenient weather. They weren't surfers, but when I recall them, I never think of them wearing anything but cut-off jeans with their faces toward a six-o'clock sun in one of those unbelievably corny pink and orange sunsets on a turquoise sea, their bare feet on cooling sand.

When the sky turns gray, the colonnade of palm trees lining the Sunset Boulevard side of Hollywood High looks cross and sulky. But when the sky was its occasional non-smoggy, dry, clean, cloudless self, Hollywood High made sense, and even teachers would gaze quietly out at the shining palm tree tops blowing in the breeze. And when summer came and we went to the beach after a dismal morning of summer school, the palm trees high above the sea on the Palisades would look black against an aggressive sky which drained away all color of anything that was forced to silhouette against it, only waiting for a moment of weakness to swallow it up completely and only let there be electric blue trying to be white. Lying on your stomach in the hot sand . . . I don't think there were any of us who seriously thought life could be any better. We *knew* "The Sheik" was a movie, we knew that the air of unreality—like an Italian Roman Slave Girl B flick, that California, the Pacific, the white beaches, the sky so blue it yearned, that the palm trees, the banana leaves, the rounded Thirties buildings, were part of the trance. We were hot, the sea was one long wave to be ridden in, our skins were dark, and time even stopped now and then and let things shimmer since time, too, is affected by beauty and will stop sometimes for a moment. We didn't know, as kids in other schools seemed to, what we were supposed to be, but we knew that somehow we were being taught something about life and that it couldn't get much better. And when the sun began to set and we'd gather our things and walk silently back to the cars, we only wondered how the waves would be tomorrow in baked, half-conscious curiosity.

In the fall, around the middle of September, school

would start again for real. The 20 were more beautiful than before, but then we all were. The two immune guys wouldn't show up, though, until it got too cold to go to the beach—which is why, undoubtedly, they were both expelled before they graduated. Wait—one of them was expelled for trying to burn the school down one night with a girl who is now a movie star but was then mischievous and alertly beautiful. Tom, his name was. And then I remember he haunted the beach until about November, when he got a job on a freighter and went to South America, which was the last I heard of him for years.

The other guy, Mark, wasn't expelled, now that I think of it—he quit, got lonely, probably. He had always had this magical air of tragedy beneath his carelessness and grace and charm. Where Tom was funny and sarcastic, Mark was illusive and quick. Tom was dark and strong; Mark was blond, green-eyed and lithe. All the girls' parents were smart enough to sense anarchy in those two, and most of the girls were forbidden to see them. And we, of the chorus and audience, would watch and appreciate and know. Fans.

It is ten years since I took my last final in summer school at Hollywood and graduated, since I dropped a cigarette into the toilet in the girls' room or silently watched one of the 20 perform. . . . Still, though, when the sky turns gray and a certain smell tinges the air in Hollywood, I can make Carolyn stand there just from the scent. If I told you what she looked like, you'd say I was too extravagant, that there is no such thing. But people who went there then will tell you that I'm not exaggerating and that Carolyn existed just as I describe her. They might say that maybe they didn't recognize how unanswerable her beauty was because of her almost complete silence and lack of vitality; they might confuse beauty with popularity, but they would not be able to argue with my description since it isn't a flight of fancy. Out of the 20, Carolyn was my favorite, and she proved absolutely that beauty was power since her power could have come from nothing else—not imagination, kindness, wit, not anything else—only her face.

Carolyn possessed the colors. She *was* the colors of the Arabian Nights, dusk in Cairo . . . a children's illustration. She had one talent—exaggerating the colors until everything else in sight looked faded; maybe she ate colors when she entered a place and took them all in her. Her skin was dark and warm—flawless, clear with mauve cheeks like hidden roses. I was amazed once to find that hazel eyes meant eyes that changed colors, too. Carolyn had hazel hair; her hair was thick, silky, waved carelessly and slid with a separate gravity. . . . forward and . . . back. Her hair was hazel or opalescent—it changed colors in different lights or depending on what colors were nearby to fade out. Her lashes were dark, so her hair must have been dark, though sometimes it looks, as she stands here and I breathe the smell of rain, it looks light green or bronze or copper /orange with her lowered eyes she usually can't bring herself to focus. Because when she does open her eyes and face you—that's when everything else doesn't just look gray or washed out; sometimes when she opens her eyes, everything else disappears.

If Carolyn owned the colors, her eyes were confusing. Her eyes were the brazen blue—the same color—as the sky in back of the palm trees on the Palisades in summer—the blue that burned away at her pupils as the sky would have done to the Palisades palms—the color blue that was so bright sometimes you had to squint. When blue's that bright, it yearns to be white—and white is supposed to be the absence of color. People aren't those colors. I know. They don't really have orange and turquoise sunsets over the ocean, either. She was a captive in the Sheik's harem, a stranger from the land beyond the sea who never learned to speak nor the purpose of speech, and it would have been more sensible if she'd been made a mute since occasionally she would unfold and stretch, her hair would . . . slide down her back, her small round hands clench, her cupid-bow mouth would unsuccessfully try to suppress a yawn, and her tiny snow teeth would show—then she'd fold back up, sigh, and say, "Fuck, man, I wish today was Friday."

People took care of Carolyn. Usually, her sorority sisters, but if they weren't there, then anyone who was would automatically assume responsibility. It wasn't that she was retarded; it was just that she couldn't scrape up even a sliver of interest in the proceedings and couldn't see why she should, and no one else could think of a good enough reason, either—at least, one that made sense when you looked at her. Her friends would make out her program, schedule her classes, choose her on gym teams and not require participation, take her to the beach with them, take her shopping (her clothes were subdued—gray or dark greens or maybe they just looked that way to me).

On days when it starts to drizzle and the cars slip by like paper tearing—days like today—we all had to stay inside during lunch. Inside in hot, sweaty rooms getting cranky and driving unlucky teachers to madness. Our

hair would fall and lose its curl, our skin would shine—
our tempers would go, or we'd just start giggling eter-
nally and trying to murder the person in front of us.
Carolyn retained perfection because very little of her
depended on artifice—her hair never went straight in
the rain, nothing like that. She would sit, stare straight
ahead, yawn, stretch, and sink back with her chin in her
hand and again stare. She was a C student; she passed
from grade to grade with total apathy. Was she staring
into another country? Was it warmer? Was she draped
in silks, did she have alabaster cases scented with jasmine and filled with pearls, rubies, emeralds—gems
who owned their own lights and couldn't fade? Women
like her were carried, their rosy feet never touched the
streets, only touched the cool marble hallways or
scented waters of their baths in that country beyond
the sea in whatever land where she belonged.

Immune Tom seemed to have an understanding with
Carolyn and could even make her laugh—he had an
instinct with aliens. Mark was unsympathetic to Carolyn and even closer—she would be near him and Tom,
and Mark, who was sharp and sensitive to conversation,
saw not only color fade by her presence but also sometimes words. They were often with her, she was one of
the 20—*that* nobody would argue about. In fact, if you
asked anyone in school who the most beautiful girl was,
mostly, I think they would finally say Carolyn, simply
because she was nothing else. We who watched were at
first captivated by the blondes, the curls, the bouncy
and vivacious smiles—but in time, we became jaded
and blasé with ordinary heiresses with American fortunes, and Carolyn inherited orange and pink sunsets
on turquoise oceans and a couch carved of sandalwood,

a husband of mythical wealth and peculiar and subtle tastes . . . but even in her own country Carolyn would have been of doubtful origin, even if her own country were on this planet.

The time from the end of summer when we returned to school—the time when we lost our tans and watched the sky turn gray—was a downhill season and would worsen and worsen until Christmas, a sad and hopeless occasion imposed on an unwilling land by the rest of the country. Banana leaves and reindeer. Hollywood, the master of spun-out fantasies, gave up on Christmas with hardly a shrug. A 70 degree Christmas morning put us out of sorts; try saying "Merry Christmas" to someone watering his lawn in shorts. Hollywood has attempted and even succeeded with the impossible many times, but Christmas has never been one of them.

I saw Mark not long ago for the first time since those days in the Troubadour. I didn't recognize him, but he remembered me. I wonder if I've changed so little in ten years; he was unrecognizable. His hair was past his shoulders, he had a beard, a thicker body, he was losing hair on top—the same green eyes. And he still had a kind of charm and elegance and a reminder of sadness. I felt strange talking to him, letting him buy me a drink, as though we were real people now and not the fans and players I had once taken for granted.

I imagined that Mark had become an adventurer, but, in fact, he had been a junkie. When he quit school, he traveled around and it just sort of happened, he told me with the humorless intensity of an ex-junkie. Tom was now a successful painter with a painting in the Museum of Modern Art, Mark told me, and Tom lived in a remote, difficult town on the Mediterranean coast

★ 87 ★

and had married a Sicilian eight years before who spoke no more English now than when they were first married, which was about three words. We laughed. He recounted other stories—mundane, unworthy squanderings of inherited fortunes of beauty, mostly. I asked about Carolyn.

She was dead, he told me. Died only two months before, in fact. OD'd.

She had bad monthly cramps, he explained, and, as I remembered that unlikely piece of information, I was surprised; I hadn't thought of that in so long, but one of the facts of Carolyn was her violent cramps which kept her on the nurse's cot every month for three days. She had very strong pain pills which she took more of than were prescribed even then, but they never really took away the pain. On that day, she took three times as many pills as she was supposed to, and some amphetamine because she had an appointment. She had been unhappy, he said, she was on her second divorce. Anyway, she took the pills, got dressed and put on her make-up. When her friend came in that afternoon and found Carolyn on the couch, at first she thought Carolyn was asleep. But she had been dead since eight a.m.

"With her make-up on, though," I said.

"Yeah," Mark said, "she was always a bitch with the old turquoise eye shadow, no matter how many downers she'd been taking."

And so now it's raining and the scent can make Carolyn appear. I keep hearing Jim Morrison sing over and over, "trapped in a prison of her own devise," and the cars on the wet street outside. The lesson of the Sheik —determined to carry on despite pain, not to stay home, too proud not to venture forth—the power of physical beauty creating a tragedy instead of just a shame, even if it's only a Hollywood devise. Now, no one will sit, staring into Persia—now when it's raining. The Sheik is extinguished by dark skies and forecasts. And now it's almost Christmas, an impatiently suffered imposition tolerated only until the hot clear skies return with shining palms, and the beautiful, scornful eyes of the new 20 gaze out of the windows of Hollywood High.

SANTA SOFIA

The way to a proper understanding of a people is through their art, they say.

There are Greeks in L.A. They are here as part of the settlements of Mediterranean people who came to California because they were starving where they were and had heard California was like home, only fertile. There are a lot of Basque sheepherders up around Bakersfield. So many, in fact, that they have a Basque Catholic priest to hear their confessions. There are Italians growing grapes and just plain Italians. And there are the Greeks.

The Greek Orthodox Church down on Pico and Normandy is in that section of town where none of my peers would ever find themselves because it's not near any freeway exits and besides, what's down there? It is still filled each Sunday at High Mass with Greeks. The choir when I went was led, to my surprise, by the man who used to teach "Orchestra" at Le Conte Jr. High. I hadn't thought he could be Greek when he led the band at school, but here he conducted the a cappella voices in their intricate quarter-tones like heaven from the rafters.

My parents encouraged my interest in Byzantine mosaics and knew of the Greek Orthodox Church where there might be some, so we went to High Mass the next Sunday.

It was a florid ceremony in English mostly with a podium that looked like a baroque gold ship's mast. The sermon was about greed and my adolescence rankled against this topic delivered from gold plaster of Paris. There were no mosaics, just paintings and cigar-box-esque murals all over inside of the domes. We rose and sank to our knees like everyone else and kissed the priest's hands on our way out like everyone else.

Then we followed everyone across the street to the Greek Delicatessen and waited amid older ladies in tight black, little kids with large, eyelashed eyes, modern married girls with almost fashionable hairdos and dresses, handsome men and older men and real old, old men.

We bought white crumbly feta cheese, ham, rolls, another kind of cheese and olives. My father got half a bottle of cold retsina.

We took our booty back across the street to the car and, like everyone else, tore open the packages and ate. High Mass had made everyone hungry and I broke apart my roll and stuffed it with ham and feta and the other cheese and tasted the green oily olives which must have been the same on a Greek cliff tending goats as they were on Pico.

"Try this," my father said, handing me the retsina.

"Ew, it smells like turpentine," I said squeamishly.

"That's what it *is*," my father said.

"Oh."

I drank it and the day changed colors. I tasted Athens and I knew what it was like to be Greek like everybody else that day after High Mass, and for me, the way to a people is through assuaged hunger.

The resin keeps the wines from spoiling when they're up in the mountains with the herd. It tastes like pine trees and goes with craggy mountains. Greeks must be wonderful, I thought, as I took my second gulp from the bottle and acquired a taste more primary than art considers proper.

★

INGENUES,
THUNDERBIRD GIRLS
AND THE
NEIGHBORHOOD BELLE:
A CONFUSING TRAGEDY

Even today I am cast down by not being invited to things, but in high school I was so damaged on the subject that I knew that I wasn't going to make it if I had to go through on the prescribed route. What they had in mind for kids graduating from Le Conte was that except for a few kids who weren't in the district, everyone went to Hollywood High. In Hollywood High your first year was spent taking English, History, Math, Spanish and electives, but if you were not suffering from the protective covering of being a wallflower, you were at the mercy of your cunty peers who whispered and squealed and giggled and screamed about who was being rushed by what sorority. Even today I am sometimes nearly heartbroken not to be invited to something, so you can imagine how the prospect of sororities looked to me at the age of 14 when I had no control over my sanity. The only way out of it was not to be there, and I was not schizophrenic enough not to be there while I actually physically was there, so I removed myself physically and lied. I gave a fake address and went to a peaceful residential school called Marshall High, which was out of my district but not too far by bus.

My first year of high school, therefore, was spent at Marshall where I got good grades and a vague idea of what it must be like to grow up in a small town and go to a small-town high school. I was a little too dramatic for that place—my high-school picture shows that—but there was not the power plays and sharp edges that I saw inevitable at Hollywood, and it was a gentle, coddling, evasionary tactic which I recommend to anyone whose nature is not to face hard things. Skip town.

"But how will you toughen up and mature?" they ask.

"No," I say. "Who says you have to mature? I don't want to get old and die. I just want to die."

"But . . ."

"Why mature?"

"But . . . you can't do that!" They are scandalized.

"I'm doing it, though."

I've always done it. I don't believe in facing pain unless it's the kind you like.

At the end of "Death Takes a Holiday," Fredric March drapes Grazia, the ingenue played by Evelyn Venable, in a cape, and before our eyes they disappear into a glow of light at the top of some stairs. March plays Death, who has disguised himself as Prince Skirki to take a few days off, leave his Kingdom, and come to visit

Life in order to discover why people cling to it so much and what Love is. No one, during Death's holiday, dies. Even a guy who jumps off the Eiffel Tower survives. The house Prince Skirki visits belongs to a wealthy American family (in the middle of the 1934 depression) who are innocent and flattered by this Continental guest. At a party in his honor a neighbor belle flirts with him on the patio until she looks into his eyes, sees death, shrieks and flees. She is too practical to love Death, even though he is so beautiful. But Grazia, the excruciating camellia petal of a daughter of the house, is such an ingenue that she decides she sees beyond what is in his eyes and to prove her love, she insists on following Death into his kingdom and abandoning her fiancé who is a nice guy. The solemn inevitability stays in the air long after the television has moved on to other things.

Thirty-six years after Evelyn Venable saw past Death, I sat in Schwab's drinking coffee with my actor/race-track friends whom I've known all my life but can't remember where from and we're discussing impossible possibilities, frittering away the afternoon. The question is: "What would you do if you were going to the gas chamber and instead of giving you a last meal they gave you a last movie?"

" 'Lassie Come Home,' " says Eddie immediately. Eddie is pure of heart.

"No, no, no," says Louie who's a sharp cookie, "get one of those interminable Warhol flicks. That way you die of boredom before they can nail you."

"How about 'Death Takes a Holiday'?" asks Jimmy.

There is a pause while the perfection of this idea is appreciated. Not only is there the miracle hope of reprieve, but there is also Evelyn Venable as a possibility on the other side.

"She married her cameraman," Jimmy imparts.

"Jesus . . . she was beautiful," Eddie recalls, and we all think of her strange eyes until Eddie, the pure of heart, brings us back with "Do you think they'd let you have a double feature? Then you could see 'Lassie Come Home' too."

Only I remember the neighborhood belle who fled from the patio. She was a kind of brazen girl; she flirted and insinuated shamelessly. But flirting with disaster is not the same as courting it like the ingenue did or not noticing it like the sorority girls. The sorority girls have no place in their souls for the unknown.

The neighborhood belle is all I'll ever be. Knowing where disaster lies and getting as far away as possible from it. I had no qualms lying about my address when I went to Marshall, though usually I'm a coward about being found out.

You would not have found me in Berlin after the Reichstag fire for longer than it took to pack. Cowards are the fittest, it must be, since they're so adept at avoiding extinction.

Heroes and Ingenues must be mutants because they never last past the middle of Act Three. (If this is a tragedy, and it usually is.)

Meanwhile, I entered Hollywood High in the 11th grade with enough plans going so that I could skip a grade and get out early. I knew that Hollywood was going to be hard even without sororities, because the absolute necessity of high-school life I had chosen to renounce—the best friend.

If I'd gone to Hollywood that first year, I would have

had a chance to wind up, if not in a sorority, at least with a best friend. Avoiding the whole rushing torture meant that by the time I entered Hollywood, everyone would already have paired up and so I'd be lonely. Sane but lonely. See, a mature person would have faced the music and gotten a best friend for their efforts instead of having the ant and the grasshopper Calvinistic morality play ending of "Well, since you didn't plan for winter, you're going to starve, so there." So I planned to escape at least half a year early, knowing that my immaturity had to be paid for and that now it was winter, no best friend.

According to Calvin, Sally should not have shown up at the very moment I entered Hollywood, but she did and there was my "best friend." She was an ingenue and they're always screwing up the works, which is why she came just at that moment when I rightfully deserved to be, friendless.

If Sally had been ugly or socially retarded, maybe it wouldn't have been such a coup for my side, the side of evasion. But Sally was beautiful and in the high school she'd transferred from she'd been in the best sorority and one of the most popular girls. She was also smart. And she was rich. It was love at first sight.

It was a romance. Everything to do with Sally was a romance, that was how she was. She wasn't one of those cheerfully sunny girls who bring spring into the room with them. She was way too Garbo, sullen and tragic. Ingenues are tragic. It's their best friends who flee shrieking from the patio.

Because Sally was so quiet, hardly anyone saw her at first. I also think it was because she willed herself to disappear that the sorority sisters who sometimes made

an exception and rushed a newcomer in the 11th grade
forgot to look at her. With me, she came dramatically
into focus on the third day because I saw her smile and
her smile from that Garbo sadness broke the heavens
open in choral arpeggios and the guy sitting next to me
just sat there after she'd gone past. Just sat there.

By the time Sally had finished the play she was doing
at night and had the energy to look presentable at
school, it was too late for the Deltas. She had decided
that clubs were "bourgeois" (her favorite word besides
"depressed") and, besides, we had begun our long association with the Thunderbird Girls that outclassed Hollywood High as though it had never had any power at
all. Though it took me some getting used to realize that
instead of trying to talk to peers about hair, I was now
in racy Sunset Strip hot, fast company talking about
Sally. Because right from the start it was my friendship
with Sally which made me accepted in that heady mi-
lieu. Ingenues are what make the world go round, un-
fortunately for Calvin.

She was also an actress, which made the discussions
of her even more real because her future could be
anything. She was a good actress, she was brilliant at
pretense. She was more real in suspended disbelief
than most things are just standing there. Her body, the
one that you touch with your hands, unfolded into
other people, and she was so sunk into performance
that things got funneled into moments as hard as diamonds. The moments shimmered and hung in the air,
they were at her fingertips, they were her craft.

In the room where Monroe died there were boxes of
unopened new clothes stacked haphazardly on the
floor, and there doesn't seem to be any furniture other
than an unmade bed. My family was passing through a

provincial French vacation spot, Nimes, in bourgeois August Holidays—things were so bourgeois, in fact, that I could hear Sally saying the word. She savored French and spoke it well. The streets of Nimes were crowded with summerers, but the newspaper headlines greeted us blackly: *"Marilyn Est Morte!"* They didn't say which Marilyn because everyone knew which Marilyn. Her startled face tried to smile from the newspaper to us. It was as ingenuous as a caged angel only now she was smashed from within. An accident, they decided to say.

Sally had that same missed beat in her face from which Marilyn derived her special tragic wonder. But they both fell into the "torch singer" category, loving the wrong thing, loving beyond what they see in Death's eyes.

On the other hand, Sally and I had fun nearly all the time. We never fought or felt the other had done something slighting. There were no misunderstandings.

Sally, though, never had misunderstandings.

Ingenues don't.

Sally's acting class was where she met Wendy and from Wendy we got to know all the Thunderbird Girls. Like those Mexican sandpaper boxes they rub against each other as musical instrument to make the sound of whhhhhisssssh, we were in Café Society at night and school in the daytime. We were both virgins, too, as we drank in the Garden of Allah bar with fake I.D.s and tried to be clever around men twice as old as us. We had no more business suddenly finding ourselves in Wendy's jaded, fast world than we did on the freeway on foot. Things whihhissshed past us dangerously and we watched, as though through a glass shell like unborn twins.

Wendy was 24 and she had a kind of open-handed

nature and was flattered when such an ingenue as Sally showed guileless admiration for everything Wendy was about. Wendy was exotically birdlike and unique. They were all similarly unique, those girls; they all drove the same kind of car. Wendy had very small bones and the face of a tempestuous and beautiful child. She had a beautiful figure, which was cinched in at the waist and squashed together at the breasts, and she bought all her clothes at Jax, which made sexy-starlet clothes. Her hair came halfway down to her waist and was dark auburn and tangled and like a lion's mane always. I never saw it combed. It always looked like she'd just risen from a bed of passion that only she could have inspired. And finally, she was the master of brilliant mean tricks, and the recounter of past coups.

Wendy's sister married so well that she could afford to put a private detective on her bridegroom's trail the morning of their honeymoon and when, six months later, her husband at last committed an indiscretion, she cleaned up. She even got a house with a lavender pool. Wendy's sister was a myth and spoken of with respect; she had won in a hard gate.

All of Wendy's friends were perfectly gorgeous. They were all pioneers of diaphragm libertinism and they all, except for Wendy's sister, who cleaned up and finished with a Mercedes and a Continental, had Thunderbirds.

It was all wrong in the movie "Butterfield 8" because Elizabeth Taylor was a kind of promiscuous New York one of those girls and she should have ended in a Thunderbird, not a Sunbeam. A Sunbeam just looks like a Thunderbird and everyone knows it's the details that matter in things like that.

The only ones who don't have to pay attention to the

details are the ingenues. Current styles are beneath the timeless flames of love into which they disappear in the end. So Sally, who moved among those girls and who was loved and taken care of, only acted like them as much as she needed to for their acceptance.

Wendy and I became friends over Sally and long after we both had to give Sally up because she was too hard, we remained friends. Sally was too tragic to appreciate Wendy's raw anecdotes of the mean tricks accomplished over the years, the mean tricks she'd played on the schmucks. Wendy classified men into two categories—Nice Guys and Schmucks. 90% were Schmucks.

Sally and I used to be Wendy's guests at the Beverly Hills Health Club, and there we would lounge around naked in the sauna and Wendy would tell about the time some schmuck had the gall to not just stand her up but to telephone the next day with hardly an apology and then tell her he was bringing a friend over that night and would she please make guacamole because that was his favorite thing. Sally's friend, Lois, came over that afternoon to best plot revenge, and so that night came to be called "Remember the time we peed in the guacamole."

"Oh, God," Sally would say, experiencing the actual taste through her actress senses.

"And then, my dear," Wendy finished, "we told him right when we were leaving what we'd done and locked the door on him and his friend!"

"Tell about the douche powder," I'd say. I liked to hear them over.

"I told you that one already," Wendy would say, her auburn tangles damp from the sauna. The other ladies were all ears, waiting to hear about the douche powder, as we sweated together and rubbed Braisovol on our faces to annihilate pimples.

"Tell it again," I'd say.

"I haven't heard it," Sally would say, though she had, she just never listened.

"That was the night I picked up Jean-Paul at a party and the next morning I woke up and he wouldn't let me into the bathroom, he took almost half an hour. Finally, he let me in and I took a shower and douched with this special peppermint douche powder that I kept in this prescription bottle in case it fell out of my purse at a party. I was just putting on my eyelashes when Jean-Paul comes in and looks at the bottle and smells it and asks what it is.

"I just looked at him and then I said, 'Tooth powder,' and he believed me, so to make it really good I told him it was special prescription tooth powder from the doctor. He's such a health fiend anyway, he was dying to use it, and I let him!"

"Oh, God," Sally said.

Sally and I were both captivated, we longed to do mean tricks too. Lois was even brazener and was whispered to have an I.Q. of 168, which was a weird thing to whisper about someone whose black hair curled out around her face like jet clouds and whose green eyes gazed so purely as she said the worst things imaginable.

"Fuck you, Grandmother," Lois would shout over her shoulder as she was leaving during the short period of time she had to stay with her grandmother. Sally and I had come to take her to Cantor's for a Sunday lox and cream cheese. Lois shouted yenta obscenities up the street at her grandmother, who ran after her, trying to get her to put on a sweater.

Meanwhile, back at Hollywood High . . .

It didn't take me too long to figure out that the Thunderbird Girls were a souped-up version of the Deltas and at last, since I was given a choice and not herded into a railroad car to the slaughter, I got to decide if I even liked sororities or groups at all. When I was in the Brownies in the 4th grade and we went to Griffith Park for a Hot Dog Cookout, they wouldn't let us wander in the hills alone. We had to go in groups. I'd always wandered in those hills alone. They were right in back of our house, and now it turns out, because there was a group, my style is cramped.

In grammar there is a noun and there are adjectives. Adjectives modify the noun, they alter it and cramp its style. I didn't want to be a Brownie girl, I just wanted to be a girl. So I quit the Brownies. Everyone was very concerned over my decision except my mother because I was the only girl in the entire school who quit the Brownies.

Friends were all right. I loved Sally and our friendship was simple because it was as though we'd both quit the Brownies and each other was the only person to play with. Only Sally was willing to go hide in the Thunderbird Girls, let the older ones take care of her and make it so that she didn't have to make any more choices. They got her "dates" and chose her clothes and she just let them.

And for Sally, it was easier to let someone take over the controls, whereas for me it was the patio scene all over again. Marilyn kept putting herself in people's hands, believed them. They let her think she was just a shitty Hollywood actress and Arthur Miller was a brilliant genius whereas he was just another modifier in her already corseted life. No wonder she liked to sleep.

★ 103 ★

Sally found mornings so impossible that it was all that she, four cups of thin coffee and a 15 mg Dexamyl could do to get her into class.

"Oh, Evie," she'd say each morning as I got into her car, "I'm *so* depressed."

But to be in the Thunderbird Girls, for me, was at last the final test of who I was. To my dazzled teen-age eyes, their fur coats and blue eyelids were almost overwhelmingly tempting, their "dates" and their weekends in Palm Springs with people like Lenny Bruce or Sinatra.

I began to get headaches, my first and last. After half an hour with Wendy as part of her circle a headache would come over me that nothing would cast out except vacating the premises. I was not in with them. There were too many modifications, too many things you couldn't do.

There were a couple of other things the matter with them as well which I couldn't avoid because they were elementary in my life. One was that they didn't read, they didn't know about art and they didn't know about music. Elmer Bernstein was as far as they went musically. Modigliani was on their walls between horrible Hugh Hefner pieces of bronze sculpture, and *Lie Down in Darkness* was the Bible because they all thought they were the girl. The second reason was that they were so brittle, so stylized and so modified that they were on the brink of being over with, finished. They'd perfected a way to be that made them obsolete from just two strokes of God's Japanese paintbrush—Marilyn dying and the Beatles.

And besides, you can't go mountain climbing or on other adventures when you've got all these people in back of you trying to decide who's going in whose car.

It is the girl who fled whom I remember, the one who skipped town when she saw something she was not about to acquire a taste for no matter how ingenuous it would make her or how much everyone would remember her in Schwab's 36 years later.

And though her lesson seems trifling, I'd advise anyone who'll believe me to avoid pain they don't like or they're liable to acquire a taste for new pain and think that they like it when in reality it's only a movie (like watching Stanley Kowalski hit Stella and then thinking, "Gee, maybe I'd like to get hit," when you wouldn't really at all). If you'd rather have your back rubbed than your front hit, skip town at the slightest suggestion that someone's about to do the latter.

As we both drifted out of high school, Sally and I saw less and less of each other. Once I saw her on the beach and we ran into the ocean with vodka martinis on the rocks in our hands until she was knocked down on sharp shells and cut her leg. Another time I saw her standing on Hollywood Blvd., looking blond and beautiful in a white pleated skirt on Easter, but we had driven a block past her before I realized that that was Sally. Wendy told me that she'd gone to Las Vegas, Sally had, with a pimp junkie, that Sally now had to have four Dexamyls to wake up in the morning and that she'd burned 2 holes in her mattress falling asleep with cigarettes . . .

Sally's whole huge future, the one we all had seen for her as an ingenue, an actress and a Garbo, just trickled away like the gold dust in "Treasure of the Sierra Madre."

"Your father saw Sally yesterday," my mother said. No one had remembered her for about two years; she'd disappeared.

"What's she doing?" I asked.

"She's a lesbian," my father said.

Sally was always such a torch song in one way or another. But my father must have been wrong.

Torch songs are all right at the end of tragedies or in a sad café in Sumatra, but hardly anyone has the strength past new youth to try to talk the girl out of seducing Prince Skirki, though when Marilyn died I knew that all across the world people were harboring grudges against Hollywood and thinking, *"I* would have saved her, *I* wouldn't have just let her die like that. Those insensitive Hollywood people killed her." People who think that have never been around an ingenue. The logic of an ingenue is to court disaster. I never tried to save Sally because the neighborhood belle doesn't. The Sorority girls try to because they always do the conventional thing. Wendy tried to for a long time, but finally Sally slipped away beyond the pale even for the Thunderbird Girls.

Down, down, down she went is her tragic law.

"She's working as a manicurist," Wendy told me, "a buck sixty an hour. What are you doing these days?"

"Oh," I said, in a bad mood that day, "I'm working in an office full of male chauvinist pigs."

"Yeah?" She paused, her timing always perfect. "What do they look like?"

So my character remains in its untried stage and the few chances it has had to prove itself, it's faced with tears and shrieks and not a trace of bravery. I'm always trying to get people to rub my back and drink champagne with me out in the garden at sunset with jasmine scenting the air, and I feel bad when I'm not invited. The Thunderbird Girls are obsolete. Sally's gone with Death, and the Neighborhood Belle will probably have to get old and die instead of just die no matter how many towns she skips. But maybe winter won't ever come, and now what, my darling, will you have to drink?

PRURIENT INTERESTS

The other day I was driving past La Brea and Sunset. There are a lot of hookers around there and the competition's gotten pretty stiff, so you're liable to see anything coming down the street. I live around there and the stories about the 43-year-old millionaire hacked up at the motel on the corner and being found in three shopping bags in Baldwin Hills as told by the guy at Consumer's Liquor, ". . . and the lady at the reservation desk, she told me she'd seen blood before in the rooms but this really . . ."

It was a quiet Thursday afternoon and coming across Sunset, I saw her waiting for the light. She was a tall, slender black girl with a bandanna around her head and big gold earrings. Her bodice consisted of another bandanna artfully contrived, and between it and her tiny bikini/cut-down jeans lay about a foot and a half of midriff. From her left hand extended a leash from which an ordinary medium-size dog was also waiting. And she was wearing skates, roller skates. I wondered to what prurient interest she was trying to appeal, or maybe it was all of them.

The light changed and she skated across the street. Perhaps she was just out skating her dog.

THE FANTASY

God is full of mean tricks and one of them is the fantasy.

I had a lover who told me his fantasies and the ones I felt up to, I went along with, but I was always at a loss when he'd ask, "But what are your fantasies, my darling?"

I knew what he meant and labored through pornography to tickle his fancy with tales that never rang true, because I didn't want to do them, I just wanted to do his. I loved him.

The man Brando is in "Last Tango" reminded me a lot of that lover, who I could easily imagine renting a room and persuading a girl that no names were allowed. And in the movie I was not surprised when the girl went along with it, for after all it was a lark and no skin off her nose since she had a nice fiancé, youth, beauty, her family's money and her childhood memories. Why not see what else she could have meanwhile? And she could love Brando, too, like I loved that man.

But in order for real life to continue, there must be a few compromises in the fantasies of us all.

To have a child is an event that God in his evolutionary wisdom figured out this way. A woman must know the future. That is the fantasy a man must provide her with, otherwise it is only a lark. And love can be in the lark, but women cannot have children or a life out of safety—it's bad tactics and we'd go out like the dodo. Now men could go along with this quietly, but they don't; they are somehow born with fantasies that say, "She must love me even if I don't tell her my name or where I live or anything. She must overcome what it means to be a woman and adopt the fantasies of a man."

Now, that's impossible.

It won't work. It's fun for a lark, but if suddenly in the middle of it the man, like Brando, gets up and says, I believe you love me enough to keep this up forever, let's get married—any woman, but especially a bourgeois French woman, is going to back off and say "What?" because now it's into her territory, no longer a lark. Now it's a quadruped heavily rooted to the earth and she'd like to know more about him, like how much money does he have and will the kids be able to go to nice schools, is he the type to fuck around and, above all, is he the type to live out his fantasies so fully that he does really weird things like rent rooms and have bizarre affairs with girls he doesn't know?

So what does a woman have that will make a man give up his fantasies of no names and get into her fantasies of the future? More fantasies. The man must think, She'd love me even if I didn't have this job and didn't say I'd stay forever. The woman must think, He has given up his childish ways and realizes that stability is the main thing.

"Tell me your fantasies," my lover asked, once again.

"Take me out to dinner," I said, directly opposing his fantasies which depended on him never spending longer than half an hour at a time with me. And never in public.

"Not a chance," he recoiled. One of the only times he was ever truly hurt.

It was the last time I asked; it wasn't meant to be real. And without the compromise of fantasy exchange, real life cannot go on.

It's another of God's mean tricks—that if it weren't like that, nobody'd give a fuck.

THE EARTHQUAKE

Last year we were suddenly awakened, we being everyone in L.A., by the house not standing still. I saw the tv fall off the table and dance across the floor like a marionette. There was nothing for it but to wait. I had already explored fully the ways you can suffer thinking about earthquakes. It was one of the lessons of childhood.

"Now do you believe in God?" a friend telephoned immediately to ask.

The sky was flashing like lightning and the rumble had barely subsided, but I'll be damned before I'll believe in God just because of earthquakes, I've seen where that can lead.

"No," I said and hung up.

An aftershock rolled under the house again and the man I was with trembled in terror. He had never thought about earthquakes and had only been in L.A. for a few months.

"Stand under the doorframe," I told him because he was grabbing his clothes and would probably run outside in a minute. The worst thing you can do is run outside, phone wires being what they are. The earth rocked beneath us like a cradle and if God wants me to believe in him, I'll do it, but only for the Pacific Ocean and sunsets. Earthquakes are only earthquakes, but a good sunset . . .

When I was growing up in L.A., I heard people talking about earthquakes but I was always sleeping when they happened so I had to take their word for it. It wasn't until Dancie became our governess/baby sitter that my sister and I ever got interested as a full-time occupation.

There was a spare room downstairs in our house, and throughout my childhood there were various governesses/baby sitters who lived with us. Women answered the ad my mother put in the paper and my sister and I had them at our mercy and vice versa.

One girl came who was only 14 and stayed almost a year before getting married to a man with a trailer. She brought a small hand luggage case for her clothes and toilet articles and a giant trunk for her comics. We gazed in amazement as she opened the trunk and there were stacks and stacks of comic books which she piled up on the floor in three piles—love comics, mysteries and funnies. She took her comics with her when she got married.

Dancie came when I was 8 and my sister was 5. She

came one night after we'd gone to bed. In the morning when we woke up, she had already unpacked everything except one large tin case which stood mysteriously in the center of the room. She was waiting for us before she unpacked it and we sat on her bed to watch.

In the trunk were marionettes. Marionettes, she carefully explained, not puppets. Puppets were manipulated by hands from beneath and were not anything like marionettes, which were controlled by strings and sticks from above. She held up a jerky figure, which became marvelously graceful and controlled and did a little Irish jig. We were speechless converts.

Puppets would always be out of the question; marionettes were the true art.

She had marionettes that did everything. They danced in a chorus line to Offenbach and stuck their bottoms out coyly in unison at the end, they drank orange juice and they blew soap bubbles while they rode unicycles. We practiced but never got as smooth as Dancie, who was truly inspired.

She showed us how to make papier-mâché with flour and water and newspapers (which was all she ever used) and she showed us how the strings were measured and how the sticks fitted over each other. She even showed us the secret hollow plastic tube which went from in back of the marionette's mouth and sucked up the orange juice into Dancie's invisible mouth, or where she blew out to blow bubbles.

Even as children, we knew she was more of a child than we were.

It didn't matter that she was a frumpy overdressed powdery forty-five with too much dark red cupid's-bow lipstick and orange-blossom water, we knew. We knew she was with us only because of a belief in the devil, and even as young as we were, we knew she was superstitious and misguided.

Dancie had come to Southern California for the express purpose of indulging her religious peculiarities. She would never have been able to get away with what she was intent on indulging in any place else. It was murky ground she craved.

She was a member of a sect. The sect and her marionettes were her entire life except for a nice middle-aged man who somehow discovered her and wanted to marry her. She let him escort her to dinner, but in the end it was Yahlway who won.

Yahlway is what they called God. She never told us why. She just said that if you said "Yahlway" enough times, the earthquake that was coming would let you off.

"But why do that?" we asked, innocent.

"Because in a real earthquake," she breathlessly whispered when our mother wasn't looking, "in a real earthquake, the whole earth splits apart and people fall into the cracks in the world and then it closes back up over them while they die in the fire."

My sister and I got scared.

My mother and father had gone away for four days and this was only the first, and it was also the first we'd heard about the earth cracking open. She showed us pictures of people trying to get out of the cracks like quicksand with their mouths open in terror and their hands reaching out to loved ones (who were apparently saying "Yahlway" and so were immune).

By the second day my sister and I were both sick. She

had a temperature and I was throwing up. My mother had to come home, and a short time later Dancie packed her marionettes into the tin trunk which turned into a stage and went to Texas with the entire sect. The fiancé was left behind since he did not want to go to Texas.

For almost a year I thought of earthquakes, had nightmares and cried and screamed myself awake. I was afraid to walk, the earth might crack open.

When the real earthquake came and I awoke in a house shaking and the skies flashing lightning above an ominous rumble, I found myself looking at the television bouncing like a jerky marionette. And even if the earth were to crack wide open, I refuse to have God dance me off to Texas or blow my bubbles for me. If God wants me to believe in him, he'll have to do better than that. I'll wait under a doorframe.

THE BOUTIQUE

"No, really, Eve, have a bottle. My father's real cool. Last month the bill was Five Hundred Dollars and he didn't bat an eyelash. . . . Hey, Sylvia, do you have French champagne?"

"Dry," I added as long as we were doing it.

"Look, Michael Caine! This place is a fishbowl."

"Yeah and we're the fish," I noticed. We sat in a booth of which two sides were glass at right angles at the corner of Little Santa Monica and Beverly Drive. "I mean, who are we if not the fish?"

"Don't get smart, Eve, I can always tell them to rescind the champagne."

The best thing you can get at the Boutique aside from the devastating chocolate mousse is a Leon Salad and glimpses of people you never believe live. The Leon Salad is a chopped affair made out of Swiss cheese, ham, salami and lettuce run through something that turns them into the cheerful consistency of linguine.

"Oh, my dear, I can't believe it, not again today," my friend with the father groans.

Every day she comes to the Boutique and sits in the corner table when she can get it throughout the afternoon. Around her neck she wears a medicinal-looking medallion like the ones they make for diabetics. Hers says, "I am emotionally retarded." Her favorite and only writer she reads is Sylvia Plath. She read Joan Didion too, but she snickered through the movie because she knew how much all of Tuesday Weld's clothes cost. When *she* went to the mental institution there were no cypresses in sight, and, not only that, no one wore trench coats. So every day she comes to the Boutique, and if I'm in a particularly delicate and brazen mood, I go see if I can find her.

She, today, has carefully positioned herself so as not to be facing an ex-lover, but in order to do this she is now facing a terrible red-headed girl who looks mean as hell and interferes with your digestion, she's so unappetizing. Like a wicked stepmother. She, too, it seems has been coming lately. And her lipstick is a philosophically incomprehensible shade of chalky orange.

My friend with the father never wears make-up, she wears turtleneck sweaters and plaid skirts and she looks about as rich and conventional as is possible unless you look closely at the medallion. She is a Bach fugue of a commentary to the reality of what passes in front of her.

★ 119 ★

". . . and, my God, a Gucci bag, my dear," rollicking into her iced tea. "I always say there's nothing so useful as a black purse."

Styles come and go at the Boutique and the rest of the world adopts a few of the more obvious ones that filter down a year or two later.

The redhead is showing off her $300 black suede accessory, her Gucci bag, in front of Doug McClure. Doug McClure is in between series right now and spends his canceled afternoons in Beverly Hills, drinking after tennis.

"The first time I saw her, I knew she was evil, didn't I?" my friend with the father who is up to 92 lbs. leans over to ask my other friend, who I have known since she was the receptionist at a rock-and-roll magazine and who is now a fixture of sanity, 10 years later, in the Boutique and other places where the children of Hollywood gather. "Didn't I say she was evil?"

My old friend looks doubtful and I fill the gap grandly, "She's not really evil—it's who she's trying to be that's evil!"

"Is that what they're saying now?"

"No, but it seems to go, don't you think?"

"Oh, thank god, the champagne . . ."

The waitress comes and opens the bottle flawlessly. She pours into three long-stemmed glasses that sparkle in the fishbowl and says, out of the side of her mouth to the friend with the father who she knows well, "I got stuck last night with a puller and pincher, jesus, what do you do with one of those?"

She is called away before any of us can do more than laugh, and my friend with the father sips the champagne and comments on it, "God, it's rough. . ."

"Rough?" I ask.

It was dry French champagne and cost thirty dollars a bottle for her father.

"You have to be up for it," she explained.

"For champagne. . . . doesn't it just get you up?" But before I know it: "Isn't that . . . I mean, is that Daniel Ellsberg?"

"What's he doing with that woman?" my frequenter of the Boutique friend leaps. "She's got a wedding ring on and she's not his wife, what're they doing?"

"Probably a business associate," I supply. I hadn't known I had any illusions to shatter and right there was one.

"Where's his wife?" she asks.

Illusions shatter at the Boutique daily.

I drank more champagne.

The fancy restaurant, La Scala, is where you go if you want dependable, expensive, high-class Italian food in Beverly Hills. It's an institution. About 10 years ago they opened an afternoon "sandwich shop" for their customers who were cancelled to come to after tennis. The Boutique is popular because the food is unwaveringly good and so it has never gone out of fashion, just as La Scala is always there at night.

"Where's M?"

"He's trying to stay home. He turned the phone off. He said if he ever had another party like that Christmas thing, he'd kill himself."

"He's always going to kill himself," my old friend says with her perpetual mixture of awe and cynicism. Her cynicism never seems to quite encompass her continual awe that is her reaction to what they do. That is why her sanity, in the end, begins to appear so attractive. It takes time, though.

"Well, what about S?"

"Do you know what that cunt said? I helped her escape that night in a hail of bullets with her lately estranged and his brother shooting out of that Silver Cloud at our tires. We'd just barely had time to get the baby's things and she told me that the only reason I'd helped her was because I was selfish and liked her company!"

"More champagne?"

". . . that woman's here," my old friend notices.

"Oh, that one! I asked her what she did since she was sitting next to me all through lunch the other day and no one introduced us. She said she was a socialite!"

"A socialite!" Another illusion bites the dust. Did people say they were socialites?

"Yeah, and it turns out she's Henry Fonda's wife. An ex-stewardess! Ha! Socialite!"

And so as the sun sinks slowly in the west where all that remains is Hawaii until it finishes with America, we come to our last drop of champagne and the warm glow of my friend with the father's gold medallion dims at last into the fishbowl shadows of the Boutique. Across the room the tables are empty and Daniel Ellsberg and his friend were gone.

"Shall we go?" I ask.

"Yeah, let's." My old friend gathers her things.

"I'm staying," our friend insists. "I want to see who's here for dinner."

My old friend and I walk to our cars, parked in back in metered spaces, and say goodbye, feeling a little tired and drunk and shocked and disillusioned and wonder how she can go every day. Everyone politely overlooked Daniel Ellsberg, the way they do with all celebrities, even the ones who have cancelled written across their futures.

ROSEWOOD CASKET

Death, to me, has always been the last word in people having fun without you. I suppose I got this idea when I listened to "Rosewood Casket," a song my mother sang because lullabys bored her and she didn't think that I'd notice the words since I was so little. But the song is about a man who is dying and meanwhile his true love, who can be seen just outside the window, is having fun with someone new. The whole tone of the song is the terrifying melancholy of knowing that here you are stuck in bed dying and there she is, having fun. So, though he was not yet dead, he was as good as dead.

The Catholics thought up a terrific dodge for this entire thing by having there be a heaven which you could get in if you were good or if you were rich. The

Pope issued dispensations to the country club of heaven where everyone would be having all the fun, still, and not only would hell be where there wasn't any fun, it would also be full of torture, just in case you weren't the type who thought it was bad enough that other people were having a party to which you weren't invited, never mind burning your toenails.

The only way to get around any of the above is to be having your own private party going on with just you continuously. So when I was in kindergarten and the two teacher's pets EVERY SINGLE DAY got to play in the Doll House and the rest of us just watched, I learned that not only could I have fun painting, I could also infuriate the teacher by wanting to paint because it made such a mess. And finally, I began to paint so well that the brattiest of the teacher's pets got jealous. She began wanting to paint and had a tantrum when it turned out she was only second best.

So you can change the boundaries of heaven, just so long as you don't really believe in it or anything that anyone tells you. And whatever you do, don't give the Pope one cent unless he is extortionate and your army isn't big enough to fight him.

My mother once told me that in high school she won the state championship for catsup making. The girl with whom she'd shared a kitchen only won 4th place though they'd made the catsup in the same pot and there was no difference. My mother put hers in a glass jar with flowers painted on it that she painted herself. Packaging is all heaven is.

It's the frames which made some things important and some things forgotten. It's all only frames from which the content arises. Van Gogh had to be a dead madman in order to be the right frame for his pictures, no one could have stood him rich and mad. And Picasso was always rich as was Stravinsky, because they were charming, strong and sane. People believed them; it is packaging.

Of course, the Vatican has always enforced its efforts by continuously playing up that it was hell not to be in heaven until finally everyone forgot the entire point, which was that they should be at their own party in the meantime, just in case . . . Just in case death is other people having fun without you.

Groupies are like dispensation believers who pay with their bodies in order to be invited to heaven, or what looks like heaven from their seat. But instead of figuring out that if they want a star, then the actual person that the star has grown out of would probably like a little suspension of disbelief too and not just an easy lay. Mick Jagger became a Catholic in order to marry Bianca, and that did not amaze me. Mick Jagger believes in creations and Bianca created a Catholic figurine. She's let the Doll House come to her.

What I wanted, although at the time I didn't understand what the thing was because no one ever tells you anything until you already know it, was everything. Or as much as I could get with what I had to work with. I wanted, mainly, a certain kind of song.

Like scents, certain songs just throw me. And I wanted to be thrown into that moment of perfume when everything was gone except for the dazzle. It doesn't last long, but in order to have everything you must have those moments of such unrelated importance that time ripples away like a frame of water. Without those moments, your own heaven party can die of thirst. They're like booster shots, they make you stronger. You know it's worth the twinge of envy when you've recovered from the dazzle because the mystery of life fades when death, people having fun without you, is forgotten. Time escapes unnoticed and time is all you get.

If you live in L.A., to reckon time is a trick since there are no winters. There are just earthquakes, parties and certain people. And songs. Though most of the songs indigenous to the city are similar because of their quality of smoothness which carries into the other entertainment/arts—the technical sheen of the movies, the "Finish Fetish" artists who spend the last month before their show opens making hingeless metal frames that look as though no mortal man had ever had a hand in it. The Byrds and the Beach Boys and the Mamas and the Papas all sounded as though they came out of a Frostie Freeze machine pipe organ. And Van Dyke Parks (a record man) gets so smooth if left to his own devices that the content drops away in his concern over the frame so that nothing could ever go inside the structure and no one knew where to look.

A friend of mine, an artist, once became so infatuated with frames that he made a huge piece about 10 feet square which began on the outer perimeter as a frame that framed only smaller and smaller frames until finally in a narrow 6-inch by 8-inch space in the center was a blueprint for the structure itself.

So sometimes, though you are not connected with a song or a person, they assume an importance which is almost impossible to tell to anyone else, especially if they live where seasons make a difference.

In my life there have never been seasons except for the year in New York.

So it is with this explanation that I first fastened on James Byrns. His importance in my life is not that of a friend, a lover and hardly even an acquaintance—he was a clock, an alarm clock that aroused me from sameness.

Marjorie was still living across the street from me on Formosa in those days and it was she who told me about James. She, too, felt some of his importance and though her taste and mine rarely coincided, I finally acquiesced one day and drove her to James's house. Marjorie was to baby-sit for Celeste, James's 19-year-old mother of his child. Celeste, Marjorie told me, was not happy, and I thought to myself, I wouldn't be either with a baby at that age, but on the other hand it is not my style to hang around in "unhappiness" because it assumes that other people are having fun without you and that's being as good as dead. Nevertheless, I went because the whisper of Marjorie's voice when she said James's name attracted me. And besides, the days had been unbroken by anything back to back for so long that it was time to force it.

James, she told me, had a great house. We were all living in fairy tales then, but nothing so much as the house James and Celeste had discovered.

It was one of those English-countryside houses in May during the Crusades where Richard the Lionhearted stopped over for a meat pie. Richard the Lionhearted would have only thought it was a dream, not a nightmare, when he saw the turrets and leaded glass and overgrowing flowers except that all around him lay West Hollywood in the middle-class Jewishness of the plain Spanish stucco. There were only a few houses on the block that had those things on the roofs that soldiers used to hide behind to shoot arrows out of and which are sometimes on the tops of castles in chess, those little ⎍⎍⎍ type things. It was Ivanhoe time.

So Marjorie brought me to this house at dusk and inside I waited while she went upstairs to find Celeste and James. I had never been in a room like that before, their living room. I knew that James was a musician and now I realized that all musicians' houses were alike and I only realized it because James was intensely different. Instead of being furnished in LSD/Cowboys & Indians where the only place to sit was amps (or LSD/Victoriana like San Francisco, where the only place to sit was chaises) this place was to stay in my personal history forever.

The floor was covered with a dark blue Persian rug, the walls hung with Chinese tapestries and the furniture was oak and polished, there was even a highboy with crystal glasses inside. And on top of all the surfaces were silver frames with flowers, roses, etched or embossed on them, and aged sepia faces smiling out from farther and farther away in the past until they seem to come equal with the very beginning of photography. The silver frames held me until James, himself, came in and was the prince to whom the room belonged.

There is a statue of Hermes that has all my life been my idea of masculine beauty. He is broken, but he's holding a baby on one arm and the other arm is outstretched where he apparently was once teasing the baby with grapes, the baby is reaching for the grapes. The face of this statue had been floated up through time, tempered by the South, and now James had it. Instead of recalling games and Plato, James moved in a spell of plantations and verandas, the content beyond the Mason-Dixon Line, and there was something almost too much about him. His eyes were too blue, like periwinkles from the sea.

He stood there in the doorway as though just recently home from the Civil War Crusade. He moved into the room with such elegance that all the things that Marjorie had told me, that he was 20 and that he was an iron theology student—all those things just made more sense in this strange room that had no precedent.

His hands were narrow and steady. He was the heir to a strange kingdom, and suddenly I thought of his father, who must pass on duty and privilege to his son who was a little too beautiful.

It was like the scent of wet asphalt on a summer night that suddenly makes you think it's rain. The stability was a scent illusion because only one month later the house was dismantled, Celeste was banished, paid off and took the child and Marjorie home to Portland (James was rich; he got money "quarterly" from his family). Her Rose Red beauty could not survive unhappiness.

Or it may have been that just then Jack Hunter telephoned for James to join him in his rented dry Palomino-colored ranch in Ventura. With Jack Hunter, James abandoned himself to worldly toys.

In L.A. when someone gets corrupt, it always takes place out by the pool. And even the most flagrantly flaunting ex-Christian nevertheless takes a lot of Vitamin C. James did not do what we do here at all. He instead embraced a wholesale debauchery that was as out of the question as though he were Dmitri Karamazov. They only went out at night.

Jack Hunter was the leader of a band that played jagged rock and roll and not the finished creamy local productions at all. In fact, his music survived on no room for errors, no margins, just an infinite depth that went snagging into everyone's history so that each of his important songs throws you as only he can, into an anxious rush which awakens that feeling that he's having fun without you. Jack knew of James Byrns because of the almost pristine reputation James had of incorruptibility insofar as his music was concerned. Of course, James did not have the temptation of money to be a reason to play music that would make him a star, but he did have the temptation of youth to just be a star. He did not bow to it, of course, since the songs he wrote (James wrote and played in a small band which he also abandoned once he moved from the Crusade House) were part of his out-of-time, out-of-place aristocratic wholeness. Hunter telephoned James one day to come visit the ranch and James never went back, to Celeste or the life.

The ranch in Ventura was just perfect for Hunter's band. They'd come to L.A. to make a summer record, to avoid the taxes and to forestall the enticements of their own country.

James was the only person they invited to their ranch aside from the groupies. At night they would come into town and rehearse and record at an undisclosed studio. Sometimes, if they finished early enough, they'd go to the Whiskey and catch a last set. I saw them once.

I would have been afraid to live in such dry, inflammable hills like they did in the summer. Of course, I heard that the beach was nearby, and for me that meant that when the fires came, you could always run out into the ocean. It dries you out, though, that kind of heat, and the night I saw Hunter and James they were almost hollow and sere themselves, their hair dried from the ocean into layered segments and white lines of salt down their necks. They were both skeletally thin, fleshless young men, but Hunter made you think of evil, not yellow moons and magnolias like James.

That was the year everyone, all the rock stars, were wearing satin pants which looked like cloissonné colors from China. James and Hunter wore translucent India cotton shirts, the kind with embroidery and mirror sequins and all the girls wanted to lick the salt off their unbuttoned fronts. When they came into the Whiskey, they changed everything and again a moment made time valuable like a newly cut diamond.

The Whiskey hushed at the sight of the two of them and no one dared claim past friendship with James, not in this company.

I saw a kind of formal strangeness in the way Jack Hunter treated James and the way James behaved back. It was as though death could be tomorrow morning and it certainly, when Jack lit his friend's cigarette, made a small flame of jealousy go up. Who among us, after all, treats their friends so well? And why don't they?

That kind of party, though, is too foolish to go on.

They diminished each other like Picasso and Stravinsky sharing an apartment.

They looked beautiful, but you couldn't look too long.

You could see that Hunter had chosen a true diversion. I wondered what they had for lunch and if they were lovers and what Sin was and other questions that hadn't come up in that stock summer from which nothing dazzled.

I heard that James was going to make a record, but

by the end of the summer when Hunter went home, nothing more was said about it.

James then was going to form a new band and find a house, and meanwhile he got a suite at the Chateau Marmont. He never looked for a house; he gradually just began to think of the Chateau as home.

The open boom-town quality of the Monterey Pop Festival days had passed, and now some of the groups had grown rich while others had split up and fallen apart. The older rich stars, people I knew, I watched as they all followed such an easily predictable path that you could have closed your eyes and known what they were doing. They all decided that "the city" was simply out of the question and they wanted to be ranchers like real men. So they all moved to ranches.

The rock stars who had no money either went to Hawaii and took drugs or went to Topanga Canyon and took drugs and meanwhile they waited for the next thing.

The next thing was James, who gathered the motliest, most outlandishly worldly and jaded bunch of them together and from this came the innocence of James Byrns's music. How those guys sang "Give Me the Christian Life" and made you believe it, I'll never know. And there was James, salty and famished-looking from the summer, standing like a raped angel with these dark blue eyes throwing southern aristocratic landscapes all across dark smelly nightclubs where we sat in front of the impossible.

The rock stars came in from their ranches and listened raptly, all ears, trying to figure out where to steal, because James was still so pure that he could not be a star and the stars could take his songs and pasteurize them into hits.

Backstage afterwards they would greet with fashionable horror the news that James lived in the weird Chateau Marmont. But in spite of James's drugs and in spite of his ambiguous friends and in spite of his money . . . in spite of his torn satin pants, James was still the same. Pure.

I as yet hadn't met James, really. He'd just been these strange moments that helped to know the time. As for myself, I listened and watched and wondered what he'd do. The group he'd assembled never recorded and only stayed together a little while before one of them quit and then the next to go back to Hawaii and Topanga.

James stayed at the Chateau, and it was there that we met one afternoon by the pool. No one was out except for some kids, the guy I was visiting was away and James was there reading a paper. It was the *Wall Street Journal.*

"My God!" I said.

"Hi." He shaded his eyes and looked up.

The *Wall Street Journal* went with the Chinese Tapestries and the Oxford digs.

"Oh," he said. "I met you before . . . Where was it?"

We started talking and I insinuated myself into his life by telling him that I was a photographer and really wanted to take pictures of him. I had a Brownie.

The way I looked at it, anything past a Brownie was an invention of the Germans to make life impossible. All those numbers. I'd actually taken album covers with the Brownie, so it wasn't really as much of a scam as it looks to the naked eye. However, I always brought along this other hard camera so that people would think I knew what I was doing. (I'd sneak the Brownie ones in between.)

We arranged for me to come over the next day and take pictures. He said that he would need some because he was going to make an album soon and, besides, it would be fun. We were going to have fun, then, in spite of the bleak season.

The next day I arrived with both cameras in my bag, but suddenly I felt shy when I came to his door. I wondered if it wouldn't be better just to let him be an alarm clock rather than try to make him come out in a photograph the way I saw him. I'd parked my car downstairs and felt the uncut dullness of another L.A. afternoon with the sky casually smoggy and the temperature its usual 75° and it was going to be like that in the future and it had been like that for as far back as I could remember. There was a danger that I'd spoil things by knowing too much and I wasn't used to being shy.

But I rang and he came to the door, half finished with what he was doing at the coffee table, which was chopping up some pure cocaine that came in sealed vials from Germany. I had hardly sat down, my shyness blocking my vision, when he said, "Now, close one nostril and take a real deep snort of this."

Cocaine came in with Jack Hunter that previous summer.

There are only three things to say about cocaine. One, there is no such thing as enough. Two, it will never be as good as the first time. Three, those first two facts constitute a tragedy of expense in ways that can't be experienced unless you've had cocaine. Its expense lies in knowing that someone's having fun on Mt. Olympus without you and that should you try to stay there always. Your brain will settle into a puddle around your sinuses and you will die.

"Get it?" he asked, a host.

"The thing is," I began, my shyness evaporated like a tear in the sun, "everything about you is just like F. Scott Fitzgerald."

How I could have brought up literature to a rock star without any further ado is one of the easier mysteries of cocaine.

"Yeah," he said, "he's my favorite writer. In fact, I just finished rereading my favorite story by him the other day—'The Diamond as Big as the Ritz.'"

"Why that one?"

We were standing; we'd forgotten to sit down. The cocaine had illuminated the world so much that we just hung there in the middle of my dream adventures I'd been nurturing along now coming true.

He was now going to tell me why that was his favorite story.

Though it was perfect anyway since it was about a kid at a fancy boarding school who meets another kid who's exactly like everyone else only he's subtly better dressed and no one knows where he comes from. The kid is invited to the rich kid's house for summer vacation and the rich kid lives with his sisters and father in Colorado atop a diamond as big as the Ritz Hotel. At the end God cracks down on the father with thunder and lightning and the father tries to make a deal with him as the sisters and the kid escape.

"I liked it 'cause of the end," he said. We were standing on the little balcony almost all the rooms at the Chateau have overlooking the city in what would become a salmon sunset, whitely orange. It was now still white, a usual white day glittering from cocaine of white crystals while my mind recalled the story's end.

"You mean, when the father tries to bribe God with the diamond?" I asked.

"No," he said. "When all the sisters took with them were rhinestones."

"Oh."

To the sisters, the rhinestones had been the rarest treasure.

I looked from his black lashes back out to the white city and heard him add, "I don't know why, but I always think about those rhinestones."

People who live without winters all their lives may not know the need for rhinestones. I never have. Maybe it goes on and you don't know.

We talked on that cocaine all afternoon, sometimes drifting out to the little balcony and sometimes talking in a kind of coke code. We drank bourbon and smoked a mixture of Lebanese and Pakistani hash. When it got dark I left, my illusions intact.

Had it been anyone else, I would have assumed we would have wound up in bed. With him, I knew it was an impossibility even before his girl friend came home from being a starlet in a new movie. She was a beautiful 17-year-old with a constant easy laugh and white teeth. Her reddish hair followed her around and she looked at you with mint-green eyes. Before she came home James had told me that she satisfied his taste for "street girls."

If she was a street girl, then Grace Kelly was a scullery maid, I thought to myself, coming down the elevator and off the coke at the same time and remembering that I had forgotten to take any pictures.

A few days later I went back with determination and got the picture of what I saw. People who know him, upon looking at the picture, say, "When was that taken?" It looks Long Ago.

I thought I might be friends with James, and when he told me he was negotiating a record contract and would be making an album, it sounded like this time it would happen. Jack Hunter came into town and was about to do this major tour of the country and after to go for a Greek Cruise, and so James and Teresa (the girl) put their things in the Chateau's storage room and were gone.

"Have you seen James?" someone asked.

"James who?"

"Byrns . . . I thought he was your friend. Anyway, he's here."

"Where?"

"Here, in the bar, right now . . . I couldn't believe it was him."

"Why?"

"He's fat."

"What?"

"Fat."

James Byrns sere off the Ventura mountains fat? I couldn't believe it. He'd been gone for so long that I could believe he was dead—but fat? Never.

Of life in Rockdom, part of the privileged existence and scorn depends on being slender as a thread. Old people are fat and ugly people are fat, but even the children of rock people are gracefully slender and the fat babies of the past are no longer. It had been 2 years since Hunter had toured, so it was 2 years since James had been in L.A., and I scanned the bar until I landed on the face of a mean-looking Southern cop and that was James. Sitting next to him looking washed out and famished was Teresa, wearing a Dior jersey floor-length mauve gown through which her ribs showed. But James was fat.

Of course, outside of the Troubadour Bar and *Vogue* magazine, no one would have thought that James was anything but just a little overweight. But we weren't anywhere else.

"Hi," he said, noticing me. I'd lost 20 pounds since we'd last met and was vamping the world in consequence, but I would not have vamped James out of a feeling that I still got from him no matter what course he'd now adopted.

I sat down and smiled at Teresa who coughed back and then gave me a thin little smile before she leaned on the bar, exhausted. She was 19, I thought, and he's . . . 26.

"How are you?" I asked. His hand shook so badly he dropped his cigarette on the floor and didn't even pick it up but tried to light another.

"I'm in town to make a record," he said.

"Oh."

I wondered if you could play guitar with your hands shaking.

James was soon surrounded by old friends and I saw Teresa take a seat by the wall, alone.

"He's a punk," his manager told me.

"What?"

"A fucking punk," his manager, an old friend who'd been around always, repeated. "The first day we were supposed to record, he comes into the studio so on pills and drunk that when he drops his pick it takes him 30 minutes to find it."

"So . . . what are you going to do?"

"Nothing. We're making a record. His friends came

in after that first night and beat the shit out of him and ever since then he's been fine."

"Oh."

It was another night and another restaurant. The sameness pervaded, and I was living inside my own private party when a disturbance in the front of the bar caused me to look up and there was James. He would have been unable to stand had he not been leaning on a three-day-old binge of a groupie who'd probably heard about Jack Hunter and thought she could get to him through James. The maître d' was looking worried at such a tequilaed and tuinalled pair, and I felt sorry for the maître d', who I knew, so went over.

"Hi," James said just barely.

"Jesus Christ, James." I suddenly flew into such a rage that I wanted to beat the shit out of him. "Can't you the fuck . . . Look at you!" My mother's childhood songs sound like a Southern Cop drunk. "What the fuck would your family . . . your father think?"

I so shocked myself with that admission of fantasy that I fell back amazed as James squinted through his drugs and looked at me with his beautiful eyes.

"My father," he pronounced softly, just for me, "died in jail drunk."

"What?"

"Haven't you ever heard of Jackson Ryan? He was just about as good as Hank Williams. Some thought he was better. Anyway . . ."

He forgot what he was saying; he was always doing that now.

"But what about those pictures and the silver frames with the roses . . . ?"

"That wasn't *our* money, that was *their* money," he

explained tortuously. "Once . . . my father died, we were poor, you know? Poor? My mother got married and . . . It's always been their money."

And so now the album is finished and out, and it sounds as easy as a crap shooter winning, fast and chancey. As though sung by a gentleman who didn't have to try.

On the cover he told me he didn't want to use the old picture I'd taken because it didn't show him as he was. He said, too, that he wanted to wear the belt that Jack Hunter had given him, but it isn't on there in either the front or the back picture, so he must have changed his mind. The belt he showed me was made out of rhinestones and would not have gone with that plain voice so pure it just throws you. Other people's rooms at dusk have the value of a freshly cut diamond in the city where time's texture, life, depends on earthquakes, parties and certain songs.

> In a little rosewood casket
> Sitting on a marble stand
> There's a package of love letters
> Written by my true love's hand
>
> Go and bring them to me, brother
> Come and sit upon my bed
> Read them gently to me, brother
> Till my aching heart goes dead.

I telephoned my mother for the exact words of the next verse and all she remembered was this:

ROSEWOOD CASKET

Last Sunday I saw him walking
With a lady by his side
And I thought I heard him whisper
You can never be my bride.

I always thought it was that she was having fun without him and that that was what death was. So it turns out that what I got from the words was never there either.

The photograph, like James's songs, is a recording of a past that only exists in private histories. The days lie back to back in the sameness of smoggy afternoons, levelly maintaining a comfortable temperature of 75° except summers that are sometimes remembered for unbroken heat. Perhaps it is just my illusions that have made some days seem different from others, maybe I save the rhinestones and just don't know.

I wonder what that song is about.

★ CENTRAL MARKET

At the bottom of Angels Flight, you turned right and went a block and came to Central Market. This market covered an entire city block and had entrances on two streets at either end, Hill and Broadway, I think. In Central Market there are about 50 stalls. Unlike the Farmers Market, where tourists and Angelenos get cheerfully gypped daily, Central Market sells fresh produce and fresh fish and every kind of edible that could appeal to any faction of population minority that is in L.A., cheap. It's like Baghdad.

THE WATTS RIOTS

I spent the riots in a penthouse at the Chateau Marmont with this ex-philosophy major from Stanford
whose family owned all the more oily pieces of land in
Arizona, Mexico and California and who had taken up
the profession of herding cattle. He was a Stanford
Cowboy, is how I always thought of him in my mind. He
showed me his spurs so I'd believe him and his saddle
bags. In his saddle bags he kept his prize possessions,
books on magic and the works of Alistair Crowley. His
horse must have felt like a roving library. The police
shot this guy in a car while he was taking his wife to the
hospital to have a baby just as Nicky, the Stanford Cowboy, must have been checking into the Chateau that
evening, having driven from Indio, the desert where
the Santa Ana winds came from.

The guy getting shot in Watts made the winds, I think, like escaping gas, explode.

L.A. was closed.

There were no cars out on the streets. Everyone was home watching tv, where Joe Pine had dumped a satchelful of guns out onto his podium and explained that he was not about to let anyone try and get *his* stuff away from him, never mind his wife and daughters.

Nicky laughed soundlessly and begged me to drive with him down to Watts. The tv was with its back to the French windows which overlooked the city, and tiny needles of smoke arose in the distant distance. What Nicky thought was so funny was that "they" were shooting at planes with .22s.

"Are you crazy?" I wondered. I'd only just met him once the riots had started. We'd been alone outside at the Four Oaks Bar, an artists' bar in Beverly Glen and I'd assumed he was an interchangeable Californian. Even if he did have these huge magic books from the Horace Greeley Mann collection or something and even if he was a cowboy. We were drinking bourbon and eating potato chips, delivered from the Liquor Locker right next to the Chateau. It was nice spending the Riots in a penthouse. It seemed asking for trouble to go watch them shooting at planes.

At night we saw a couple nakedly entwined in passion two stories below us, but we slept in separate beds and changed channels to mostly watch old movies. We only turned on the Riots during the commercials.

"Tom Wolfe's here," Nicky said.

"Yeah?" I said. Nicky had gone to Schwab's for magazines and so knew what was going on outside the room in our immediate vicinity rather than just what we could see on tv.

At first, when I'd first started talking to Nicky out in the winds that smelled of eucalyptus and jasmine in Beverly Glen, I'd thought he was an actor whose series had just been canceled. He had eyes of canceled blue and he was too handsome and too tan and too tall to be much else. When it turned out he was the heir of a huge California fortune, I took his word for it.

"Why are you a cowboy then?" was all I'd asked.

"Oh, I don't like cows," he explained.

"Well, why then?"

"Horses. I want to find out as much as I can about horses before I start racing them."

"Race horses cost a fortune."

"I know where I can get one cheap for $60,000."

"Oh."

SINS OF THE GREEN DEATH

I got deflowered on two cans of Rainier Ale when I was 17. It's a local product sold up and down the Coast originating in Seattle (where Mt. Rainier is) and in those days a small can cost about 26 cents. So all this time a handsome, flashy young man had been pouring Courvoisier and champagne into me only to become the tool, in the end, of a can and a half of Rainier Ale. He'd pursued me, done everything—told me he loved me in 8 different languages, introduced me to café society and movie stars, covered me in gardenias and telephoned me 4 times a day, besides which he had a convertible and was rich and had tawny curly hair. It was the Rainier Ale that did it, though, and in the end he became just a pawn of the fancy properties known to exist by coastal natives who have always called this special liquid "The Green Death."

They'd told me I would bleed and it would hurt and it would turn me into a woman. But it didn't hurt. I didn't bleed, and instead of turning into a mature person, I began to wonder what else there was out there that was like Rainier Ale.

At the time, I was trying to shorten my stay at Hollywood High by skipping a grade so that I graduated in summer school, half a semester ahead. On my last day there I got summoned to the girls' vice-principal's office and thought, "Oh, no, they're not going to tell me I can't spell and now I can't get out, are they?" but instead Mrs. Standfast (Mrs. *Bertha* Standfast) gave me the "You are now about to embark upon the road of life speech," which, I hoped, would keep her mind off the fact that come was dripping down my leg, hardly appropriate, but I hadn't known they didn't skip the amenities even in summer school. Usually when you have a diploma handed to you at Hollywood, it's off the stage of the Hollywood Bowl. The Hollywood Bowl seats something like 20,000 people. It must really be a smattering little ceremony with just kids and their parents there, but I suppose nobody can resist. At the time, it didn't occur to me that I'd already embarked on the road of life.

At the end of her speech she handed me a handsome black diploma case and told me my diploma would be coming in the mail since it was still at the printer's. And then she became less formal. "And what will you do now, dear?"

I'd always liked Mrs. Standfast because she had a sense of humor and she tried to keep out of people's way. (She once was tipped off that the girls were smoking in the girls' room in the Arts Bldg., and she took a delegation and the place emptied out like a clown car, and all she did was laugh and laugh, she didn't even pretend it wasn't funny. I always liked her.) So I didn't want to hurt her feelings by telling her what I planned to do. I had been one of the girls in the girls' room.

"Do?" I asked, trying to rub my calf dry.

"Yes," she said. "You have good grades but you seem to have changed your major a number of times . . . Will you go on . . . ?"

Going on meant going to UCLA, which, like Everest, was there.

"I don't know," I said. "I thought I'd go to L.A.C.C. until I decided, you know?"

"Well, dear . . ." she said, not hiding her disappointment—they liked you to "go on" and not just dodge the issue by going to L.A.C.C. "Good luck."

We rose and she shook my hand.

I stuffed the diploma case into my big, open-topped purse and half fled to the girls' room, where I had a cigarette and stuffed tissue paper into my pants to be on the safe side.

Feeling more confident, I stood on the steps in front of the Administration Building, struggling in my overcrowded purse to find my sunglasses before walking up Highland to Hollywood Blvd. to take the bus, for the last time, home from school. My purse was full of its usual scandalous reading material, cigarettes, contraception and make-up as I stood beneath the hot August smoggy sun unshaded by the surrounding banana trees. Hollywood High always was unshaded by the banana trees that grew in profusion near the buildings.

My sunglasses were down at the bottom next to the beer opener. I never called a beer opener a church key; the association never seemed right. I always had a beer opener with me in those days, like lipstick.

I didn't tell my flashy young man that I'd graduated from high school. He was too removed to have understood the American import or to have thought an empty diploma case after a speech in a room with only two people was anything to wonder about. He was a "serious" composer and had instilled in me his attitudes about things like the Four Freshmen singing "Graduation Day" and the sentimental oosh of " . . . we'll remember, always, Graduation Day" would have fallen into his scorn. I was so instilled with his world that one night I spent 15 minutes telling a nice older man at a party that all popular music was crap and then the nice older man turned out to have written "You Make Me Feel So Young," which was my favorite song, secretly, in the whole world.

What I'll remember always was not the flashy lover, who is a watery valentine floating translucently in a half-forgotten resort of souvenirs, nor the relief of getting that diploma case. What I'll remember always was the Rainier Ale.

For the Green Death, I have reserved a kind of dazzling and cherished intensity that you hear in the voices of Frenchmen in movies when they speak of their first love, an older woman who is no more but is savored in memory to the day they die. The trouble with Rainier Ale is, it's still there. They haven't changed it, it's just a few cents more, that's all. The Frenchman can go on with his life, get married and have grandchildren—the temptation of his first love is out of reach.

★ 149 ★

Only with me, every time I go into a liquor store . . .

My flashy lover was ideal for the kind of love-comic virgin that I went as until his texture began to conflict with who I really was which had to come out sooner or later. I was not the sweet flower petal of femininity we'd conjured up for me to be when we first started and it was just as well that he got another Fulbright and was swept away to learn yet another language in the beds of yet another nation's girls. And by that time I'd begun to realize that a life of rehearsals, jam sessions, eccentric old men writing 12-tone serial pieces and being introduced to everyone as Stravinsky's goddaughter was not the life for me.

I looked like Brigitte Bardot and I was Stravinsky's goddaughter. There was nothing I could do about being named by Stravinsky and I had a feeling that no matter what I looked like, he would have had to have me just for that, for Stravinsky reasons. So I could never get too in love with him and, anyway, it was ridiculous to imagine going to concerts for much longer. I, being Stravinsky's goddaughter, spent my childhood growing up hating concerts.

But in liquor stores now when I go to the refrigerated section to pick up some Vernor's 1 Cal (Vernor's Ginger Ale is another regional thing of beauty and unending quality, only not our region—Detroit it's from), now when I stand by the huge glass doors and search past the Cokes and Cold Duck and Squirt, sometimes as they are gliding over the rows my eyes are suddenly rooted to the emerald green-golden monarchial crests which adorn the cans of Rainier Ale. And then they boldly whisper the rapture of secret desires consummated in passion that we once stumbled upon together in the days when we never thought that such a thing as "irreconcilable differences" would have to do with us. Rainier Ale, you see, is too fattening.

Now I drink champagne.

Sins are the ones you have to give up, not the ones that don't make any difference. Champagne doesn't make any difference. Half a can of the Green Death equals five pounds. I never give up sins until the last moment, hoping that modern science will figure it out. But true sins are never ironed out either by science or art, so since all either of them could come up with was champagne, it tides me over. Sometimes, just in the first ten minutes, you get almost a hint of Rainier.

Anything that's your heart's desire, I've noticed, sooner or later turns into a sin and you're only going to wind up with hints, so you'll be lucky to get even half. Desire something enormous, the road of life being what it is.

I decided through and through on Marlon Brando. That's why I couldn't tell Mrs. Standfast and covered up with L.A.C.C.

Marlon Brando is not included in talks with your school counselor or the brochures about what to do once you're out of high school to safeguard your life against coming out a blank. But how're you going to get them to UCLA after they've seen Zapata?

It was an irreconcilable difference in a nutshell.

People like me with high scores (except for spelling) were supposed to turn right and march down Sunset to UCLA and take, if we were practical, education or, if we were socially conscious, psychology, or, if we were romantic flowers, English Lit. I was sick of everyone by that time and couldn't imagine doing more time with them with even more kids like them from farther and wider.

"Gee," they asked me, concerned, "don't you wish you could graduate off the stage? How come you're just getting your diploma in summer school?"

Their heart's desires were really paltry, and I guess they decided to take their chances with not taking any chances.

They didn't even care about sins.

It was "Viva Zapata!" that did it. I remember coming out of a theater alone one Saturday afternoon. It was still daylight. I was 15 and it was as simple as that. In the end, when Zapata walks into the fort where his white horse awaits him and he is ambushed by hundreds of rifles until his body is convulsed in bullets and they fling this lacy reminder to the peasants, the peasants turn their eyes to the mountains where the white horse has fled. The white horse whinnies, his long sexy mane in the breeze, and we know that Zapata is not really dead but hiding back in the wilderness and will return.

When I walked out of that nearly empty movie house on Hollywood Blvd., Marlon Brando it was. UCLA didn't stand a chance.

"But what will you *do*, dear . . . ?" the counselor kept asking, looking at my Iowa Test Scores, which were all incredibly high and not just because I cheated.

If I had been about to weaken, though I was not, then "One-Eyed Jacks" would have nailed me permanently to the cross of indifference about the minute variations between Psychology, English Lit and Education. "One-Eyed Jacks" came out that summer, and Sally and I were first in line at the Pix and stayed to see it three times. He was too fat in that movie. That was the only thing wrong, but a too fat Brando was much more Everything In The World than a university could hope to even be a hint of. It hurt me, though, that he was too fat and that the people in back of us were laughing at him because of it. I decided never to get too fat.

"But what *will* you do," the counselor's eyes leave my test scores and focus on my face, "if you don't go to UCLA?"

"I was thinking of becoming an adventuress . . ." I mumble.

"What?"

"Maybe I'll . . . " I chicken out, only 17 and not Brando enough yet, "go . . . to L.A.C.C."

"Oh."

She is disappointed.

They don't like you to go to L.A.C.C. It fucks up their record. They like a huge percentage to go to a real college. It wasn't a "nice" college, L.A.C.C. For one thing, it wasn't hard enough to get into. All you had to do was say "yes" when they asked you if you spoke English. If you said "no," they put you into a remedial English class. And besides, the place was teeming with undesirables and had been thrown open to the masses in spite of the Watts Riots being so far in the future.

There was no attempt at L.A.C.C. at anything resembling scholarly deportment or school spirit, and the only sport I remember them excelling in was soccer. Soccer was not "nice." The school was located about 4 blocks from the hospital I was born in. It was on Vermont near Melrose, which is an indeterminate lower-middle-class sort of neighborhood with no delusions. Westwood, where UCLA is, is so insanely crappy you could throw up. It's so WHITE and it's so clean and it's so impervious, and the closest I ever got to that feeling of Westwood was when someone took me out of the Lower East Side in New York one horrible summer day to their mother's house in Westport, Conn., and their mother was so shocked and repelled by me (she could tell I was Jewish, where her son hadn't noticed) that she ran slides of his ex-girl friend for 45 minutes after dinner. That's what Westwood is like. You could slam its teeth down its throat. Anyway, L.A.C.C. didn't even make a stab at school spirit even in jest. It just tried not to get too irrevocably entangled about who was in what class, that was the best it could do. It was a nice school. I went there for three semesters and no one ever asked me what I was doing.

Everyone else went to UCLA from Hollywood High and became "educators." Except Sally, of course, and a few other of the ones who just didn't see how they could go do that.

My parents were still living on Cheremoya then and I lived with them when I first started going to L.A.C.C. The flashy lover had been granted out of the country and we wrote letters pledging fidelity but I knew he was already probably fucking the stewardesses on the plane out and that it didn't matter because he wasn't my heart's desire at all.

I was looking for something in Brando, I would have said if a saleslady had asked to help me, something outrageous and grandiose.

I didn't want a vine-covered cottage, stability, children, a college degree or a dog. If the horse was in the mountains, I would follow it to Zapata and stay with him.

My mother never asked me what I was going to do,

nor did my father. They both thought universities were where people went who didn't know what they were doing, which is how, I suppose, the idea took root in me too. And then Zapata came along and Rainier Ale and so by comparison everything paled. It was my mother who discovered Rainier Ale and she would sip it from a blue Mexican glass before dinner as she stood by her kitchen window looking out at the sunsets and sighing, "The pink light of Hollywood . . ." (She thought it was a tangible reality, the "Pink Light.") Sometimes she'd look at me happily, so I suppose she did not regard with alarm the fact that I was so Zapataed out that I was on the verge of doubling up on everything to stop it from seeming like half.

"Mother . . ." I said one night as we sat outside watching the cats play on the lawn.

"Yes, darling . . ." she said.

"I think I'm going to be an adventuress," I said. "Is it all right?"

"We'll always think you're wonderful," she said.

"O.K.," I said. Poor Thomas Wolfe.

So there I was, nearing my 18th birthday, so Hollywooded up that I aspired to be a kind of Scheherazade/Sheena combination with Mme. Récarmier and Elizabeth Taylor thrown in. I hadn't really liked Elizabeth Taylor until she took Debbie Reynolds' husband away from her, and then I began to love Elizabeth Taylor. It wasn't until I got to Rome and Elizabeth Taylor's dalliances made 20,000 extras be paid ten thousand lire a day for six additional months and the rents skyrocketed that I began to wish Elizabeth Taylor would calm down, but still . . . it was worth it. Every time I thought how the rent had been so much cheaper

EVE'S HOLLYWOOD

before "Cleopatra", I remembered those horrible bones in Debbie Reynolds' eye sockets. Elizabeth Taylor served everyone right.

L.A.C.C. didn't interfere with my plans to be an adventuress by inflicting its personality because it had no personality; it couldn't even get the lawns to grow right. The classes I took had no sign of future intentions, they were just ones I liked, and for a while I thought that it would be fun to be a history major, but I met some history majors in graduate classes at UCLA and their white pudgy skin reversed my decision.

After a suitable period of faithfulness, I found out for sure that my flashy lover had gone to the Alps with an old girl friend, and then I felt free to indulge myself in the huge, new, unbelievably diverse world of men who wanted to sleep with me. The second one was an architect from San Francisco who had a penthouse and fed me scotch (no Rainier, though I tried to get him to buy me some); the third was another too-old millionaire who sent me home in a cab. (I was later delighted to learn that he was busted for grass and actually had to go to jail for 6 months. You'll never get any sympathy from ex-lovers who've been sent home in cabs.) After that, I forget. All I remember was that they were too easy, too callow and my initial belief that people liked to have fun was proven all wrong, though how I could have thought people like to have fun when most of them were going to UCLA is something I should have not overlooked. In no time at all, I was cornered in my old place where all I had was the Rainier Ale and Marlon Brando as proof of a better world.

I was a bitch.

The day I was 18, Sally and I had a reunion because

we were still friends though we saw less and less of each other. We went to Pupi's, a place devoted to cake, overlooking the Strip. I invited her to this surprise birthday party my mother was giving me that night (though she never would do anything so unforgivable as actually surprise me; I *hate* surprises). Sally told me about her new acting class and how the guy who was teaching it was fantastically adorable but wouldn't give her a tumble and also about how she'd contracted this case of "chronic gonorrhea" which I thought was unfair, especially the chronic part.

She licked her fork of lemon icing and scowled, "Shit, I'm so depressed, I haven't been laid in 3 months."

"You're not missing anything," I said, having recently come to that conclusion. Our 18-year-old vast jadedness came out in little puffs from our ears, like steamboats. "They're all assholes, they got no class and I actually met one guy who thought going down on a girl was something called "muff-diving" and only perverts did it."

"Really?" she said. "How bourgeois."

We watched the fashionable traffic go back and forth on the Strip for a while and felt fantastic. Sally had become a platinum blonde, which made her look like Kim Novak with a brain, and her career, as she referred to her life, looked like it might do something. She actually could act.

Neither of us knew what I was going to do, but it didn't matter.

"You know, Evie," she began, "I think it would be fun to be in love."

"Love?" I scoffed, as cupid hovered above me waiting for just the right moment to take aim.

★ 157 ★

"Yes . . ." she said.

"Who would you fall in love with?"

"Oh, Evie, you should see my acting teacher . . . He's so adorable . . . he really is."

"Actors!"

"But he's different . . . He's . . ."

Since we both were almost twins about Marlon Brando, I shouldn't have been surprised if her acting teacher was adorable. But all those Thunderbird Girls were in his class and that whole thing was already decided upon when it turned out I got headaches if there were more than one in the same room with me. My idea of the word "love" anyway was something that other people did to get themselves into the right frame of mind to have children. I'd be satisfied if it were only Zapata and I could appreciate it from afar, the way things were going.

"You know," I said to her, "I'd just like someone who didn't make me feel old."

"That's love," she said.

"Oh."

I finished my Mocha Almond Crunch and wondered at Sally's definitions. In those days, I still ate cake.

My surprise birthday party was filled with a relaxed mixture of relatives and friends. Sally and I left out of the back door without saying goodbye because she heard of a party in Laurel Canyon that wasn't relaxed. I told my mother I was going and she said goodbye, and to have fun.

Sally dressed like the Thunderbird Girls. She wore all that garter-belt, Merry Widow, boned stuff and black cocktail dresses. Girls of 18 were still trying to look "older," and then I sort of wished I looked older too, but

I wasn't willing to do anything about it if it stuck into my waist. The party was good and not relaxed. It was a fast crowd.

It was a house in Laurel Canyon where this guy who knew everyone was having about 2 years of winning at the race track, so he threw parties all the time and lechery for young girls was de rigueur.

We were used to it.

Sally and I had been going to these things since she met Wendy, and sometimes you could meet someone who wasn't an actor. For me by then, anyone who was an actor was automatically an empty space and didn't count. Nothing they said registered in my brain and nothing they did ever was mistaken for a true action.

All I had were students at L.A.C.C. and these actors. I didn't know any artists yet, and even though I had nothing to choose from (actors and students being nothing), I stuck to my guns and held out. I wasn't going to change my mind and think an actor or a student was Zapata or that it didn't matter. Rainier Ale existed. You could buy it in the store in case you forgot what real stuff tasted like.

Sally's acting teacher came in with a friend from an overcast night, so how is it that I remember him *still* as coming in alone from the stars? Cupid let go with a spear dipped in purple prose, not just an arrow, and then he drew another one, so there were two, one conventionally through my heart and the other through my head. They were both about 8 feet long and two inches thick. They were crude.

I half rose up against the impact and he saw me across the room as he came in alone from the stars and then he disappeared. He was swamped by girls, deluged in

★ 159 ★

a tangle of beautiful arms and feminine exclamations of flower-petal softness. Three of the prettiest had twisted free of their conversations and it was like Santa Claus in an orphanage.

I, it turned out, wasn't the only one.

Graham, as he was to be called, was one of those people who distinguish certain handfuls of time—like Brando—in the rare arrangements that circumstance occasionally allows so that life is made to seem worth living. At least for people like me. I have girl friends who have met him and are actually frightened of him like people used to be afraid of witches. Not me. Anyway, I think witches are kid stuff.

Graham wore black and had black hair, long and shiny, that fell over his face and got pushed back from his listening brown eyes as you talked to him. His eyes were the true eyes of a liar. The hands that pushed back his hair were the hands of someone who loves women and who knows what to do. His eyes listen to you, carefully watching to see what you want to hear so that it shortens the time until his hands can undo your clothes and touch you back into heaven, into blue heaven and lies. Lies that weren't lies because there was a blue heaven, the white horse gallops back to the wilderness where Zapata, who is not this lacy corpse, is waiting and if you doubt, there is Green Death at the liquor store.

All really enormous charm, the kind that Graham exuded, does much more than it needs to. It gushes out so much that you can live inside it. That was the reason that Graham didn't just mow down women, which most men would have been satisfied with. Graham had men friends who might have died for him and even gas-station attendants felt it and did his windshield better.

Animals woke up and came and sat on top of him when he came into a room. Plants that were dying in my house would get better if Graham fixed them. My grandmother met him accidentally one day and still asks about him.

I sat back on the couch to watch Graham and the girls.

They did it all wrong, those girls. With hair spray. When I found out that hair spray was horrible just like everyone knew in the first place but went ahead and did anyway, I was careful to never do any of that stuff if I could help it again. Just because it's simpler to forget what you're doing is not a good reason to put gook on your hair. But they were doing it wrong with nylons and pancake make-up and those Merry Widows on their already slender waists. They were cluttered up with too many formalities to ever get the thing off the ground.

One of the main Brando things is dispensed formalities. If you stand around waiting for the guy to open the door for you, you'll suddenly discover you're with Ernest Borgnine and that Marlon Brando has gone to Ensenada with the car hop.

Graham, whose name I gathered from hearing it cried across the room, looked at me.

I looked away and then back, he was still looking. He was going, I thought, to play it all the way through. Sally pulled him from the crowd and brought him to the couch next to me where she'd been sitting. It was a strategical error, though how she could have missed those two huge spears sticking out of me, I don't know. She introduced us.

"I'd like to talk to you before you go," Graham said

with this intimate Manhattan chocolate-kisses voice which reminded me of the "Dead End Kids", all of whom I loved except for Mugsy, whom I was enslaved by. Graham reminded me of Mugsy and I'd loved Mugsy since I could see.

"You would?" I asked.

"Are you old enough?"

"I was 18 today," I said. Jailbait was still a consideration before the Beatles.

"You're old enough," he said. His voice was exactly like chocolate, it was like chocolate chocolate chocolate. One of my dreams of childhood was opening a door and finding an entire room with nothing but chocolate in it, no air, all chocolate so that you had to chip off a piece with a knife just to begin. I have never wondered how the chocolate got into the room. His voice was what he used to tell the lies with, but it didn't matter, I suppose, since blue heaven and chocolate noise make distress over lies pathetic.

It was like a skipped formality when he lied, to see if you were true.

Nobody was looking like Brigitte Bardot yet but me, except for beatniks, and that's no fun, they threw ashes on the spirit of the thing. So what Graham must have seen when he looked at me was a tall, clean California Bardot with too much brown eyeliner, too messy hair and probably too young. I wore my lavender sheath and sandals, no stockings or bracelets. I was dying to kiss him.

"Let's go," I said.

"Where?"

I dragged him into a back room where the coats were and locked the door. I'd absconded with everyone's heart's desire.

"What's your name?"

"Graham Thomas."

"What's your real name?"

"Graham Thomas."

"Why are you an actor?"

"Who told you I was an actor?"

"Sally."

"I'm a director. I used to act but they make you ride horses all day and I got sick of breaking my ass. Besides, horses are so stupid you could hit them with a stick."

I laughed.

That was the trouble, I suppose, he always made me laugh. I changed the subject. "Do you give head?"

"I'm captain of the Olympics. Why? Don't any of the kids at school go down on each other these days?"

"No. They're callow," I said. I was sitting on the bed of coats and now leaned back on my elbows so that my skirt hitched up to a point that would be fashionable only a few years later but was then unheard of.

"Do you give head?" he asked. His hands resisted me, he was always very smart.

"Not very good," I said.

"Somebody should teach you," he said.

"Oh."

"I'll pick you up tomorrow night."

"Where?"

"Near where you live."

"How come not at my house?" I asked.

He paused.

"You're married!" I said. I accused, accurately.

"Yeah," he shrugged.

"Are you in love with your wife?"

"Madly."

"You *asshole!*"

★ 163 ★

My lavender dress and I rose from the coats and slammed into the bathroom, where we doubled up deflated from "married men." Like the hair spray, I just used it. I drew the line because that's where the ones who used hair spray and went to UCLA without question said to draw it. There was this huge "married man" neon sign that read like a Times Square newspaper ribbon about "ruining your life" and "only bring unhappiness" and "they only want to use you." I looked in the mirror—no tears, fortunately for my too much brown eyeliner. Shit, I said to myself, if I stop now, I'm liable to wind up with a fucking picket fence.

He was waiting.

"You asshole!" I said again, under the circumstances.

"Well, darling . . ." his hot-fudge voice trailed, "I'd rather *be* one than in *love* with one."

"What time tomorrow?"

It lasted a long time and was worth it.

When Kennedy was assassinated, Graham and I'd been having a fight and I hadn't seen him for 2 months. I went to Santa Monica Blvd. to look for him and even now that he's got all this money and power, I still think of him in the Arrow Market or Carl's. He loved walking through markets and making remarks about the products, and I would be stuck to his side, laughing. So I thought, with Kennedy assassinated, he must be in the market because there is, for some people, nothing more of a solace than certain markets.

He was standing out in front of the Arrow Market with an armful of groceries when I finally found him after wandering up and down Santa Monica for two hours. He was talking to friends.

"Hello, darling," he said. They were always my fights, he never was in them, he used to just wait until I stopped being mad.

"Listen . . ." I said. "I mean, what do you think? . . ."

"Oh, about Kennedy?" He laughed. "Well, I'll tell ya, it *is* terrible and a tragedy and all that . . . but it sure does pick up daytime tv."

Nowadays I drink tequila when I can't get French Champagne. Graham's in London in limousines with violent beauties, though I know he'd prefer rumpled 18-year-olds just as I'd rather have Rainier. Sometimes he telephones from some studio in the middle of the night 9,000 miles away and tells me he has always loved me and really loves me still.

"Yeah, well, send me some money," I say.

"What? I can't hear you, there's something the matter with the phone."

He lies and I'm broke.

But when I hear that liar's chocolate voice I am, each time, thrown into a confusion of the night he came in alone from the stars.

My cousin Polly is graduating from high school out in Long Island this summer. She was visiting here on New Year's Eve and shared that can of Rainier Ale with me, the one where I gained 5 lbs. In spite of her sophistication about drugs, I was glad to see that she got knocked for a loop over just one glass and went dancing on Olvera Street with the Mexicans and my parents, something far beneath her acid dignity. She told me she hated school and didn't know what she wanted to do and I said she could come stay with me if I had any money by that time. She's never seen "Zapata."

Graham said he could screen it for us when he gets back.

Mrs. Standfast would not be happy with my record. It would not do credit to Hollywood High, whose motto is "Seek Honor Through Service," and here I am with no children, no dog, no husband and no divorce, even. But as an adventuress, it is to be said that sometimes I've ridden a white horse, clutching its mane, into blue heaven and tasted the sins of the Green Death.

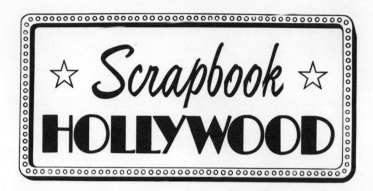
☆ *Scrapbook* ☆
HOLLYWOOD

Valentino

Football field of
Hollywood High
with Sheik painted
on Boys' Gym.

PHOTO BY SOL BABITZ

One of my father's more fabulous photos, Stravinsky descending from boat staircase.

Mother,
Mae
Babitz

PHOTOGRAPHER UNKNOWN

The $5.00 picture
(grandpa piece)

My father's sister, Thelma Babitz being Isadora as a teenager in some Hollywood ruin.

Agnes and her brother in Louisiana long ago, attesting to author's half-Cajun ancestry.

Mother, father and author
in 1943 — author disgruntled
in spite of beautiful parents.

Author, 1944

Below:
author, age 14,
reading
biography of
Elinor Glyn
(author of
"It" and
"Three Weeks"
and other '20
classics).

Sister, mother and author in Petrified Forest.

PHOTO BY SOL BABITZ

Mother and author

Mae Babitz
(author's mother)

PHOTO BY SOL BABITZ

Mother and father
in early 1940's, taken
by author's father.

Mrs V. Sokoloff, Vera Stravinsky,
Igor Stravinsky, Vladimir Sokoloff,
Mae Babitz, Germaine Prevost (who
commissioned Stravinsky to write
an Elegy in memory of Laurent
Halleux for Viola),

Darius Milhaud (seated) and
author dressed in purple and
white checks.

Author's sister at
Watts Towers.

Mother and father with birds—
1972

Photo of Hollywood High
by author.

Sane and peaceful
Marshall High.

Little
girl
on
Olvera
Street.

One-and-a-half
taquitos!

Hollywood and Vine at 9:15 a.m. - Friday morning

Below: View of Hollywood and Vine photographed by author hanging out of Taft Building.

*Malevolent banana leaves and palm,
photos taken by author at Hollywood High,*

PHOTO BY EVE BABITZ

*Hollywood High lawns facing
Sunset Blvd.*

Author at Polar
Palace during
Tweed Days
(photo by booth)

Author, age 15,
in school photo
from Marshall
High.

Author in booth
in New York City
perishing from
Consumption of
Claustrophobic
environs.

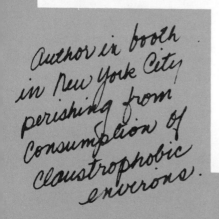

*Rosie
looking
aggrieved*

Rosie Nosie

Rosie looking "irresistible"

LOS ANGELES - Bunker Hill 2nd & Grand

MAE-49
BABITZ

Bunker Hill Drawing
by Mae Babitz

Plaza Drawing by
Mac Babitz

Angels Flight Drawing by
Mae Babitz

★

GRAMMAR

I know how to draw a face.

According to Greek anatomy, the perfect face is 1/8 the size of the whole body (in the Renaissance, it's 1/7). So if you draw a face, you measure 7 more down and there is the bottom of the foot. The eyes are in the middle of the head, exactly. The mouth is measured precisely from the top of the upper lip at its points to the center of the mouth. The breasts of the female nude are exactly between the chin and the waist and stick out just so far.

Picasso knows how to draw a face, only how come half the face is over there and the mouth is this huge hole and it's blue? And real faces, even beautiful faces, are sometimes not 1/8 the size of the human body. Sophia Loren's all wrong.

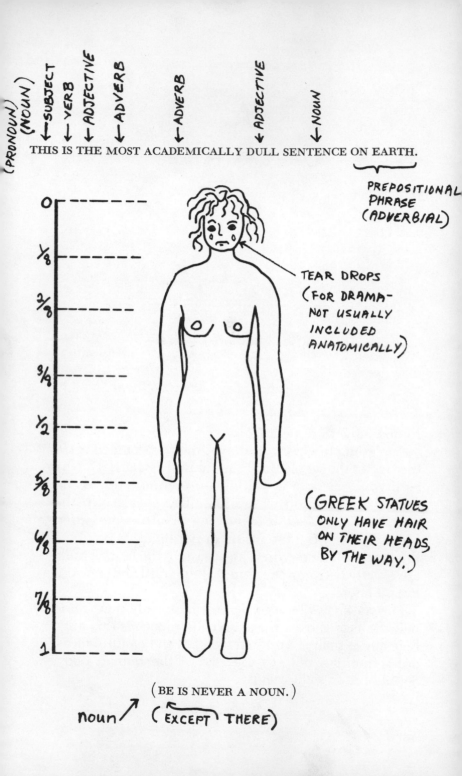

(PRONOUN)
(NOUN)

← SUBJECT
← VERB
← ADJECTIVE
← ADVERB
← ADVERB
← ADJECTIVE
← NOUN

THIS IS THE MOST ACADEMICALLY DULL SENTENCE ON EARTH.

PREPOSITIONAL PHRASE (ADVERBIAL)

0
⅛
2/8
3/8
½
5/8
4/8
7/8
1

TEAR DROPS (FOR DRAMA—NOT USUALLY INCLUDED ANATOMICALLY)

(GREEK STATUES ONLY HAVE HAIR ON THEIR HEADS, BY THE WAY.)

(BE IS NEVER A NOUN.)

noun↗ (EXCEPT THERE)

GRAMMAR

In the 10th grade I took a test and got the highest grade in the city in grammar. I had learned the kind of cozy mathematical sense of well-being you can derive from a parsed sentence. I liked the way a sentence looked all Royal Familyed up with blood lines and right angles, all those reasons. But it seemed to me after looking at it that a point that parses is a point that people'd rather go to the circus to avoid seeing than hang around and appreciate. Though I can't stop saying "were" with "if" instead of "was," I've tried to let a little more of the confusion that comes with looking at Sophia Loren rather than the cozy 1/8 size of the head.

Picasso's faces are confusing.

I know how to draw a face.

I wonder if he felt the same way when someone said, "You can't draw a face like that," when the fact that the person could tell it was a face meant you could, as I felt when an instructor said, " 'Be' is never a noun."

If I knew how *not* to draw a face, I might be doing that instead.

EAST IS EAST

There are certain aspects of the East Coast that are inconceivable to someone who has lived his whole life in Los Angeles and vice versa. A friend of mine is head of his alumni association from Harvard and he lives in Boston. Alumni association, Harvard and Boston are all inconceivable to me, but my friend, nevertheless, exists. He asked, "What does it mean?"

"What?" I needed clarification. The Beverly Hills Hotel poolside was mostly Fag-Rock entourage that day and Miss Plumbkiss was sitting in a Cabana with a snood on and silver shoes. I thought my friend might have meant her, but didn't want to chance it. "What does *what* mean?"

"When I called my friend who is a producer, I asked

him what he was doing tomorrow and he said, 'I'm either going to do some work on my plane or go to New York.' "

"So?"

"What does it mean?"

"It means he's rich and he'd like to work on his plane but he'll probably have to go to New York."

"But . . . *I* always know at least a month in advance when I'm going to fly to the opposite coast . . ."

"Yeah?" I never know in the morning what I'll be doing at 6.

Miss Plumbkiss got up and I said hi when she went by. She stopped to chat about a mutual friend in New York, one we both knew well. Miss Plumbkiss said, defenselessly, "I'd give, God, I don't know, anything, to see him right now . . . Anything."

Her face was completely taken with wistfulness and she slung her silver purse over her shoulder with a sad shrug before she went on.

"God," my friend groaned, his flesh crawling from the proximity of Miss Plumbkiss beneath the afternoon sunshine. But I thought Miss Plumbkiss was beautiful with her perfect white skin. And sad. And though I'd only met her once briefly in our mutual friend's weird motel room at the Tropicana Motor Hotel years before, we both remembered each other at once.

Not like at lunch.

This man across the patio at the Polo Lounge looked at my friend with the "don't I know yous?" wondered so hard through his squinting eyes that I made my friend look over at him. Something he never would have done as a matter of course because he noticed no one.

"I know that guy from some place," my friend said.
They'd been roommates for their Junior Year at Harvard.

He knew exactly where he'd be in a month, but he didn't know who he was with at the time. It's an East Coast attitude, it seems to me. To spend a year in a room with someone and not remember who they are is inconceivable to me. Yet he exists to ask what does it mean when a guy might go to New York tomorrow unless he could stay and work on his plane and he was annoyed with me for saying hello to Miss Plumbkiss.

His ex-roommate is Californianized, a movie director. He looked at my friend with withdrawn uncertainty. He would never go to the next reunion of the alumni that they spoke of, I could tell. In fact, I knew his ex-roommate much better than my friend. I couldn't really describe it to you except to say that three months later, in another restaurant, sitting across the room, we saw each other and nodded, acquaintances.

There are some aspects of the East Coast which people from L.A. regard as color-blindness, just as I cannot understand, ever, about Harvard or Boston, a certain tunnel quality that cuts off periphery vision and stops one from looking across restaurants, I guess it is. Or not knowing where you'll be in a month.

NEW YORK CONFIDENTIAL

(NO FICTIONAL CHARACTERS— THEY WERE STORIES ENOUGH WITHOUT IT)

I went to New York on March 6th, 1966, and left on March 5th, 1967. One year.

Because what I was supposed to be doing was being the "office manager" of the *East Village Other* (an underground newspaper), I had the advantage of knowing everyone and everything at once. It wasn't like I came from Kansas and went to work at Woolworth's. John Wilcock (one of the founders of *EVO*) talked about me so much that some girl who got around started calling me "Wondercunt" before I'd even shown up, I was so famous. John had some idea that I was going to stage this party, the *East Village Other* April Fools Ball (or something), and he convinced Walter Bowart, the Editor, that I was just the one for the job. I have never considered having a party a job.

★ 173 ★

When I arrived in New York, John it turns out is in Chicago, so Walter Bowart, whom I'd never met before and who didn't believe there was such a place as California and who was suspicious of John anyway because John liked Andy Warhol and Walter thought Andy Warhol was the Death of Art, Walter put me up my first night in New York in the apartment of a friend. The friend had written speeches for Senator McCarthy and spent 5 years in jail for changing his mind. In New York, everybody was a story.

Walter and I were born on consecutive days. We always understood each other perfectly and had a wonderful time pulling the wool over everyone's eyes until he saw the dove of peace on acid, which was a drag. But anyway, we are friends. He's an orphan, it was part of his story.

The second morning he took me to Carol's and it was love at first sight to this very day, only she's up in San Francisco with children and I can't stand children. Carol was perfect. She looked exactly like me, only she was black. She was from the Bronx and was a proofreader and she'd once been one of Walter's girl friends when he tended bar at Stanley's, a Lower East Side Bar. Carol and I took acid every chance we got.

While I was in New York Donovan's "Sunshine Superman" album came out and so did "Revolver." The poet Frank O'Hara got run over on Fire Island and died.

The party I had was one of those things where everyone who wasn't there wishes they'd been, but actually at the time it was like a Bruegel, too sweaty and people hanging from the rafters. I invited seven bands, and since it was held in the Village Gate or whatever that

★ 174 ★

place is called on Bleecker, there was only a tiny dressing room. There were seven drum sets, never mind
amps. Right before the thing was to start Buzzy Linhart, who is my friend, handed me a piece of colored
paper and told me to eat it, and 20 minutes later things
started to get real shiny and then I was completely on
acid and couldn't handle a thing for the entire rest of
the party. Carol did everything.

LSD was not illegal in those days.

It was all right that I was out of control because the
party was completely homogeneous, Everyone knew
what to do, I was pleased to observe. The seven bands
played, Timothy Leary stood on that stage and gave a
speech about levels of consciousness (I snickered behind my hand as he turned into Billy Graham and the
rest of the room started pulsing), television cameras
interfered beautifully with everything and Flexus, a
group who staged happenings and from whence we
have Yoko Ono and the husband who's skipped with
the kid, Tony Cox, Flexus were all dressed in overalls
and had tall ladders and throughout the night they put
up crepe-paper streamers in that den of iniquity like a
high-school gym. Nobody saw them, it was like they
were invisible. There were about 700 people there. The
room fit about 500. And all those amps, tv cameras and
sweaty bodies.

"How could Bruegel stand it?" I demanded of a girl
standing next to me. "How could he live?"

"Like this," she said and pushed her blouse ruffle
away from the inside of her wrist, where I saw a sun
tattooed in every color. But just then we were dragged
onto the stage under all those tv lights, and the businessmen decided there had to be a fake Slum goddess

crowned. The word "Slum goddess" was Ed Sanders' from the Fugs (he played their band), and these fat men with mustaches and cigars had decided the gimmick would be to crown a Slum goddess, so there I was holding Carol's hand and trying to hide behind the girl with the tattooed wrist on the stage with all these lights. Buzzy Linhart, Gentleman Buzzy, strode manfully out and took the crown from the man and put it on his own head. Buzzy was shirtless and his hair stuck out a foot in every direction and it was just the right touch to give the men with cigars the slip.

"You can ask me anything you want," Buzzy whispered to me, "except what's happening."

Buzzy played in a band called the Seventh Son or Sun and he was a vibe player and guitar player of astounding genius who, in those days, abused drugs so much that I'm surprised he's still alive, but he is. He doesn't even drink any more. He has a face of beauty and a soul of Olympian goodness and, boy, could he play the guitar. Everyone stole from him.

Buzzy's story now is that he wrote Bette Midler's theme song.

The girl with the tattoo turned out to be my friend. She used to have cats that would leap right through the glass of her ninth-story apartment window and live. She once told me, "Marianne Faithful has 36 pairs of shoes and goes around barefoot. She's the kind of a girl who is always carrying books about witchcraft, only they're *new.*" This girl with the tattoo, Suzanna, wore kohl and dressed like Bip by Marcel Marceau.

I wanted to be Slum goddess. That was the sort of Playmate of the Month the *East Village Other* came up with using Ed Sanders' name. There was a girl who was supposed to be it that issue, but since I was right there in the office, I aced her out. We have been in a stage of ambivalence toward each other since that moment, and when she tried to take my boy friend away from me at a party, I was not surprised. I paid her back later. I am sure she'll get me again someday. It's the fortunes of war that Robin, who is a girl of enormous deadpan talent (she's an actress, but not an L.A. kind of one), should forever be out to get me, but somehow simultaneously we have maintained what would pass as a friendship to an observer. She was more beautiful than me and should have been the Slum goddess.

The Fugs used to rehearse every day at the Astor Theater up in Cooper Union and I used to go watch them. Ed Sanders, Tuli Kupferberg, Ken Weaver and this kid named John Anderson were in that weird thing together. The only one who knew how to play really was John Anderson, and then he allowed himself to be drafted (Weaver never got over it and neither did I). Everyone said that Ed Sanders was a poet.

I met tons of poets in New York. There are none whatsoever in L.A.

If anyone in L.A. said they were a poet, everyone would get mildly embarrassed and go look for someone else to talk to.

I ran into Ed Sanders when he was doing the Manson book later in L.A., and I don't know about poetry, but prose he can write.

When summer came, I found myself a boy friend who had air-conditioning. He was one of my favorite kinds of men—German. Is it because I'm Jewish that German accents do it to me? He was the third name. There were three names on all the material, and his was always the third—Leary, Alpert and Metzner. I cannot believe that either Timothy Leary or Richard Alpert ever got in the way of Ralph Metzner doing the hard part. They all grew to loathe each other, it seemed to me, as time went by, but they were stuck in it together because their three names were on all the papers and books. And they had to have Ralph there. The German accent gave the thing an air of authenticity you couldn't get otherwise.

One Friday, Ralph suggested we leave the City and go to the Country. The Country was Millbrook, the Castalia Foundation where Tim had settled into this rich-kids mansion that had about 40 rooms in it and a place called the bungalow. Somehow a Victorian mansion with Buddhas everywhere wasn't really the Country, but it was different. Timothy Leary's Rosemary used to cook or supervise breakfast, lunch and dinner for 35 people a day. They got crates of Velveeta cheese. Everyone smoked Pall Mall Menthols.

The life in the Country was slow, so Ralph and I went to bed at about 10:30. At 1:00 there was a knock at the door. We were in the attic, so it was unlikely that anyone would be knocking on the door, but they were.

"Who's there?" Ralph asked.

"Police."

The man came in with a flashlight, and I sat innocently up in bed, letting the sheet slide from my naked body and pretending I was 10.

"Oh," he stammered, shining the light away. He was a gentleman from Poughkeepsie who had been deputized for the raid, not a real cop. "Oh . . . I'll be back in half an hour to search the room."

Which was good.

Marya Mannes was there doing a story for *McCall's*, and she had to strip for the matron. She held my hand and we got along fine. There were about 40 adults there and 4 of them got busted. The phone was suddenly out of order and no one was allowed to leave the house, so no lawyer could be telephoned until the morning from a phone booth at a gas station, though when Ralph came back the phone was working again. They were looking, those gentlemen from Poughkeepsie, for the only thing that seemed worthwhile to them—pornography. They were positive that young girls were forced to make stag movies, and when they came upon Tim Leary's son's darkroom, they went into completely "we were right" police seriousness. They took *The Agony and the Ecstasy* as part of their evidence. Nothing pornographic ever went on around that ex-Harvard professor. He wasn't the type. What he used to do in secret was read the sports page and drink Scotch. Timothy Leary is innocent.

Well, that was the Country. We went a few more times to testify, but the charges were dropped against the four. They busted a kid who was sleeping outside in the forest because he had about enough grass to roll half a joint. They busted a married couple who were unable to dispose of the evidence because the evidence was an attache case neatly fitted out to hold bottles in which every psychedelic known to the civilized world was contained in labeled jars. They also busted Timothy Leary and actually handcuffed him. He wore white and no shoes and looked divine. Even Marya Mannes succumbed at the moment, though later she wrote this piece in *McCall's* which made me fly into a rage. They busted Tim because it was his house.

They tried to get Rosemary to testify before a grand jury about Tim, and when she wouldn't answer they put her in jail for a month. They were going to keep her longer, but at the end of the month Tim just kind of came and got her, smiling, and they figured . . . Rosemary was innocent.

Because they questioned us without lawyers (which couldn't be reached on account of the phone), they had to let everyone go. Which was lucky. That whole weekend was not very Country.

I never liked Millbrook.

The kid who got busted with half a joint became my dearest friend in the world and now I can't find him and no one knows where he is and no one has even heard anything about him for about 4 years. He is the only person I know like that.

I didn't know him until later, months after I'd moved away from Ralph and back to my own wretched 40-dollar-a-month slanting-floor Polish–Puerto Rican home. While I was at Ralph's they used my apartment as the headquarters of the Timothy Leary Defense Fund, and a girl, a secretary, put her cigarette out in my antique papier-mâché bird box from Persia. She was much more guilty than most people. The whole time I lived in New York I knew I was going back to L.A. so I never believed I was actually living there and never furnished my apartment with more than a bed and a chair. Once I started making collages, the magazines took over and then the place was really really ungodly, scraps all over the slanting floor, glue.

One day Barry came down to the *East Village Other* because he was a photographer and thought they paid for pictures. They paid for almost nothing there, but I went back to the Chelsea with him. He lived in the Chelsea Hotel on the 4th floor, so you had to take the elevator with all the old women with turquoise jewelry. The elevator was the slowest in the city of New York.

Barry was extremely young; he was only about 21. He was from Detroit and wanted to be Avedon. He was one of my obvious inclinations; all women simply adored him. He would have adored me if I'd weighed 109 and was two inches taller. As it was, I weighed 145 and was 5' 7". I was way too fat. But I had to do something in New York, and eating seemed less evil than the other alternatives, like Bellevue or the needle.

On Friday, I would call Barry (by this time I was working uptown as a secretary) and tell him to get up, I was coming over. Oh, he'd say, what time is it? Four, I'd say. He sometimes slept for weeks and wouldn't go out of his room unless someone called him. Why doesn't anyone call me or come over? he asked me once after three weeks of total divorce from the world, which had only been broken into because I thought he might like me even though I was fat. Barry, I told him, everyone loves you. It's just that you never have any beer.

The next time I came over five people were sitting on the floor drinking beer.

"Do you think I should get Fritos?" he asked, worried. The young host.

"Not unless you want them to hang around forever."

"I do."

"Well, I'll go down and get some for you."

The beer was outside on the window ledge, freezing.

On Friday I would call him and after work I'd take the subway down to the Chelsea and go and wake Barry up again. He was one of the most darling men I ever knew. His looks were all tawny and nice. He used to wear polo coats and could have worn spats. He had tawny thick hair which he didn't wear too long and he grew a mustache so that when he smiled and you saw one front tooth was missing. It was really funny. He used to write LSD in Magic Marker on the walls of uptown elevators very neatly in small capital letters.

He used to make me kiss him on 22nd Street and 7th Avenue when he was eating a banana.

For Christmas I gave him a cane with an ivory wolf head on top, and he developed a limp without further ado.

On Friday I would knock on his door and he'd come groggily to let me in before going back to bed. I'd turn on the television and get things going until finally he'd feel it was safe to get up. There were proof sheets everywhere. He shot fashion.

By about 7, we'd be downstairs trying to get a taxi. Either I'd blow all my money or he'd blow all his money. It was the only sensible thing to do. Once when I was mortally depressed and thought about dying, Barry got a check for a thousand dollars and we spent the entire thing in one weekend on champagne cocktails. It seemed the only sensible thing to do.

I'd run up to my horrid apartment and dump food out for the cat and run back down again and the world was our oyster. We usually went to the Koh-i-noor, an Indian restaurant on like Second Avenue and 4th Street or around there.

"Andy Warhol's having a party," I'd turn over delicately. The evening lay naked before us. We could go anywhere or do anything. It was New York City.

"Yeah?"

"Yeah, and they're having one at the Dakota too."

"Oh, boy!"

"And 'Un Chien Andalou' is playing." (It was Barry's favorite movie.)

"Oh, well let's go see that."

"O.K."

We'd get let out at the restaurant and go across the street and get beer to drink with the food. Ale. Ballantine. No Ranier in New York City. By the time we were halfway finished with dinner an almost unearthly sense of well-being would lift us both to the highest planes of food-gladness.

"Ahhhhh . . ." Barry would say, leaning back and smiling.

We never went anywhere. We'd think when we were done that we might go to Max's, but in the end we just went back to the Chelsea and watched TV. Barry had fantastic drugs and sometimes we'd go onto the roof of the Chelsea and smoke DMT, but mostly we'd just smoke hash and watch tv for the entire weekend. Every now and then I'd go home and feed the cat.

We were not lovers.

Barry's friends were mostly tied up in this agency that took fantastically New York City color photographs of things like Gloom Toothpaste. I could never be friends with them and that's why I can't find out where he is. I asked Tim Leary and he doesn't know. He hasn't heard anything about any of those people, though even the straight photographers once lived at Millbrook.

Salvador Dali loved Barry. Maybe he knows where he is. Anyway, Salvador Dali speaks wretched English and Barry speaks no French or Spanish, but somehow Dali telephoned Barry the first day he arrived in New York at the St. Regis and they managed to communicate into complete madness.

It was Barry who made it possible for me to introduce Frank Zappa to Salvador Dali, one of my favorite things I ever did. Frank Zappa had been there always in Los Angeles and I have known him since I was about 17. He came to New York to do a record and we were walking down Madison Avenue one evening handing out "We Will Bury You" buttons that Frank had had made up of himself glowering over the top of his glasses, sitting behind a desk. The time was right.

"Meet us at the King Cole Bar," Barry said.

Frank wore a monkeyskin coat that came down to his feet. Underneath that he wore pink and yellow striped pants, shoes (it was cold) and a silken jersey basketball T-shirt in neon yellow-orange. His hair curled sweetly around his narrow, pointy face. The guy at the door said he had to wear a tie.

Frank tied it in a bow. It was silver satin and not a bow tie, and handed him one.

Dali took one look at Frank from across the room and rose to his feet in immediate approbation. If Frank was not for Dali, Dali didn't care; he was for Frank.

So I really had very little trouble introducing them. We drank chartreuse.

Dali said he would like to see the Mothers rehearse, which Frank was doing later on. They planned to meet at the Dom on St. Mark's Place, which was where Frank was playing. Dali was very anxious to see that act, as you can imagine.

The management of the Dom was having trouble with the management of Frank Zappa and locked Frank Zappa out so that we sat on the steps, locked out, as Dali and Gala, his wife, pulled up and got out of a taxi into the dangers of the Lower East Side.

It was a shame.

When it turned out positively that they weren't going to let us in, Dali and Gala dejectedly got another cab and went back to the St. Regis. I went to the Chelsea to find Barry and Frank went back to the Hotel Albert or whever he was staying to argue with the fucking management who had ruined something that was very delicate and could only happen once. Dali and Zappa alone together in a big empty room with musical instruments.

Barry and I went drinking.

Max's was where everyone went to drink.

Barry got a girl friend, one of those thin ones who looked like Holyoke or Vassar and horses. She didn't know what I was and Barry couldn't figure out how to explain, so we saw less of each other.

Also, I moved in with an anarchist dealer who taught art and had red hair. He had aliases. He's the only person I ever knew with an alias. I called him by it. I didn't even know it was made up.

He had red hair and a German shepherd and we talked for hours and hours and drank Wild Turkey. He had a chair which was made out of leather, an easy chair that you could lean back in, and every so often it fell over and you wound up looking at the ceiling. He thought this was a good anarchistic chair. His alias was Mike.

I met him one morning as he was walking by with a day-old pumpkin pie he'd bought for 15 cents. He insisted I come with him and eat it, so I did in spite of the fact that he had a dog and I hate dogs. The next day I moved in. I kept my apartment for Rosie, my cat, who hated dogs even more than I did.

Mike was a thief and a gourmet.

I lost about 15 pounds living with him because we only ate the finest, and being around Mike got you involved in a lot of physical exercise that didn't just come from fucking. I used to run off because he was such a shoplifter. Wine and stuff, he'd steal.

I worked on Madison Avenue as a secretary, though I could neither type nor acquiesce to my circumstances. I hated being a secretary on Madison Avenue. I hated being put on hold and I hated waiting for elevators. My boss acted like he'd just shot meth. Always.

He'd come in in the morning, his trench coat flapping, the door slamming open and him in mid-sentence in a voice too anxious and too loud, "Any messages, any messages? What do I have to do today? Where's the mail? What are my appointments like? Did you do the expense account?" Shit.

He was an ad salesman for magazines. I told him Barry was my fiancé and got a ring at the dime store. The only good thing that happened was when it snowed so hard no traffic could go up and down Madison Avenue and my boss was stuck, there was nowhere to turn. He was fat and had blue eyes like a baby and I think he thought he was crafty and maybe he was, but shit!, that "Any messages?" thing made me want to kill him.

In February on Valentine's Day Mike and I put a sticker heart on the German shepherd's forehead and went to our favorite restaurant, John's, on 12th Street between 1st and 2nd Avenues, I think. I realized that it was almost March, and in March I could go.

I wondered how I was going to get all those magazines back to L.A., the main part of my life being cen-
tered around collages. It was like the white corpuscles,
it staved off disaster. So I sent 90 pounds of *Life*s to L.A.
in a duffel bag by Greyhound Bus. It wasn't too expensive.

I took a cab to the airport without telling anyone but
Carol and Mike that I was leaving. I didn't want to call
Barry in front of Mike. I called Barry from the airport.

"Where've you been?" he asked. He was working.
You could hear rock-and-roll shooting music in back of
him; photographers play rock and roll to shoot. Barry
usually played the Stones.

"I'm leaving, I am done, the year's over," I said.

"Where're you going."

"L.A."

"You didn't say goodbye to me. Tomorrow's my
birthday."

"I'm at the airport."

"Oh . . . well, maybe I'll come see you."

"You won't. Anyway, I love you."

"I love you."

I sent him a singing telegram for his birthday. He
sent me two postcards from London. And that was the
end of him.

But I just couldn't stay in New York, though confiden-
tially, it might be fun to go back and try and look for
him. He must be around there somewhere. I should
have stayed for his birthday.

The cat, I took.

I didn't put in about how I testified about LSD to
Teddy Kennedy in the room the McCarthy hearings

were held in or about the time I woke up to someone telling me not to scream with their hand over my mouth or about how Walter Bowart had to find me an uptown job because the amount of money I was embezzling nearly floored him, but they were just stories. Everything about New York was a story.

My friend Annie told me that when she was in New York last time she'd been doing so many things that when she finally found herself alone she decided to just take a kind of a here-and-there ramble "just to think," she said, "you know." Rounding the corner, she was confronted with a wino wielding a broken glass bottle, so she threw five dollars at him and ran. That always seemed like the whole thing; they'll let you have stories, but you can't ever think in a certain way. There are no spaces between the words, it's one of the charms of the place. Certain things don't have to be thought about carefully because you're always being pushed from behind. It's like a tunnel where there's no sky.

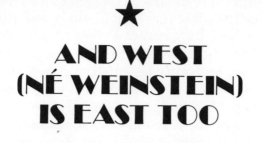

AND WEST
(NÉ WEINSTEIN)
IS EAST TOO

"Nathanael West is the best writer about Hollywood there ever was."

"No, he isn't"

The first speaker is someone from Chicago, the second is me, born in Hollywood. People from the East all like Nathanael West because he shows them it's not all blue skies and pink sunsets, so they don't have to worry: It's shallow, corrupt and ugly.

I think Nathanael West was a creep. Assuring his friends back at Dartmouth that even though he'd gone *to* Hollywood, he had not *gone* Hollywood. It's a little apologia for coming to the Coast for the money and having a winter where you didn't have to put tons of clothes on just to go out and buy a pack of cigarettes or a beer. And so people from New York and Chicago say, "Nathanael West is the best writer about Hollywood there ever was."

All the things that Nathanael West noticed are here. The old people dying, the ennui, the architecture and fat screenplay writers who think it's a tragedy when they can't get laid by the 14-year-old doxette in Gower Gulch, the same 14-year-old who'll ball the cowboys any old time. But if there had been someone, say, who wrote a book about New York, a nice, precise, short little novel in which New York was only described as ugly, horrendous and finally damned and that was the book everyone from elsewhere decided was the "best book about New York there ever was," people who grew up knowing why New York was beautiful would finally, right before dessert, throw their sherry across the table and yell, "I'll pick you up in a taxi, honey, and take you for a fucking guided tour, you blind jerk."

"But it's so manicured, I mean the grass isn't real, the plants look like plastic, they look like they're not real."

"But it's tropical here," I point out, wanting to throw Chicago freezes into their faces to remind them what they're missing. "It's not manicured, it's beautiful."

"Yeah, Jesus, I don't know, the best time I ever had in L.A. was when I stayed in a motel on the Sunset Strip."

"I know," I answer, "because in motels you don't start acquiring possessions. You don't need any possessions. You can rent anything you need and the rest is free."

I drive my friend from Chicago to his temporary abode, the apartment of some girl who's letting him stay at her house for the time he's in L.A. to play on a recording session. Where she lives is Gower Gulch, the very home of *Day of the Locust*. We have just had extraordinary rains and it is spring, so the bougainvilleas are rampant and the poinsettias which don't match are almost arching to meet each other in front of her old stucco, falling-apart house, the house of a girl I don't know. The house is overgrown, but all the houses up there are mostly overgrown.

"*That*'s manicured?" I demand. The grass is a foot high.

"That's brush." He does not see.

"But don't you think this is beautiful?" The papery flowers, a blood/magenta color black against the sky of rainswept blue, dangle in the air above us, it is like Mexico, the lushness is so simple, each ingredient of the highest quality, the air, the colors, the slight breeze.

He shrugs.

For him, still, Nathanael West is all he will see with his turquoise Chicago eyes.

"New York has a kind of push," he argues further.

"I know. You never have time to think. It's one of its charms."

"Yeah, it is."

He can forgive New York's shortcomings and think of them as charms, but he cannot forgive L.A. for the spaces between the words, the blandness and the complete absence of push. I can appreciate New York's charms, but I am speechless with rage when someone earlier that week sat across from me at a table and said, in a London drawl, "New York is quite nice, actually, but Los Angeles . . . There are no pubs here."

"You stupid asshole creep," I want to shout. "You provincial dope."

"I suppose in order to appreciate this place," he continues to the man at my left (he has not spoken directly to me at any time during the lunch because you don't talk to women where he's from), "to truly appreciate it, I mean, I shall have to visit Forest Lawn."

"No!" I cry.

"But it's very Los Angeles, isn't it?" He turns blasély to me.

"No, it's not Los Angeles, it's English."

"I'm sorry, I don't understand." He's so polite.

"All English people who come to L.A. always head right to Forest Lawn and go nuts. There's something about it that gets them. I've never been there. People from L.A. don't as a rule hang around Forest Lawn until the end."

"But there's no place for them to go, and when they do, people from L.A. have to travel vast amounts of distance."

"Lots of distance, but hardly any time, the freeways . . ."

But he's not listening, he's turned back to the man on my left, he's been polite long enough.

Like talking about uprisings in front of the slaves, people travel to Los Angeles from more civilized spots and cast their insults upon the days, only to see their own reflections sniffing down their noses back. It's perfectly all right to say, "Los Angeles is so garish and a wasteland," as they sit beneath the arbors and pour themselves another glass of wine though it's already 3 p.m. and they should be getting back to the studio to earn their money.

But the true secrets of Los Angeles flourish everywhere. All they allow themselves is their own image

★ 192 ★

reflected in a glass Nathanael West holds up for them so they won't be seduced by the sunsets.

I wonder if Nathanael West changed his name before or after he came out here, married my sister Eileen and died in a car crash. Not that it matters, since he never got seduced unless he did it behind everyone's back while he wrote how vile it all was, about the old people dying and the 14-year-old doxette balling the cowboys with condescending remarks about, "There is something not altogether disgusting about people trying to live in beauty," so that the bougainvilleas didn't stand a chance and my friend from Chicago can't see them.

★
FAIRY TALE

The first year and a half I went to Le Conte Jr. High I read fairy tales. I walked to school with a girl who was a fellow victim of circumstance because we hated each other and had grown up right across the street from each other and were the same age. The circumstance was that we were always thrown together. Even in summer.

Each morning I'd dress with resignation and excruciating care to join the enemy and walk to school, about 8 blocks. During this crucial period before I faced my real friends, she tore me apart and analyzed my pitiful life. She was older than I was, she was more physically developed and so she felt it was her duty. By the time I was 14 I had still not started my period or come even close to showing any signs of my present form and she would weigh my chances with "Maybe you can become a career woman." Finally I arrived at school, destroyed.

This last Christmas I saw my neighbor, but she's not my neighbor any more, she has to live in Brooklyn! With the wisdom of age, I see now that what she felt toward me was not scorn but jealousy and that she was terrified that I might turn out to have a future or even be great. But then, in that first year and a half, I could only counter with fairy tales about frogs turning into princes—they seemed about right and defused what she threw at me each morning as she looked at my choice of clothing from head to toe and laughed.

"Oh, Evie," she'd sneer, "is *that* the blouse you're going to wear?"

"I . . . What's the matter with it?"

"Well, if you don't know, I'm not going to tell you."

She has to live in Brooklyn!

THE CHICKEN

It has a certain rural quality, the place I lived in on Formosa.

When I lived there, there was a period during which I was often visited with bad dreams which would wake me up at 5 a.m. with my heart pounding.

It was a season of Spring and so I was comforted because even in the flats of Hollywood which have come to be overlayed by strange hookers and other things I don't even want to find out, it is still Spring when it is Spring.

I dressed and went for walks remarkable for their pastoral tranquility when you realized that the day that was to follow with smog and the kind of brazen unholiness was sure to come to La Brea and Sunset like always. The funny thing was that just twenty feet off

Sunset and you were no longer subject to men in giant cars not rolling down their windows but merely honking to pick you up for a price, though occasionally a carful of black guys would mistakenly take a side street and look at you with God knows what in their eyes. Enough hate to give you nightmares, anyway.

But in the mornings at 5 a.m., I used to take my Brownie camera sometimes and just walk through the streets meeting the cats. The cats are all out sitting on porches waiting for "them" to wake up and feed them. Meanwhile, the cats catch the first drops of sunlight and squint dopily with their front paws in the second position of ballet.

There are still a lot of trees everywhere and so the birds, too, are awake, thousands of them. All different kinds, even crows and hummingbirds.

But the cats have always been what I look for. Just to see their faces and variety. I love fluffy cats, I love crumby old bleeding tom cats and I like every description of kitten.

There are three basic personality factors in cats: The kind who run up when you say hello and rub against you in cheap romance; the kind who run away certain that you mean to ravish them; and the kind who just look back and don't move a muscle. I love all three kinds.

Near to where I was living was a park called Plummer Park, which was given to the city by a Socialist who wanted it to be a People's Park. And it turned out to be a people's park. There were old people, naturally, who came to play Jewish games and sit in the sun. But there are also little kids, teenagers, adults who lie around reading and tennis players because there are tennis courts there and tennis is what everyone's doing now.

There is a hall where the All City Orchestra rehearses, school children who play well. There are all kinds of dancing classes and other classes like Yoga. An Audubon Society outpost is nestled in the middle of the park in a tiny home surrounded by a tall fence. Inside is a birdbath and trees of every description around the tiny home which houses a museum of birds and bird pictures and is opened each day by an older woman for its allotted amount of time so that people can come and sit by the birdbath and listen to the birds. It's a minute sanctuary.

Sometimes, in my morning ramblings, I would go directly to Plummer Park and just sit. While other times, I'd go to different streets, each of which has its own special life, its own cats, its own houses. It was because of this that I fell upon the House with the Chicken.

This house was beyond where I usually walked on the other side of the park and I was going past one morning across the street from it when I spotted three furry kittens washing their faces unsteadily in the misty sun.

"Hi, cats," I said and crossed the street to sit beside them on a stone driveway embankment. The kittens fell helter-skelter upon me and purred all the way up to my ear and were joined by other kittens and three mother cats.

The house was rundown and the driveway had not been used for years. A tree in the front lawn had a bird cage hanging from it which was used as a birdhouse, and the birds flew in and out to get food.

As I sat in kitten-land, I heard in back of me an unfamiliar kind of squawk. I twisted my head to look down the street when it did it again.

It was a street that on one side had the park I just

came from and on the other had little bungalow houses, all one-story and all with front lawns. None of the houses was as rundown as the one I sat by, but they were all small and would one day fall under the ax to make room for horrible apartments. Meanwhile, they were overgrown with flowers of every subtropical invention and painted the color of Easter Eggs.

About 100 feet down this street on the residential side but getting closer with every step came a chicken.

It was really a chicken. It was walking on the sidewalk with its arms inside its wings like Toshiro Mifune playing a samurai. Each three-pronged foot followed the last, left, right, left, right, closer and closer right to me, and I watched with the kittens.

When it came even with me and the creatures, I was sure the cats would do something cattish, but they didn't even look at the chicken. The chicken jumped up on the embankment beside me and waited its turn to be petted.

The sun had risen and it was about 7 so I could see the incredibly well-made chicken close up, the beak, the gorgeous feathers, the thing on its head. It was a rust-colored one and it thought it was a kitten. The kittens thought it was a kitten. The mother cats didn't and only licked their own faces and their own kittens.

I didn't know how to pet a chicken and, besides, I was transfixed by this glorious foreigner who had taken the seat next to me without so much as a by your leave. The chicken waited. When it realized that it wasn't going to be petted, it stopped trying to purr and walked with dignity to the front porch where it jumped up the stairs and where a flat dish of chicken feed, I suppose, waited for just such consolation.

Then it hopped down off the front porch and followed the driveway to the back of the house, which I couldn't see because the driveway was planted with corn about 5 feet high and copious. The last I saw of the chicken that first day, it turned round the bend at the far end of the house.

When I got home he said, "Where were you?"

"I went for a walk."

"Oh."

"There was this chicken!"

From then on, whenever I came home from the walks, he'd laugh and ask, "Did you see the chicken?"

He didn't believe there was a chicken. I stopped mistrusting it. (Though I could never quite pet it like a kitten.)

One Sunday afternoon we went to the park in spite of the fact that he said that parks "depressed" him. Plummer Park couldn't depress anyone, it's too bustling and too full of "the people," and besides there are too many 14-year-old girls in shorts for him to hang onto "depressed."

"Let's go see if the chicken's there," I suggested.

"Are you still dragging that chicken around?"

"Come on."

We went through the park to the other side and to the House with the Chicken.

For the first time I saw a human being connected to the house. It was an unironed middle-aged man inspecting the corn.

"That your corn?" I asked by way of conversation.

"Yeah, it sure is. It's got too much water, though. It's gone to flower. The corn is all gone to flower."

"Where's the chicken?"

"Oh, you mean the chicken?"

My friend was pretending he only knew me slightly and gazed down the street raptly as though he weren't listening.

"Yeah the chicken," I said, hoping the amenities about the corn was enough for a full discussion about the chicken.

"Well, it's under the house. That's where it stays mostly in the daytime. The dogs around here . . ."

"How come you have a chicken?"

"Oh, sometimes they get out of the kosher chicken delivery trucks, you know, over by the butcher shop down on Santa Monica . . ."

"And you take them?"

"Yeah, but most of them are too stupid, they get run over. This one, though, I've had it for a year, never gets run over."

"See," I said to my friend, who was all ears and no eyes.

He turned and looked uncertainly at both of us.

A duck came out from under the corn and stood by the man who had turned back to flower problems, and we walked slowly up toward Fountain.

"I know," he said, pouncing upon an idea, "let's go to the Formosa Café and have a dry martini."

"I wonder," I wondered aloud, "if that duck was kosher."

"But how can you stand living in that neighborhood?" a Laurel Canyoner asks. "I mean, with all that rough-and-tough stuff, the hookers?"

"It has a certain rural quality . . ." I begin.

THE ANSWER

I know that there's something seriously lacking when people try to nail down The Answer more than two plus two equals four. "Where's The Answer?" they ask colorlessly. Their life must lack pink for them to mention such things. It makes me embarrassed to hear a question so coarsely imposed upon my ears, as though humans can survive such abuse. As though anything so synthetically dredged up could live. It is like dragging something dead into a party, something black and white.

The first I knew about LSD was in high school when I did a report of some length on madness for Science and read about how there was this drug . . . I went to the UCLA Medical Library to inqure further and found that it would be in a section entitled "Psychophar-macology," but there were only two books about that in 1961 and both of them were unintelligible. I read Huxley's *Doors of Perception* although even at that time I thought perception was a harsh word to apply to anything that happened during the day, and I'd always thought Huxley was another one of those Englishmen who went nuts looking for The Answer, or to serious gray lengths anyway. The way he described the colors, though, got me. I wanted to see colors like that. I love colors. I love red, orange, yellow, green, blue and pur-ple and magenta and chartreuse and neon pink and brown and turquoise and cerise. I was jealous because it sounded like he saw them better. I despaired of ever getting any mescaline of my own. The envy lay dor-mant.

The only person I knew who was in a position to get LSD was a medical student I met when I was 17. But he was so crazy, I didn't want to risk it. "Ohhhhh, be nice . . ." he used to beg me when I refused to ride on the back of his motorcycle with him. The one time I had "been nice" and gone, he'd driven 100 mph on the Freeway and I'd found myself thrust into the position of having to pray to God to save me, and God, it turned out, was Graham sitting on a cardboard throne with a quart bottle of Rainier Ale on his lap. That I didn't like one bit and never told Graham about it.

This medical student told me about Romilar, which was a cough pill made out of synthetic morphine. If you took 20 of them, you were no longer subject to the laws of gravity. They were quickly taken off the market and rethought when it was discovered by those in com-mand that the name "Romilar-har-har" was just another legal way of getting high and that you could not purchase any near UCLA or USC because the students were all dumping them down their gullets. But they didn't do a thing for colors, just gravity.

I wanted colors and I knew you could get them in acid.

The reason I knew is because when I was doing my report I read how these psychiatrists blindfolded their patients when they were giving them LSD for therapy because otherwise they could get nothing done, their patients' souls having gone out the window through their eyes. It sounded fine to me.

All of a sudden the Sunset Strip was filled with 16-year-old children with painted faces who liked to dance. They were called hippies even by themselves, though hippie is a word I've never been able to get through my lips, because like "rap" it's Wonder Bread synthetic. We made the smell of Banana in Chemistry once and I nearly cried because it actually smelled like Bananas and was so simple and so fake. "Rap" was a word invented by social workers under which no one will ever flower; it's a dead word in black and white. Wonder Bread turns to chemical sticky inside the human mouth. Everyone knows it, but they eat it as though it were food. Hip is a word, Hippie and Rap are toasted Wonder Bread with fake grape jelly on them. (Grape was as easy as banana.)

I yearned for the colors, but I'd be damned if I was going to have some "hippie" around with me, and it wasn't just because they were poor, though that was about half of it. Money and colors. The other half was a combination of repulsions. It repelled me that the art was so vile. Magic Markers were not real colors; they

were like Happiness Is a Warm Puppy. I was repelled
by an instinct that ran through me from the tips of my
toes to the top of my scalp. I was also enormously horrified by Eastern religions, it was bad enough Western
religions. But Eastern religions, all that Hindu junk everyone sank into, that piece of total shit which said The
Answer lay somewhere in a religion in which they actually *named* people "Untouchables." I mean, we all
know there are untouchables, but to name people, that
seems like true crassness of unredeemable proportions.
At least Catholics called them heathens and implied
they could be "saved." Buddhism with that fat guy in
a lotus position was faintly pornographic because I always wondered what his cock could ever be like in all
that flab. No wonder he didn't "have women." His cock
was probably two inches when fully extended in passion.

But mainly I withdrew from "hippies" because they
didn't have any money. They were always begging
from regular people. And they seemed to be propound-
ing that they "had" The Answer.

I didn't want The Answer. I wanted the colors.

My job at the L.A. *Free Press* let me meet tons of
people who were taking and had acid. When Richard
Alpert (Leary's co-professor, who didn't smile as much)
and some guy named Steve gave a talk at Santa Monica
Civic Auditorium, tickets were sold in the *Free Press*
office and I met acid heads galore. None of them
seemed to have an ounce of worldliness, and worldliness was in the back of my mind throughout my life. It's
just been there and won't go away and that's why I was
so ashamed when I had to call on God for the motorcycle incident.

Randy was worldly. He was Mr. Casual Worldly in a polo shirt, white pants and wide acid blue eyes and he asked me for one ticket. I knew for absolute certain that he was on acid.

He was surprised that I knew, but I'd been on the lookout and we went for coffee. I told him that I really wanted to take acid but I was afraid of winding up naked on top of city hall with a painted face if I took it with the S.F. "hippies" and he agreed that San Francisco was no place for a civilized person. (San Francisco has always been a place disdained by L.A. people; they drink it in their mother's milk and it never goes away.)

He said, OK, on Saturday he'd give me acid and he could pretty much guarantee that nothing untoward would happen to me and I believed him. He also told me that he'd taken it just about every day since he first volunteered for a UCLA experiment in 1961. It was now 1966. He was rich.

On Friday night I saw the Alpert/Steve thing at the Santa Monica Civic and they were so smug with their secrets they were like pregnant women who haven't told yet. Hardly anyone in the audience had had acid, was why. I went with Randy, who was rapidly indifferent.

On Saturday he came and picked me up in his maroon Lincoln Continental and took me to his house, which lay in a dale of Hollywood completely apart from any other houses so that you could imagine you were in rustic Switzerland without even having to try, much less taking acid. The maroon Lincoln Continental looked exotic in the driveway, like a speedboat in Peru.

We wore jeans and old T-shirts and no shoes. He went to the refrigerator and poured us each a champagne glass full of LSD (Sandoz) diluted in spring water. We toasted and drank. Randy was not a serious person, he drank his acid like champagne.

Then I sat down and waited. He must have given me about 250 micrograms from what I know now. Psychiatrists in the book were giving people 90 and the kids on the Strip were taking anywhere from 150 to 1500. 90 was child's play.

About half an hour later my mouth tasted like blood and things took on a shine. They became so completely beautiful and shiny that I kept being afraid that they would stop. Soon I could stand up in ENOUGH colors. Oh, at last, the childhood pain of color entered effortlessly and filled me with colors, all the ones I loved. Green, especially, stole the show.

The fear of beauty walked the plank. Beauty was all there was.

Randy played jazz, nice hip west coast smooth jazz that didn't try to do anything to you or convert you, it just tried to join up the beauty. The beauty was comfortable and not scary and rolls around now and then still whenever I'm remotely reminded of *Heidi* or Switzerland. There's a description in *Heidi* about the sun turning the mountains pink at dusk which lodges in childhoods the way that day rolls past with a smile to me still.

Children are overwhelmed constantly by not enough words. Words go out on acid, they don't work. We fell silent.

Later, I wrote long letters to my friends explaining how words don't stick.

Outside the trees were beautiful and green took over. I remembered from my Science report that schizophrenics didn't know where they left off and anything else began and I would have felt that way too only I knew I was on acid. Self-delusion is not easy, but I knew what they meant. Meanwhile, the colors kept on going.

The phone rang. It pealed actually.

Randy looked at it and it pealed again.

He extended his beautiful, narrow long hand and lifted it on the third peal and put it to his ear, a masterful achievement under the circumstances. How he did it, I'll never know.

The phone sat on the coffee table on top of a *Wall Street Journal* and the receiver spiraled out to his head and he was using words rapidly though we had both fallen silent only a short while before.

The receiver left Randy's head and went back onto the beautiful telephone and then I saw that Randy was talking to me and I shed the colors to hear him.

"I have to go to the bank," he said.

"The bank?"

"Yeah, the bank," he said. "I know it's Saturday, but a forty-thousand-dollar loan I've been negotiating has just come through and I have to go. Shit."

"Where is it?"

"In the Valley."

"What do we do?"

"What has to be done."

He took off his clothes, his blue jeans and T-shirt, and I watched him shower in beautiful warm water. I sat on the bed as he put on different clothes that I'd never seen before. First he put socks on, then boxer shorts. When he was through, he was wearing a gray three-piece business suit and a tie and a watch chain with a gold watch. He looked like a beautiful advertisement for the *Wall Street Journal* in The *New Yorker* and he was my friend with wide blue eyes. He was my friend, so he had not tried to imprint anything on me, and to this day green rolls around and I am not boxed in with a lot of reasons. It's pure green, thank heavens.

He drove me home in a world that seemed to be caving in upon itself in beauty. He telephoned me later to see how I was and told me he'd gotten the money. I suppose psychiatrists and gurus and other punks would say that it was not good of him to leave me halfway through to my own devices on the crest of acid, but to me he was always a true person with no axes to grind and an assumption of worldliness that made me feel just fine. He never even tried to convince me that money was everything. Money was just everything for him, then. Like colors.

In New York, where I went three days later, I forgot to be careful and took LSD in dark places so that the word "anxiety" wedged into my frontal cortex like an icepick. Anxiety, I thought, anxiety, anxiety, anxiety. I caught a look of those *Ramparts* pictures in color of children napalmed in Vietnam and it nearly killed me. For about six months after that I was subject to bouts of deafness and simultaneous visions of people in 2-D like cardboard Elvises. Things were as ugly as they had been beautiful. I deserved it for eating banana fakes, synthetic beauty too fast.

I wanted to die.

Back in California, I began to not be afraid of the sky. In New York it was such a cave that coming back to California was like having the top of your head exposed to horizons in every direction. Too much light, made me squint. There was a new layer of acid-takers in California, sophisticates who did not roam the Strip begging. Randy had gone deeper into the hills with his money and I hardly ever saw him.

I went to a party one night to please a friend, though I was so tired I could barely stand up. A girl gave me 1000 micrograms of White Lightning acid and told me it was half a Dexedrine, by mistake. I was so tired I went into a back bedroom and went to sleep.

I awoke in the middle of The Answer broadcasting in black and white on and off the ceiling, "Why? Why not? Why? Why not?" it exclaimed, like an idiot. It was so stupid that I got up and went back to the party. *That* is The Answer, I thought to myself, *that* dumb moosh is why all those people are banging their heads against the walls. Well, I thought, I suppose they deserve it.

In the main room of the party, my friend, an English gentleman of brilliance and inspiration saw me coming.

"My mouth tastes like there's blood in it and I keep seeing the fucking answer flashing on the ceiling," I complained.

"You're on acid, dear, I'm afraid," he said, taking my hand in worldly consolation. My haggard defenselessness was a condition he recognized. Never before had I been so under that I couldn't tell I was on acid. His hand and words dispelled my anxiety and we waited together for the dawn.

Across from us was a hideous black-and-white photograph of a hairy man and a leering girl, fucking and smiling at the camera. "Please," I said to my friend, "it's so hideous."

He took it down and hid it, though it wasn't his house and the host wondered aloud where it went.

The dawn came, the sun rose up in unendurable hori-

zons of peach from which I could not take my eyes. All
lay in beauty beneath the round orange sun and sweetness filled the air like a lake feels to a fish.

By then even my English friend was sleeping. And so
I watched alone. Two plus two equals pink.

For me, sometimes.

★

ROSIE

The cat I had most of my adult life so far committed suicide last summer and we buried her under the apricot tree in back of my parents' house.

Whatever it was about Rosie, to untangle it would take me years of therapy and study of ancient scriptures and it wasn't until I was on mescaline that I made a pilgrimage out to the back yard to think about Rosie. There, growing from the spot where we buried her three feet under, were weeds, not rose bowers, just weeds. I had to laugh. What else could grow from Rosie's heart but weeds?

She came to me in New York, given to me one day by a poet who'd gotten the mother cat from Frank O'Hara. The mother cat had three kittens. One died very young of a cranial hemorrhage. One is in Arizona with the Fugs' ex-drummer's ex-old lady, Betsy. And the third was Rosie, who stood in front of a car once and for all this last July. Poor Rosie.

Almost the whole first year of her life was spent in my tiny New York apartment, where she never saw another creature except me, so on me falls the blame for her unimaginably ghastly personality unless it's her fault—I don't know. I named her Rosie Nosie and hoped she'd act accordingly. But she never got over anything. Least of all, her one-room childhood.

By the time she grew up and I was living back in California, my life as projected by me looked like at least another 12 years (because she was healthy and sometimes cats live as much as 17 years even) of being paired with this animal, Rosie. For one thing, I could never have friends who had any animals of their own, because Rosie went completely insane if any other furry came close, most of all a dog, but cats made her sick too. And who could I give her to? She bit company, and no one liked her, even people who loved cats couldn't stand Rosie. She was foul-tempered and would complain with a Siamese voice about everything always. (The Frank O'Hara Mother was Siamese.) So my future looked spinsterish, though I was, at the start, only 24.

Why, one might ask, didn't I just get rid of her? Why and how did she get away with everything? Well, for one thing, she had a stomach so white that Peking snowpeas couldn't have come from anyplace purer. She'd lie on her back and tempt you irresistibly to touch her gorgeous stomach—and when you did that, she had you with all four claws and all her teeth. But the main fact that everyone, even those who abhorred her and kicked her when I wasn't looking, was the fact of her face. She had the most beautiful face on a cat I ever saw. Her nose was rose-petal pink and her eyes were cat green, but half her face was orange and the other half was gray striped and she was so beautiful that when she stretched out on the windowsill in the sun you knew that you'd never understand anything but that you might as well take what you could get. And what I got was Rosie.

On Formosa the cars screamed by killing small children and dogs and cats and Rosie never got run over. It wasn't until we moved to my parents' house in a very quiet residential, hilly part of Hollywood where the cars go 10 mph that she finally decided to end it all after seven years of life. The thing was, I couldn't feel bad for her, she wasn't nice.

Next time I get a cat, it's going to be from the pound and it's going to be grateful if I even give it Friskies, not like the liver I used to give Rosie, who'd then look up at me and say in her Siamese disdain, "What, liver again, you resourceless bitch . . . please!"

Which were the last words she said to me before she walked out the back door.

THE ART OF BALANCE

SANTA MONICA, CALIFORNIA: MacGillivray-Freeman Films premiered their final surfing film, *Five Summer Stories*, March 24 on a Friday night at the Santa Monica Civic Auditorium to a sold-out capacity-3000 house. The film-makers themselves, Greg MacGillivray and Jim Freeman, were there to run the projectors, deal with an onslaught of a thousand counterfeit tickets and successfully to introduce the first use of stereo sound with 16mm film. The sound, mostly music, was provided by the Beach Boys and a band called Honk, among other sources.

There were three things going on Friday at the Santa Monica Civic. First, the audience, whose median age seemed to be about 17 and who were tan, mostly blond, clear-eyed and radiated health in thick pulses you could almost hear. Few of them smoked cigarettes or wore glasses and all exhibited a sense of exhilarated urgency and impatience while waiting for the movie. Second, the surfers in the movie, who were recognized instantly by the audience and wildly cheered as they engaged gleaming green dreams of death in duels of fleeting, awesome beauty. And third, the attitude of the movie, its own essence, elaborately created for this night, this audience, by two of themselves, two guys who presume that this film will only be shown to surf-freaks but who spent thousands of extra dollars so the sound would wipe everyone out completely—they didn't have to, but they're hot, so they got fancy. "Hot" is surfer for great.

The delays brought the already straining-at-the-bit kids to a point of expectation and drama so that they could hardly breathe. Flattened-out popcorn boxes fris-beed through the air, the smell of burning grass got thicker and began to remind me of a tent circus (not too paranoid, these kids, I noticed) and a blanket of smoke settled democratically down so that everyone was exposed, no one escaped. Paper airplanes circled above like San Juan swallows, only pink and green, and I learned that they had to stop giving out programs at these surfing events because it left too much of a mess afterwards. A band no one had ever heard of was supposed to play first and they hadn't even started by the time they were half an hour late and it was obvious that no one wanted to hear a band, but they might be able to *endure* a band if it didn't make too much trouble. Meanwhile, colored gliders crashed into each other overhead; the mood got thicker with headlong impatience and whistling and stomping for something to do.

At 8:30 or so, the band came on and developed an instantaneous rapport, an understanding, with the audience that is rarely so above-board. The audience thought they stunk, despised them, booed, yelled *PLAY ROCK AND ROLL!* and was just generally horrified by this cleaned-up, Joni Mitchell-memorial-church band when all they wanted was loud jam, preferably haphazard. The band seemed to have despised the audience for weeks before this appearance and made diabolically certain that by the time their set was over all the sweet urgency and desire had been drained, scorned and snuffed from the giant room. *"TAKE OFF YOUR CLOTHES,"* one last word of advice at the end of the set from someone in the third row. "Thanks for your patience," sneered the band leader, "and now our lackey will clear the stage so *you* can see *your* movie." What a thing!

"Just wait till the movie comes on," a friend of mine assured me with certainty. He'd become my friend because he was sitting next to me and we were part of the audience and underneath and breathing the same thing. I thought he was just a kid—he was 20 and I'm 28—but he thought *they* were just kids 'cause they were 17, and the 17-year-olds thought everyone younger was a gremmie—which apparently is surfer for non-surfer, too young, adoring fan. ". . . you'll see," he said shyly.

I can't think that the audience would have actually rioted if the movie had started much after 9 p.m., but since it started by 9 I'll never be sure. Bolts of expectation slammed around the theater as the lights dimmed. A sudden roar rose up from the audience as the Christian entered the arena and the movie came fearlessly on the screen with some trance-imposing abstract unreal colors, solarized colors in slow, slow motion turning slowly, dragging us into its rhythms and gutting us into awed silence before the whole thing faded into realer and realer color and at last was bright, blazing truth—a man sliding down the inside of a 15-foot sheet of molten green with slow-motion diamonds shooting out at the top and as the wave curled lazily into itself the man drew back into that loop of air inside a breaking wave, the "tube," and vanished so that at the last moment, the final moment, it was impossible, but he pulled back out into the open like a confident ice skater breaking out of a trick. The Christian had disposed of the lions and was now sitting on top of a heap of them. We, his stunned converts, cheered our devotion and wondered if we ever had had a chance. Now I knew what everyone had been waiting for.

The movie was laid out loosely in 5 "chapters" with a "Chapter 2 1/2" or a "4 1/2" thrown in for digressions and an intermission after the second part. The beginning was about Hawaii's resemblance to a kind of downhome Paradise with frivolously sweet scenes of flowers, cows, smiling girls and a friendly voice discussing the happy discovery of the Banzai Pipeline in 1963 by Bruce Something who used to be the hot one as far as the pipeline was concerned but has since been superseded by Gerry Lopez. The friendly voice (belonging to film-maker Greg MacGillivray) rambled on as Lopez, who looks like a relaxed lady-killer revolutionary, retained some primeval balance left over from the time when men danced on water, stroking the inside of a curled 40-ton menace going faster than is truly permitted in the world, too much faster. The audience went crazy in transported ecstasy, and the tide of the film had us caught in its rhythm safely . . .

Later in the film, in a section devoted to great surfer's "style," MacGillivray's narration gave way to descriptions by fellow surfers about one another. Simple Californian accents, personified best perhaps by Corkey Carroll's non-stop monologue, served as poetry, especially describing Lopez. "He has an innate comprehension of himself in terms of the wave rather than apart from it and this enables him to exist in very delicate situations," and Lopez appeared out of the end of a long tunnel of green with his fingers caressing the inside of a 15-foot joyous threat. "I'd say his relationship to the ocean is definitely sexual."

Lopez was all alone, elegant in this brutality, disappearing, reappearing, deep inside all that thunderous depth. The next one. Tricky rage of aqua about to break and through this half-curled transparent dream flew Lopez leaving diamonds slowly trailing behind him, an unstable shadow. We were silenced in disbelief before raising the rafters.

Women have to lie on their backs and bleed and scream to come up with something to tempt the gods to show themselves. Men, on the other hand, do not have to lie on their backs and bleed and scream to brush and inhale the fragrance of heaven—all men have to do is thrust themselves into huge sheets of monstrous green amoral dreams and keep on their feet.

About halfway through the film we were dazzled by a face so abrupt in its savagery and its vestigial traces of paradise that I figured the immediate uproar in the audience was simply a reaction to the jagged class of the face itself. Out of the screen an indifferent glance regarded us uncomprehendingly from bygone island eyes. Disheveled black hair tangled around this face like a thorn frame and wove down past the shoulders. A mouth as naïve as before the invention of guilt fried, without warning, into the fierce and helpless smile of one of those rare creatures who get to be happy. Underneath the face flashed the news that this was David Nuuhiwa (New-eee-vah), but everyone in the whole place already knew that except me which was why they were screaming. The sky behind was a sunset, somber orange and dark gray, the smile vanished, having acknowledged the spontaneous roar of those who knew him instantly, and without the smile we were left with only a calm sea of that indifferent glance regarding us uncomprehendingly out of bygone island eyes.

"David," as he is referred to familiarly in surfing magazines and the movie, because in surfing *everyone* knows who "David" is, was filmed as he took first place in the U.S. Surfing Championship on a "blown-out" (rotten) day when he got one of the few decent waves. His "style" is to stay on the board and see what happens come hell or high water as though his feet were nailed down. His posture when walking on land recalls the diffident spare way that Manolete must have looked or T.E. Lawrence would have listened. There are some people who harbor myths and David Nuuhiwa, at the age of 22 from the Islands, appears to be one. Seeing him drive down the streets of his new home, Huntington Beach, in his weathered white Jaguar sedan with its two surfboards perched smugly on top evoked no jealousy from the 3000, who instead applauded and laughed at this show of perfection and affluence, though most surfers don't have much money, because David should be rich and happy. His shrug that accompanied his only and unexplained comment about the contest (". . . it's an instant replay of 2 years ago") was the confused gesture of one unused to having to say words or answer questions. On sea he's so fast he moves like a whip and never even seems to get wet though blazing, slivered water foams in amazement all around him. Don Thomas, Publisher of *International Surfing*, described him as "the natural surfer" whose ". . . uniqueness . . . is due to his instinct" and then seemed only able to describe what he was not (which is one of us, it appears). At the end of the contest there was David, squinting appraisingly out to sea at the sun going down before turning back to the crowd and dry land as night approached.

The film-makers editorialized on surfing for competition or surfing as an organized "sport," indicating that any competition is a corruption of the art imposed by geeks and morons who are fat, don't know anything and are just after surfers for their own mercenary ends. The audience seemed to be in accord with this point of view by the sound of their rambunctious applause. However, more and more contests are held every year for higher and higher purses ($10,000 sometimes) and, as one of the guys in the surfing magazine said, "It's better than working."

Of all the surfers shown, one of the hottest, Jeff Hakman, was the only one who made the word "athlete" come into my head. Maybe it was because his hair was so short and he looked so football playery and the attitude of other surfers apparently was grudging admiration because he's hot with inevitable triumph, but I could tell they didn't feel the dumbfounded awe that they felt about Lopez's "ability to exist in very delicate situations" or the sheer joy of knowing David just exists. Hakman is a wondrous thing to behold anyway as he survives like a bean bag, somehow, always landing comfortably upright. Another surfer defended him: "Some people say he's just muscle, but he's like a sewing machine drawing patterns on the wave's face." He's strong and fast and grows on you, his survival becomes art.

Terry Fitzgerald, an Australian, was described beautifully as, "Go, go, go, go—you can't stop and you can't look back. He looks radical but he defines his goals precisely and follows through." Pretty fancy. ("Radical" is a strange surfing word that I can't quite figure out— sometimes it means something good but to be wary of, sometimes it means an unwieldly wave. It seems to be a spur-of-the-moment word with good rather than bad connotations; maybe it means crazy.)

INTERMISSION

I went to the foot of the stairs where I was to meet Barbara, a special friend of MacGillivray (". . . that's capital M-a-c, capital G . . ." she spelled slowly for me so I'd be sure to get it right) and was dazed from the smoke and the gorgeous water and the young girls' beautiful stomachs which nearly all showed tanned and hollow because the tops of their hip-high Levi's failed to meet the bottoms of their waist-low clingy sweaters, though most of them had hair which reached down to the tops of their Levi's, blonde . . . Then Barbara came, an elegant, California-type casual woman who looks good in pink lipstick and who was clear and forthright like everything else had been. I remarked about how wonderful the audience was and she said, "Ohhh, God, these kids are notorious . . . They'll go crazy if you just put a white light on the screen. . . ." I thought I ought to mention that they booed the band, so I did and it turned out that a lot of the beautiful music in the movie was made by the band, the very band . . . honk.

Greg MacGillivray didn't look like a surfer nor a film-maker—he looked like a young high-school algebra teacher, and he talked like one too, clear and optimistic and cheerful. No tan, crisp-ironed shirt, economical manner—no shilly-shallying around, no digressions, no waste, friendly, bright. Jim Freeman looked like a Big Sur person who was into Big Sur but not necessarily into taking acid every single moment. He was more woodsy, he had work to do. Neither of them were especially anything and yet they'd made this night.

I feebly began asking questions and learned that Greg began surfing at the age of 15 and made his first film about it when he was 17 before he was out of high school and now he was 26 and this was absolutely his last surfing movie. "We've gone about as far as you can with this, you know, and we're working on the script of a real movie which should be together in maybe a year. Sunday we're going to Hawaii to do a commercial for Timex with Gerry Lopez—about how a Timex survives even that, you know?"

"What about other sports . . . or arts?" I asked.

"We did a short on dune buggies, and we're thinking of doing one on skiing."

He told me that the movie (2 hours long) cost $30,000 to make and that originally it had been planned for $20,000, but the sound, which was done special at

Twentieth Century-Fox, had cost a fortune and he asked me how it sounded.

"Great," I said. "Did the Beach Boys just *give* you music?"

"Yes, Brian Wilson wanted to write the theme song too, but we ran into a time thing so we had to let it go. We could never afford to pay them for the music they did."

Meanwhile Greg was rewinding the first reels back onto the reel by hand since they accidentally ran out of reels and had to let the film drop into a huge canvas basket. "It takes us, oh, about a year just to make our money back. We show like here and up and down the coast and rent prints and things like that."

Five minutes later I was back on my seat again, waiting for more, indulging in the generosity of the unparanoid kids around me who also shared their knowledge of these functions. They'd been going on exactly like this at the Santa Monica Civic for at least 5 years, "Only 5 years ago no one smoked," one of them said. I asked a number of people which surfing movie they thought was the best, but not one single one of them would venture a guess.

One of the "Five Summer Stories," called "Close Out," was about the disappearing surfing points and the plans for converting many of Hawaii's most perfect surfing beaches into harbors. A brilliant sound/visual collage went on as slow-motion surfers rolled through the savage water with pure classical music, while in the background the annoying noise of a newscast subaurally told us about Nixon's plans for America's coastlines. A straight-out song came on with shots of oil diggings and other shore rapes called "California, Young but Already Old." "L.A.," as one of the kids at the end of this segment remarked, "is *so* screwed."

Ecology was never mentioned; the word doesn't fit into this night or these lives. But the audience, most of whom have spent summers learning the guarded secrets of walking on water, who are enraptured by the sea, who keep themselves healthy, alert to their balance so they have the strength to shoot through green, roaring sheets—the audience has a personal, intimate, tragic stake in ecology. Most of the kids know that anyone with half an eye can see that it would be much better to leave the ocean alone, to not disturb its loose grip with perfection, so between them and some adversary somewhere planning a yachting harbor where he can go drink in peace is a sheet of something even more monstrous than the green walls that are a joy to defeat. It's the eternal thing about the artist and the businessman, and to stop businessmen the artist must forsake his art. Will David Nuuhiwa put on a shirt and go to Washington? David?

At 11:30 it was over and we were sated. Enough of slowly tunneling ocean myths, of diamonds rashly flying into a child's blue sky, of unstable trails boards leave on clear green mountains and of bygone island eyes. We'd screamed ourselves hoarse about Gerry Lopez, cheering him through lazy explosions that could snap him in two as it sometimes did the boards. We shimmered with pleasure from those afternoons, from the urgency and timelessness of this evening's spectacle. And even I, who, last Friday, barely even knew how to get to the Santa Monica Civic Auditorium, was able to "exist in very delicate situations."

THE ACADEMY

The Academy of Arts and Sciences is so corny, they're the kiss of death.

When I was 10, I saw "The Prince Who Was a Thief" for an entire year, I was in love with Tony Curtis. My mother had to take me downtown and sit through "The Great Caruso" four times so we could see "The Prince Who Was a Thief" again. Inside my wallet were *Photoplay* pictures of Tony Curtis which I stared at in school. I knew his brother. He went to Roadside and his name was Schwartz, but I wasn't in love with Tony Curtis any more by then. Now I know Tony Curtis. I met him at a party. He's all right. But he's not the same Tony Curtis who had the Prince tattoo on his arm (hidden under a bracelet until Piper Laurie threatened to step on a pearl unless everyone stopped fighting—see, I remember). Now he's suave and entrenched in the Old Hollywood. He's Cary Grant's friend and he and his wife have about 6 children between them.

He has a kind of smug energy which is still endearing.

But by the time I'd grown up, I naturally supposed that I'd grown up. I didn't expect it was going to happen again and not the way it did, either. First of all, "Lawrence of Arabia" was out an entire year and had won 9 Academy Awards before I got around to getting someone to take me. I wouldn't have gone even then if it wasn't for the fact that it was a "first date" and in those days I didn't argue about what we were going to do until the second date. And a movie with a bunch of Englishmen, no women, in the desert with Alec Guinness and Anthony Quayle was not my idea of a movie. Bring on the dancing girls, I always say (which they did in "The Prince Who Was a Thief").

The guy, who I have forgotten except that he had a silver Porsche and the strongest dope to smoke on the way over I'd had in ages, picked me up and we got so transfixed by the grass that we were almost late. He dropped me off at the cashier while he went to park and gave me 10 dollars. The lady gave me back $3.00.

"Jesus, it costs $7.00!" I told him, handing him the change. This was in like 1963 or something, when 7 dollars was a lot.

We staggered or skated into the theater and found seats. The place was crowded and I hate crowded theaters, I hate dates, I hated it. But I was paralyzed by the grass, so I asked him to get me popcorn. He obeyed and it wasn't until he'd been gone for a while that I looked around and realized that the theater was too ritzy for them to have popcorn, which turned out to be the case. He came back just in time because a drum boomed through the stereo speakers and I immediately fell under the spell of the ensuing movie so that for over a year, whenever anyone said, "Let's go to a movie," I'd always look where "Lawrence of Arabia" was playing and go see it. I saw it fourteen times.

Only this time I was not just in love with Peter O'-Toole, I was in love with the whole movie, especially the tricky English screenplay with all its Oxford Boy Scout attitudes and jazzed-up exchanges.

For example, Alec Guinness was heaven itself in that movie. His last line as Lawrence is leaving, after he tells Allenbe, "Lawrence is a two-edged blade, is he not, Major Allenbe? Neither of us wants him here." As Lawrence is leaving the roomful of diplomacy, Faisal (Guinness) says, "Ah—what I owe you . . . is . . . beyond evaluation." Just thinking about it makes me soggy.

Even Anthony Quinn wasn't vile in this one, especially vis-à-vis O'Toole with his blue eyes that look like the sky is shining right through his head. His eyes looked like they'd been cut out or left vacant.

But my favorite line is in the beginning when Lawrence is drawing maps in a cellar in Cairo and a soldier comes in with a letter and then stops to have a cigarette. Lawrence offers, deliberately, to light the cigarette and then, even more deliberately, he puts the flame out with his fingers.

The soldier tries to duplicate the action, but burns himself and says, "It hurts. What's the trick?"

"The trick, William Potter," O'Toole turns intensely to tell him, "is not *mind*ing that it hurts."

The whole movie is filled with Classical Boy Scout

things like that, as when Omar Sharif first appears out of the desert as a twenty-foot mirage that can be heard five miles away, a speck in the horizon who shoots O'-Toole's guide and then materializes.

"What is your name, Englishman?" Sharif smirks.

"My name," O'Toole says, "is for my *friends."*

"I will take you to Faisal," Sharif says, still smirking.

"I will go myself."

"How will you go?" Sharif asks. "It is two days in the desert. You will be lost."

"I have *this."* O'Toole holds up a compass on a leather strap.

Sharif slips his camel stick (the camel has been arched-neck ridden during all of this, while Lawrence is at a disadvantage on the ground) through the compass strap and leers, "And how if I take it, Englishman?"

"Then that would make you a thief!"

Oh, *why* is there only one "Lawrence of Arabia," and why isn't it playing still? I could kick myself for missing that first year. It was all those academy awards which made me so wary. Someone should have told me it was good.

I saw that movie until it was scratchy and edited all because of that corny academy. I thought it was going to be a Boy Scout thing.

★
THE HOLLYWOOD
BRANCH LIBRARY

My education has been untended by structure or anything else. And yet I find myself sometimes, when I'm
off in academia on one of my more decadent perver-
sions. There was the time I did three months devoting
myself entirely to physicists in order to get a crack at
Fred Hoyle, who I knew sometimes taught at Cal Tech
(Fred Hoyle is the ritz astrophysicist if you get a taste
for astrophysicists), but all I found was a nice young
man with a new Mercedes who knew C.P. Snow and
called him Sir Charles, but the young man was so boring that I eventually went back to rock and roll. Or I'll
be talking to an English professor and he hasn't read
Anthony Powell. A lot of people haven't read Anthony
Powell—it amazes me. He's much less leaden than John

Updike and he's a downright soufflé compared to just about anyone.

But my education has been through reading, which has been my salvation and backbone throughout life. The time I wanted to kill myself in New York, *Domby and Son* saved me. Charles Dickens is perfect for accidental hit-bottom. Anthony Trollope is too, but he's so divine that it's a shame to waste him just because you're in trouble.

When I travel, there are always certain books that go with me. Colette always is right there. I wouldn't trust myself anywhere without *Earthly Paradise*, what if something happened and I didn't have it? What if the electricity went out and all my friends died? Without Colette, where would I be? For me, Colette is one of those books you open up anywhere and brush up on what to do. When she describes a luncheon alone where all she has is a view of the Bois, a plum and a chicken wing washed down with a glass of cold white wine and capped with a Caporal—*you* get to sit in the Bois eating a plum and a chicken wing, sipping cold white wine and lighting a black tobacco cigarette. Colette has been there since I was 9 and discovered Claudine.

Mostly, I find myself coming out of the library with all women writers. I keep hoping the library attendant won't notice, but when 8 out of 8 of the books you take out are by women, you try not to look too dykey.

A woman who has otherwise proven a burden to my entire childhood, once, without saying a thing about it, gave me a special Christmas present, one she didn't give anyone else—*Seven Gothic Tales* by Isak Dinesen. After that, I gobbled up everything by Isak Dinesen I could fall across, even *Out of Africa*, which I was sure was going to be a mufti safari book but which turned out to be a sliver of heaven which you should keep in your house. I know someone whose Victorian sister lived in Nairobi when Countess Karen Blixen (Isak Dinesen) was there and the sister said that all the whites called her Crazy Karen because she talked to her servants. To this day I am ambivalent about the woman who introduced me to Isak Dinesen—how did she know?

Virginia Woolf is hard. But I've done it. We first read her in a Modern lit class taught by an inspired teacher called Mr. Major. It was not a usual high-school Modern Lit class like they give you in high school. There was no textbook with "The Wasteland" in it. In fact, I've never read "The Wasteland." What he did was, in order to make sure we knew what Modern Lit wasn't, we had to read *Green Mansions*, and Mr. Major, to make it so we wouldn't fall for it's soapy mush, kept saying things like, "I dreamed I fled through the forest in my spider web pedal pushers." Then we read the life of Gandhi so that in case we still *did* want to be a romantic, we'd know how to do it. (He actually led the entire class to the Vedanta Temple one Sunday to make sure we got the point.) So then we read Ibsen, about three of those plays, we read a slew of Chekhov, we read Tennessee Williams, we read way too much of Evelyn Waugh because everyone got hung up, we read a strange book called *Nectar in the Sievte* by an Indian woman about India and we read *Otello* by Virginia Woolf. We read tons of other stuff and were ordered to go see "Wild Strawberries" and a couple of other movies. Mr. Major paid for this flagrantly inspired teaching by having to teach remedial English the other 5 periods. He and the administration never hit it off too well. Thomas Hardy and Dostoevsky too we did—*hard* ones like *Karamazov.*

Virginia Woolf tantalizes me. I wish I could write like that. She is in love with London and I am in love with L.A., but London has seasons and this giant history and stratas of society . . . She wouldn't like L.A. but maybe she'd forgive me for loving it anyway. *The Waves* is the best she's written, you go crazy it's so perfect. And then, it was her *A Room of One's Own* that made me believe in Women's Lib. I never liked it when Gloria the Crass and Gross was trying to write about it—it was like reading that radical propaganda where the words are so poorly selected and so divorced from humans that you have to really discount your eyes to be able to let what they're saying get into your head. But when Virginia Woolf does it, it's easy. She's right and they're wrong.

M.F.K. Fisher is becoming my favorite writer, even more favorite than Colette. I once wrote her a fan letter and told her that she was just like Proust only better because she at least gave the recipes. She wrote back that she supposed that someday someone would do their Ph.D. thesis on madelines. M.F.K. Fisher attends to ingestions and, not only that, she's from Whittier and she grew up in L.A. when it was the farthest reaches of the civilized world. She describes eating peach pie with her father and sister in the sunset in the hills when she was about 5, which has always remained with me, as will the idea that to drive about 50 miles to their aunt's peach farm they got 5 flat tires and it took about 4 hours, there were no roads. I take two M.F.K. Fisher books with my Colette book when I go anyplace.

The only way to read Marshall McLuhan is to go straight through from beginning to end.

I discovered C.P. Snow by accident. I like series of books, hoping that they'll be by someone who's any good and then you'll have the whole series. It's the first time sanity looked attractive and the air of lucidity is just so strong it permeates your whole life while you're reading him so that you don't make any false moves. Also, I think I read C.P. Snow because everyone was saying how crappy he was and that he didn't know what he was talking about, saying that artists ought to find out about quantum physics. I tried to find out about quantum physics when I went on my physicists expedition, but I just couldn't understand it. The closest I ever got was when my friend Harry, who's a Scientific Philosopher mathematician type person (he used to play bass, that's how I know him), tried to explain to me about infinite set theories and absolute maniacal things from which I just automatically recoiled. He told me about the "Liar's Paradox," which I thought would be a good name for a book and apparently everyone in the world knew that the Liar's Paradox is this:

> THE STATEMENT INSIDE THIS BOX IS FALSE.

That really got me depressed. It still gets me depressed. I don't find it the least bit delightful like my friend Harry does. And I'd certainly not devote my life to it. Especially when scientists are so boring. Except for Fred Hoyle. Fred Hoyle wrote this book which was very easy to read called *The Nature of the Universe* and then a few years later wrote another one called *Fron-*

tiers in Astronomy, which was too hard and which denied everything the first book said. He also writes science fiction, but I *HATE* science fiction.

Max Beerbohm came into my life because it was fate. Of course a person like me would have to eventually stumble upon a person like Max Beerbohm. To say that I worship and adore Max Beerbohm and he's with me always with the two women writers is to say that if you know anything about Max Beerbohm and anything about my mania for outer shine, you already know. The great thing about Max Beerbohm is that, like Kaluha, any idiot can like it. He just slips down the gullet with nary a notice.

You know what I also drag into my suitcase? This weird book by Raynar Bahnam called *Los Angeles: A City of Four Ecologies.* Of course, I'm in love with L.A. and would be more likely than most people to weigh in with some book by an architectural historian about this place. But, still. It's a book that is everything that Marshall McLuhan thought *he* was being but never was, it's a book about forward march and the past sticks on as we hurtle through space. It makes the city make sense and I bought it for a rock-and-roll friend, who was complaining one day about L.A. and how he wanted to move into the country, so now he's so transformed, he's trying to get an apartment in the flats and out of the hills and the more McDonald's Hamburgery it is, the better he likes it. It is, then, something when someone can make you see beauty where you only saw ugliness before. He is wonderful, that man.

Which brings us to Joyce Carol Oates. I knew I was going to hate Joyce Carol Oates so I took the thickest, most impossible-looking gray and yellow book out of the library called *them* (how can you write a big book like that and not even have it in capitals?) and put off reading it until one morning when I had a few minutes before I was supposed to go to the beach. It was 8:15 a.m. when I started and it was 11 p.m. when she finally let me go. And *Wonderland* is even more fantastic. Don't let anyone tell you Joyce Carol Oates is not Shakespeare; she knows everything just like Shakespeare did. She knows what it's like to be beautiful and what it's like to be in a car accident and what it's like to be a doctor removing gall bladders and what it's like to be a gas-station attendant planning a robbery. She knows. And if you want to find out, she'll tell you. All you have to do is get the books. The only thing she doesn't know is how to be funny or charming. Shakespeare had it all over her for those.

I've read Proust all the way through because everyone said I'd like it, but Colette's little sketch of Proust coming into a room after everyone had thought he'd gone and already had begun gossiping about how he was a fag was only about three paragraphs and you could imply the other 9 million pages. Nevertheless, I liked the other nine million pages and recommend them to anyone in solitary confinement or otherwise out of commission. You can't read Proust at the Laundromat.

And last, I think, but not least is Henry James. When I grow up, that's what I want to be. Henry James is just right, not too simple like Dickens, not too impossible like Proust—just right. And my cousin tells me (she's reading that enormous biography of him that just came out) that he was always going out to dinner and to parties. So, when I grow up, I can still have fun. I don't know about being celibate, though. I don't want to and nowadays, it would ruin your reputation. And Henry James always understood the spirit of the times.

THE LUAU

In 1962 I lived in Rome for six months. At the beginning of each month my parents sent me a check c/o American Express for $80. I was 19 years old, but that was not why the time I spent in Rome was so immune to being poor and instead was flooded with end-to-end devil's-food cakes of good times and delights only occasionally broken into by empty solitude in a foreign city. The reason life was so wonderful was because constitutionally I am Roman and I know that one day I will get enough money to move there, and that that will be the end of it. My goal is an apartment in Rome, a little car and blue skies. But it doesn't even matter if it's raining, the blue skies always come and in Rome rain just doesn't really matter.

Each morning I awoke and pushed open the sixth-story shutters of my walk-up pension room, and there, beneath me in the rain, was Rome. I nearly wept out of gladness to see the Villa Borghese willows in the mist.

But Italians, Romans especially, are such children, they say. And look how childishly they excel. They feed you fresh food simply prepared, they erect apartment houses that are quickly covered by vines and do not hurt your eyes, and they make movies. They are children, they are not serious.

So, I am not serious. But like a Roman out of Rome, I try not to let on just how not serious I am and I try to become interested in serious facts. Just lately I became so serious I almost suffocated in forgetfulness and had come to the conclusion that there was no reason to live. The decade-later girl who'd pushed open her shutters onto the Borghese willows and wept with gladness was now sitting dry-eyed in a chair trying to figure out one single reason to live. The seriousness of the situation was led all around until finally I hit it—the seriousness of the situation was the whole thing. A Roman is not serious and can't believe in it and there I was at the mercy of seriousness and mercy has never been one of its virtues. In fact, mercy is beside the point once you get deeply into seriousness, look at Hitler. Suicide is as serious as you can get.

The first serious thing that happened to me triggered it off in what I thought was just more blue skies, otherwise it never would have gotten so out of hand. I have never had any money and suddenly I thought that if I sent a publisher a letter in just the right tone, I might get an advance to do a book and then I could even do one if I didn't have to worry about money. As proof that

I could write, I sent the publisher a Xeroxed copy of a letter from a writer, an extremely fashionable writer, who thought that a few short pieces I'd written in a local L.A. paper were terrific. I'd known the woman for years and always kind of shrugged off her New Yorky quality, a kind of serious professionalism which didn't allow for any fun. Her books were so brutally depressing that the only way you could be happy about them was to appreciate the style. She would never have allowed the Sistine Chapel if she'd been pope, she'd have directed another Crusade instead. So though her books were very well written, most people couldn't stand to read them.

The letter worked, the Xerox. It was nice. The Xeroxed copy of her letter got an advance from an East Coast Publisher and then all at once the sky got Swedish overcast, not plain rain at all. Questions such as where was I going to write this first novel and how was it going to be done suddenly drew serious considerations into the air. It was important and I had to treat it importantly. The publisher asked the woman to edit my book, and she said yes and her extreme fashionability was almost a guarantee of an important success. She was in *Vogue* done by Avedon, tall, with her Englishy hands half folded in front of her and her dogs at her feet in her Santa Barbara hacienda. She bought the hacienda with her depressing book money. She referred to me bleakly as a "survivor," it was a new word, all the rage.

All at once I was home writing. I stopped going out and met no one. My only friends were my perpetual girl friends and I didn't fuck anyone new.

The writing got dismal and you couldn't read it. Everything folded up into convoluted despair and the style was never that terrific in the first place to cover it up. It was unreadable.

But by that time I couldn't tell any more. I'd lost my nerve.

Lady Dana Wreaths, the lady novelist, read the manuscript and called me up to Santa Barbara for a purge. With wrinkled brow she asked me if someone had edited my previous pieces which had appeared in the local publication or what? Its implication was clear: the person who had written those first pieces was not the same person who was writing these.

She told me that everything needed a vast amount of work, that I could not have written those earlier pieces in two days like I'd claimed. Read Graham Greene, she told me.

So there I was sitting dry-eyed wondering why I should be allowed to live.

Socially things had deteriorated so that my one male friend was my only connection out. He was all there was in my pared-down life, which had been so madly eclectic once. When he was in town, I was invited frequently to dinner. At first he had housefuls of incredibly diverse guests but, later he had become serious himself (though proof that he too was a child lies in the fact that he had too many Romans for friends, princes and such —Italian aristocracy doesn't really count though, it's not hard enough to get into). He had taken it into his mind to go into business and his business friends began to soak up his time, but with him I didn't mind business friends since he himself was an invisible Italian just like me. We laughed often. So I went as "the girl" to business dinners and looked beautiful and made clever remarks because I loved my friend and would abet him in his deception. He could duplicate seriousness as good as a Roman in church.

He was friends with Lady Dana and often fought with her because she could sense how basically insubstantial he was, though she had to confess once to me in private that our connection friend did have the best parties in the whole world. Not really a virtue, however. Parties.

"Come over for dinner," my connection friend said.

"O.K.," I answered. I had stopped asking questions long ago about who would be there because I just liked my connection and that was enough to get me dressing. It was the day after I had decided that the fault lay in the seriousness and not in me. I had decided I could go ahead and live and I had also decided that Lady Dana was not going to edit my book, it was a contradiction in terms, mutually exclusive. She liked Paris and I could never stand it there, everyone was too short and too private. I decided suddenly that her life was ridiculous and her worried brow was merciless and that she, in fact, knew nothing about what I knew. I couldn't remember how I ever forgot so much as to have wondered why I should be allowed to live.

"Hi," my connection said and kissed me.

Behind him a business associate and his wife sat in the comfortable living room which belonged to my connection and which I knew as well as my parents' house. The business associate's wife I remembered never let anything get so much as an inch off the ground, but that was O.K. Dinner was dinner.

Just then a knock at the outside gate brought a bunch of my connection's recently arrived Italians. They were beautiful Romans. The girl was so beautiful that it was difficult to believe, her hair swung tawny to her waist, her eyes were green, her mouth was red and her body was lithe and sexy. The men were laughing and well dressed, young. The sound of Roman Italian made me go sit next to them just to hear the consonants and vowels I could sometimes understand. This might be fun, I thought. But the wife of the business associate didn't blink and my connection told his friend, Gianni, that it was business and maybe Gianni could take his friends out somewhere away.

"Come with us," Gianni said to me.

"No, she's coming with me," my connection said. I was glad to because I loved him so I forwent gli Italiani. But just as they were leaving my lately recaptured past leaped out and I got one of those "How long are you going to be here, why don't you let me take you around L.A., why don't we go to the beach tomorrow if it's not raining, what's your phone number I'll call you over the fence." I had once been good with strangers, especially ones who liked things. Not like the business associate's wife, who I wouldn't take to the drugstore for coffee.

I had been to dinner with this particular business associate before, and always at about 9 o'clock the decision about restaurants began. By 10:30 one starving evening I got up, put on my coat and said, "I'm leaving" since no compromise had been reached. So when the Italians had gone, I took destiny and recriminations (which were sure to follow) into my own hands and suggested we eat at a restaurant I knew of in Beverly Hills because at least I knew the food was good there and since they'd never been in that restaurant, they couldn't say they didn't like it.

★ 243 ★

I had been there before with two separate lovers and had pleasure just because the food was so pure, the wine list fantastic and the color of the inside so agreeable.

And besides, they have these hors d'oeuvres made of fried Gruyère, which are not the most heavenly thing on earth but are nice.

The business associate and his wife drank Cokes and left their plates barely tampered with and had not had the hors d'oeuvres because for some reason they had something against Swiss Cheese and Gruyère tasted like Swiss Cheese to them. My connection wouldn't stop talking about business even when he was being funny. And there were strange cruel insults I'd never heard before which were supposed to be funny flung back and forth across the table which interfered with the hollandaise, but then nobody but me noticed the hollandaise.

We left the restaurant in a bleak desultoriness, and the waitress who I remembered and who had approached with a kind of élan was glad to get rid of us and I hoped she wouldn't remember me from that one. I'd done the restaurant a disservice by bringing them there.

My connection and I stood alone in the living room.

"That was just awful," I said.

"Yeah, well, Mrs. Business Associate was tired," he said.

"God," I said. My emptiness was all that remained from four humans in good health having dinner in an expensive restaurant together. "Well . . . I'll talk to you later."

I got up the next morning with a hangover and a

good idea for a story. The story was written quickly and fell together like a just right deck of cards being shuffled and had the kind of crazy deftness that my other stories had always managed to run away with. But now that I'd disposed of Lady Dana, naturally that would happen.

At two, I had finished the second and last draft of the story and so I telephoned Antonio at the Beverly Hills Hotel. Antonio was the Italian I'd gotten the phone number of the night before and I was feeling so good that I thought an evening with strangers who don't speak English very well would be fun. After all, they are Roman, so it will at least be that, fun.

"I have," Antonio said, speaking brokenly, "been walking in the rain with my friends today. We went to San Fernando Valley to Nudie's Cowboy Store and we bought cowboy clothes. It was very much fun. I bought a horse."

"A horse!"

"Yes, a quarter-horse."

"But what will you do with it?"

"They ship it for you," he laughed. He was delighted with the entire thing.

We arranged to meet in the Polo Lounge at 10 and the English was so difficult that I didn't know who would be there but I didn't care. By that time I just wanted to listen to Romans.

He was 20 minutes late, which was good for an Italian, and he said that Ilsa, the girl who was so beautiful, and Gianni would be down soon, they were packing. They were going to New Mexico the next day, they were in cowboy heaven. Italians are such children.

Before joining him I had thought about where we might go for dinner. Since I was in my own city, I should suggest some place nice, but I'd been so roughed up about my suggestions with the business associates that it scared me to offer one. If I were a stranger, though, I'd have liked to be taken to the Luau, a ratty old crazy Tahitian place in Beverly Hills with blue lagoons and gardenias in the drinks, the Scorpions. When I'd suggested this to my connection one night he'd recoiled in ridicule, "The Luau!"

I never offered it again, but I went with a lover and we had fun.

On my way to the Beverly Hills Hotel I stopped by a girl friend's and asked her where she thought I ought to take them and she gave me her plastic card for the horrible Rainbow, which was the only place in town to go those days, the very only place that anyone considered when they considered going "Out" for a drink. It is a hellish place, desperate and crowded and it means you aren't satisfied with your friends if you have to drink with them at the Rainbow. It's no fun.

But maybe gli Italiani might consider it necessary to go to the Rainbow, and so I had a card which proved I was a good city hostess. Maybe they wouldn't consider it right. But it was getting too complicated, going to dinner with strangers and my newly dropped seriousness wondered what the fuck I was doing going with these people I didn't know who didn't speak English and who were so beautiful and what were they doing in America and who were they and I was alone and . . .

But, I reigned in, they were Romans and I am a Roman and I *knew* it was at least going to be all right.

We drank three drinks before the others got down and by the middle of the first one I was telling slowly and in short words this darling man who made industrial films in Milano, to Antonio, that he should come with me and see a surfing film I'd reviewed. I told him about the waves and he came right straight through to me like I remembered it was possible without reservations or seriousness. He adored "to see theeeeese movie" and he told me about his new horse and his apartment in Milan and it was not just all right, it was terrific.

Ilsa came then and electrified the room with her St. Tropez beauty, and I never found out if she was a model or who she was or how come they were all three traveling together or anything like that. My frank and truthful analysis of the situation is that one night they were all three having dinner or oysters at the Café Rosatti and decided to come to see the cowboys. Gianni began to discuss the fall of America and Vietnam, but that only lasted for about two minutes when he discovered that I was Roman and didn't need to be serious.

We went to the Luau.

They flipped over the blue lagoons and ate the gardenias. The food was heavenly, I knew what to get there, we took with chopsticks from each other's plates, the talk ran high and I don't remember what it was about but by the end of dinner Ilsa had embraced me three times and they all begged me to come with them to New Mexico and, God, I was tempted.

"We have to go to the connection's," Gianni said.

"It's so late," I said.

"But I must say goodbye because we are leaving in the morning."

My connection was angry, it was 2 a.m., but he let us in and gleaned information.

"Where'd you go?"

"The Luau," I said.

"The Luau!?" he recoiled. "Did you find anything edible?"

"We loved it!" Gianni interceded.

My connection had spent the evening again with the business couple. A "deal" had been transacted. I didn't see why he was so frowning since a "deal" had been what he'd been doing it for. Gianni knew him well. Better than I did.

"We are going to New Mexico, come with us," he smiled seductively.

"No!" my connection said.

"Just three days," Gianni persisted.

"Ahhh, yes," Ilsa sighed, flopping down on his couch and looking like a hopped-up Botticelli. "You must come with us."

"I can't," he snapped.

"You should have come to the Luau," Ilsa said. "The drinks are wonderful."

"I don't know how you can stand that place," my connection said.

"You are jealous of Ivy," Gianni said. My name had been changed to Ivy somewhere along the way that evening, not Eh-vah like Italians usually do.

"Who's Ivy?" My connection stopped.

"Her." Gianni pointed at me.

My connection looked at me in pure fury. He was completely crushed that anything like "Ivy" had happened with him not there, that people were having fun without him as he finally remembered what fun was. He was forlorn that I'd ditched the business couple and stayed with the children and he lashed out as only he knows how to do. "You talk to Lady Dana?"

"No," I said.

"She's taking your stuff with her to New York to show Ira," he whipped.

Lady Dana had in her possession the unreadable stuff I'd written under the influence of seriousness. And Ira was an ex-lover of mine who wrote and who thought I'd taken up writing to ruin his life and that I'd probably get more critical acclaim and sell more books to mortify him. My connection was telling me that these two were going to evaluate me.

"You know something." I faced him, livid. "*You* know, you *know* that Dana's a fool and a jerk and wrong and not beautiful, you *know* that and you know Ira is too. How can you even pretend to be in any of that and use it against me?"

"I . . . I mean, she didn't *say* she was going to show it to Ira." It began to dawn on him that he'd gotten in deep.

"*You know* she's wrong and *I know* she's wrong. She's not real, she doesn't exist. And they're both . . . They're not one of us."

"Don't tell her I said any of it to you, O.K.?" He is a coward. But children are and we are both children. And I love him. But, God . . .

Antonio and the rest of us got into the car. It was raining cats and dogs made of wet fur, the water was in lakes in the streets. We all loved each other and I gave them each a tin pin from Japan, my last tin pins. They loved them.

Ilsa and I had saved our half-eaten gardenias, which blue-skied the car.

They said they will come back. But that's O.K., because we'll see each other anyway, when I go to Rome.

THE SECRET DANGER
OF BEING
MARK SPITZ'S COACH

Besides death and moving, there was the additional
danger in growing up in Hollywood of having your
schoolmate be "discovered." A "discovered" kid would
reappear beyond recognition in a movie. It wasn't the
same kid. Like Linda Lou Rogers, Roy Rogers' and Dale
Evans' daughter, who sat next to me in the fourth
grade. It did not make sense that she in her fringed
cowboy jackets was the same little girl in those soapy
Roy Rogers adoption stories (he adopted her and lots of
other children). She was a brilliant kickball player.

But everyone knew Yvette Mimieux was a movie
star, even when she butted in front of you in the cafeteria line. In junior high she wore a white linen sheath cut
low with her long blond wavy mane haloing her des-

tined face. It was plain to see she was a movie star, there was nothing else to be.

Yvette had a sister who looked exactly like her only she wasn't beautiful, or maybe she was but you couldn't see it. Her sister and I used to walk home from school and she told me she wanted to be a gym teacher, which I always remembered because it seemed such a modest goal. Meantime, Yvette was turning into a classy movie star who I met later in New York when we were both long gone from Le Conte's cafeteria lines, Yvette having been discovered and me having discovered other lives to try out.

I wonder if her sister became a gym teacher and if she still lives nearby her parents' house and teaches around here. I wonder if she knows the local danger of having her best volleyball player succumbing to "discovery." A local danger.

BUMMER BOB

"Hi," I said. What was her name?

It was another one of those faces, a friend of Karen's, I pieced together, and someone else, too, that guy Bob. She and Bob had been close and I always saw them at Cantor's together when LSD was the rage. Everyone would leave the Strip at 2 when the clubs closed and go to Cantor's en masse so blasted out of their heads that if you asked someone what time it was they backed away, wide-eyed, as though you'd presented them with a philosophical impossibility. Bob was adorable but so obnoxious that he wore his nickname on his lapel. He'd had it made into a button and it said, "I am Bummer Bob."

Bummers were when the acid had something in it

that didn't agree with you. It was anything else disagreeable and a drag as well, so you can't say he didn't tell you. Except that he looked like an archangel. Bright.

People said he was a narc and a thief, but I knew he wasn't sophisticated to be either of those when I let him stay at my house once for a week with his white dog. He needed someplace to stay, nobody would talk to him, and even though I didn't sleep with him, he was beautiful and couldn't help it that he was such a bummer. He never understood anything and always asked the wrong questions. He was so unable to understand anything and he shorted out so many trains of thought that people thought he was a narc. He never took anything from my house when he stayed there, he even tried to buy food.

He left L.A. and I had heard that he'd moved to the country.

After I came back from New York and was up in San Francisco, I ran into him one night in the Fillmore. He was playing guitar in a band, and the leader of the band, my friend, had complained of him and how disruptive he was.

"What else can you expect from someone called Bummer Bob?" I asked.

"I never heard that before," he said.

"That's what he's called," I said. We were upstairs at the Fillmore, and there was Bob, dressed dramatically in black with a top hat and a cape. A look of sudden surprised hospitality flooded his face when he saw me, completely the opposite of the black cape, and he said, like a kid, "Wowie, Evie!"

My friend, the leader, was amazed later, he'd never

seen him look like that before. Shortly thereafter, Bob
left the group in a lurch and quit rock and roll or said
he was going to.

"It's just as well," I told my friend.

Now, I faced this girl in Ohrbach's and I couldn't
remember her name. She'd just been, like me, a friend
to him when no one would be. She'd been more than
me because she'd loved him, I thought, and he had
telephoned her from my house every day because he
cared about her. It was a time when no one cared about
anyone, so I noticed.

"Have you heard from Bob after he went to San
Francisco?" I asked her. It was 5 years later, but she still
had this dewy kind of thing about her.

"He sent me a Christmas card," she said.

It was sweet, I thought, that no matter how much of
a bummer he was, he held onto the amenities like
Christmas cards and daily phone calls.

"How nice," I said. "Where is he?"

"Haven't you heard?" she asked. She looked struck
with pain.

"What's he done?" I knew he must have done something terrible from her face. Something . . . really terrible.

"He's been . . . in San Quentin. He's the one they call
Cupid in the Manson family, the one Manson's supposed to have tried to free by the other murders . . ."

Bobby Beausoleil had romped with his dog in my
house. He'd worn a sign that said "I am Bummer Bob."
I'd let him stay but hadn't slept with him because anyone who called themselves that, I figured, must have the
clap or some other expensive social disease. He didn't
understand. He sent Christmas cards from Death Row.

"What'd he say?" I asked.

"Merry Christmas."

"Oh, God," I said, helplessly thrown back into the archaic idiom that even he had used to describe what he was. "What a bummer!"

She looked away quickly, she was crying in Ohrbach's. I still don't remember her name and I just touched her shoulder goodbye.

THE GIRL WHO
WENT TO JAPAN

"The privileges of beauty," Jean Cocteau said, "are enormous."

I have this pasted to my icebox and thought of adding, "so don't you be," but that would be sacrilegious, touching up Cocteau with my diet strategies. Rarely, anyway, does beauty reduce itself to truth or homilies. And the possessors of beauty are reticent about their privileges or act as though it was luck that the cop didn't give them a ticket, that it was just a "nice man" who let them through customs without having to wait in line. Beauty, unlike money, seems unable to focus on the source of the power. Even talent knows they are special and why they were invited.

But beautiful-looking people, girls especially, act like

"oh, isn't the world just the sunniest place," skipping the middleman of their own face which made everyone so much better all along. Perhaps they skip it out of superstition. And then, sometimes, they decide to be miserable like rich people who bewail around saying, "Money isn't everything." Sometimes they say, "Just because I'm beautiful doesn't mean I'm not miserable," which is one way of thickening your life, but it makes your face get lined and then they *really* get miserable. Trying to fool the gods into thinking they didn't know what they'd been given is one thing; crow's-feet is another. Cocteau said death was the mirror.

The use of beauty to gain privilege is usually called something else (like "nice man"). Except with this girl, Nellie, who Karen introduced me to.

"I just don't know," Karen said once when Nellie had gone to the ladies' room in Schwab's and the whole lunch mob found themselves with their forks halfway to their lips, transfixed as Nellie swayed out. Karen sighed again. "I just don't know."

"But, I mean . . ." I turned to Karen. "How did she . . . How did you meet her?"

"I don't know. Shit." Karen scowled and thought back. "Remember, I was married to Terry then and everything and he wanted me to see if David was back from being on tour and so I phoned David . . . and this *girl* answered. And it was Nellie."

"Yeah, but so, and then what happened?"

"It just happened. She said she was a friend of David's and that he told her any time she came to L.A. she could stay with him, so she took a cab from the airport to his house, which took up her last money and no one was there—David hadn't come back yet—so she broke in and she'd been there all day with nothing to eat and no cigarettes and it was too far to walk anywhere and she was only 17 and she really sounded, you know, only 17 and everything."

"So you fell for it . . ." I deduced. Karen was an old friend of mine who had always been so fragilely beautiful that it was all I could do to squash my natural envy and just like her. She seemed to collect girl friends that all weighed 100 lbs. and ate candy. I was her only friend who wasn't a size 5. All my life I've been a nice, healthy, ordinary girl and all my life I've wondered what it must be like to look right in a Dior. It must do something to the soul to look like a work of art and I wish I knew what it felt like.

However, in reality, I can't complain. I don't believe in pickiness, and I am beautiful enough. And sometimes, I'm almost thin enough.

"So . . ." she continued, "Terry and I went over to David's" (she chomped down on a potato chip dunked in potato salad as I sipped my tea) "and there was this . . . this *girl!*"

"Nellie, you mean . . ." I tried not to think about the potato salad.

"You know what she did?" Karen remembered. "Within 20 minutes she had us both out of our clothes in this sauna and three seconds later we were in an orgy."

"But, Karen . . ." I was shocked. We love beautiful girls but we do not fuck them, as a rule. "How *could* you?"

"You saw her, didn't you?" she argued. I had. "I mean, it was like the Uffizi all to yourself. Not to would have been a crime against nature. Anyway, Terry . . ."

"Yeah," I said. I'd never been able to stand Terry.

Terry was someone who assumed the privileges of beauty only he was not. One of the privileges is that you can be cruel, and with him this cruelty and misery were so pronounced it reminded you of what beauty could get away with. It reminded Karen of it anyway until she got a divorce. It only reminded me of cheap sham.

And like Stanley Kubrick movies, it was not the kind of cheap sham I like. It was mean and ugly and I always walk out after about 10 minutes.

"Nellie was over at your house one time," Karen reminded me.

"She was? When?"

"About two years ago, before she went to Japan."

When Karen had dropped by unannounced that day to take me out for lunch and had brought Nellie, I'd been so torn open from throat to pelvis that I barely had time to stick my kidneys back in, much less remember a quiet girl who had sat passively in my apartment ages ago while Terry and I got into an argument and I kicked them all out. But it came back to me now that this was the same girl only more clearly defined. Twenty pounds thinner was what she was. And blonder. And now she swayed back into the lunch mob, dulling the talk to a hush when she hulaed past the booths and dropped down next to Karen.

I wondered what her life could be like.

Like Beauty in "Beauty and the Beast," did all the doors open by invisible hands? But Beauty wasn't like Nellie, because Beauty acted like she didn't know why the doors opened or why she got through customs without having to wait in line. Beauty was a dope.

Nellie wasn't like that. This was real life.

She had gone to Japan, this girl from Foxglove, Idaho,

who'd met a rock star and come to LA and had to break in. She'd gone on borrowed money, which left her 10 dollars when she got off the plane in Tokyo without that surefire snap she seemed to have honed down to. Before she had gone to Japan she was simply a puddle of beautiful groupie, and now, in Schwabs, she was conscious.

She was no dope, even before. Because a dope would not have gone to Japan to become what she eventually became.

She looked like Carole Lombard. She had the same kind of translucence, only instead of being in black and white and having that ladylike blonde blonde hair, Nellie was in color and had hair of sunbursts and gold. Her eyes were dark blue like Swiss flowers just at twilight, and her skin was Gainsborough vivid. In the meantime, she sashayed around like the girl from Ipanema and weighed 107 lbs, which, because of her delicate bones, didn't look too thin on her 5′ 9″ flawlessness. She could have been a willow branch if she'd been green, her translucence was such, and yet her breasts, which you could hardly tear yourself away from once you'd accidentally strayed from her face, were Botticelli done better. She actually looked like Venus rising out of the sea, but she was less stupid-looking. Venus is as stupid-looking as Beauty, acting like she doesn't know the "nice man" is blowing roses on her shoulders.

Nellie would have looked like she knew, this being real life.

"You should see what happened when I took her over to George's," Karen told me later. "He just kind of stood there with his mouth open and you could tell there was this girl back in the apartment. I mean it was obvious. And Nellie said she didn't want to be any trouble, so when would the girl be gone so she could come back? He said 15 minutes. It was his fiancée too. Nellie told me she hoped she hadn't upset anything . . . God."

"La belle dame avec merci," I couldn't help noticing. Nothing *sans* about Nellie.

"I think it's so wonderful that you're writing," Nellie said. We still sat in Schwab's. "Karen sent me one of your stories, I thought it was terrific."

"Oh."

Over the table a strange bridge was being constructed by her to me which I was powerless to burn. I felt like a spider's anesthetized lunch, or a future one of those who sees the spider coming. I didn't want this girl showing up in *my* life the way she kept showing up in Karen's.

After her divorce, Karen found a beautiful man on a yacht and, fortunately, he was raised by Jesuits and so did not fall under Nellie's rationale, the guilt kept her at bay. But Karen was always extremely nervous about Nellie's relentless friendship. I had enough trouble not eating potato salad without knowing that all the uneaten potato salad in the world was never going to match this perfection. Now I see her coming at me, liking my writing, and I am helpless.

"Oh . . . thank you," I say, uneasily.

She smiled. Perfect little teeth, perfect nose, tiny hands and feet, perfect youth. She lived in a perfect youth and I wondered what it was like.

"When I read it," she continued, smiling, "I felt I wanted to give you something. I thought about it a long time. Before I go back to Japan I'll drop it by your house."

"No, no," I said, not my house! "Not my house! I'm going out of town, so could you just leave it with Karen."

Once Nellie had gone back to Japan, Karen brought me a package wrapped delicately in tissue paper. It was an antique hand-painted kimono, just the perfect color for me and worth about $500. In Japan, Nellie had amassed a fortune by modeling twice a week in the mornings. I don't think I ever thanked her for the kimono.

When she wasn't modeling she was growing more beautiful in her small paper house in Kyoto. At night, she told me, she would sometimes go alone to a local club and choose "one of those . . . oh, they're so beautiful . . . young Japanese boys" and in the mornings, I suppose, she licked her delicate chops from the feast and left the bones out for the garbage man.

Now she was sitting across from me in Schwab's throwing silence in her wake and on either side wherever she went.

"You know the great thing about Japan," she said suddenly because we'd been talking about writing, "when you wear clogs and are 5′9″ like me already, you can really see. I'm so much taller than everyone, I can see right over the top of any crowd."

She smiled.

"You should come visit me there," she added.

I imagined her blonde head rising like the sun out of a mob waiting for a light in Tokyo. Japan is supposed to be subtle, to place value on the discreet. I wondered what they thought of her sticking up out of them like a translucent beacon of proof that they were wrong. With no talent or money, Nellie had situated herself into a position of privilege beyond the outposts of the Occident. Even the most beautiful daughter of the East was bound to be woven into Nellie's Oriental frame.

Like Admiral Perry introducing the firearm that could turn a woman into an unsamuraiable opponent.

If she'd had a gun in her purse, she could not have been more calmly invincible. That was what Japan added. Her memory of it, concealed behind her eyes, dissolved that stupid look of Botticelli's Venus and the cheery dopiness of "nice man" let me through customs.

It worked, Japan.

"You're so tall," she went on, "you should really come back with me. I'll give you the money."

"Oh, no really . . ."

After she left I lost 20 lbs. To her and her unworkable offer of Japan, I owe my present almost-all-right state of affairs so that if anyone else comes up with a suggestion like that, when I say "no" it won't be from thinking that should I happen to say "yes" I'd not be taking full advantage of the situation. I want as many privileges as I can get, especially in Japan, where you're living in a frame. If it's going to be unfair, I want to have it all.

It's funny, since I lost all that weight, my face has changed and sometimes it looks like a beautiful mask behind which I stare out, a spy in the land of the privileged. (Once I went to a hypnotist and told him I wanted to be good and beautiful, but it only worked for a week.) I find people handing me lines which leave me stuck, like, "What's that perfume you're wearing?" when I'm not wearing any. It's a disguise.

Karen, meanwhile, tried to disentangle herself from Nellie's conception of her as a "best friend," but it was like trying to get gum out of your hair. Nellie wrote regularly, though Karen never answered, until Nellie wrote that spring had come and the violets were showing through the snow in Kyoto and that she had slashed her wrists in the snow among the violets on three separate occasions. Karen and I started calling her the Suicide Girl.

Karen wrote her a terse note explaining that only fools slashed their wrists and none of us thought it was funny at all. It was boring, Karen said, so if Nellie didn't mind, would she please stop.

No one wants a friend who goes around slashing their wrists.

Nellie kept on writing and canned the blood on the snow *haiku* which no one had liked even just on an aerogram.

"The Suicide Girl's coming," Karen told me one day, having just sailed back from Hawaii and received her mail. "Jesus . . . she's coming tomorrow!"

The message I got said, "Nellie. 4 p.m." I thought it meant that she had called at 4 p.m. of the previous day or that she would call or something like that. I did not expect, when the doorbell rang, that I'd open the front door and find Nellie standing there at 4 p.m. in my wildest dreams, but there she was.

She was more, which is to say, she was worse.

She had become completely doubtless. It was a force, her doubtlessness, which could usher her into the Kremlin. All rules vanished when she smiled and money, even, became unimportant and charmless.

"Hi," she smiled, coming in.

I had been writing in junky old clothes, my hair hadn't been combed, and I paled by comparison and did not know what to do except back up. She followed me to the room where I had been writing and settled down on the rug with an ashtray and her Sherman cigarettes.

"I didn't know you were coming over," I said. "The message . . ."

"I told them 4," She lit her cigarette. "But it's all right. You just go on doing what you were doing. I just need to sit down. I've been sick."

"Oh." I looked at her. She was slightly ivory. "Flu?"

"Yes, in Guam."

"Guam?!"

"Yes. I had to go there to visit a lover. He has been disowned by his parents because of me or I wouldn't have come back stopping off in Guam. I owed him time."

I couldn't think of anything to do but hate her.

"See, he helped me get away from the Japanese Mafia . . . You know, drugs. I mean, they weren't even my drugs. They belonged to some gaijins—you know, foreigners . . . Americans."

She leaned back against the wall in ivory languor. She was like a piece of uranium. The last time I'd seen her she had shown traces of doubt. Now you could hear her heart like a clock, ticking away the time she spent on you.

"You look terrific," I said.

"Well," she said, "you know, I've been noticing that as I get older, now that I'm 21, even though I have gotten stretch marks, I think I look younger or unchanging, you know?" She held her tiny hands to her undoubtedly perfect breasts where she found stretch marks. "When I first saw them and I knew I was getting older, I couldn't stand it. That's when I slashed my wrists."

Her hands left her breasts and she held out her naked

wrists where those almost imperceptible slash scars left by razors were the only other flaw. That and the stretch marks.

"But then—" she narrowed her eyes—"I don't know . . . I started to like getting old."

"What will you do, now that you're old?"

"I think I'll go into business," she said. "I've got the capital and there are people who will help me."

"What kind of business?"

"Oh—" she yawned—"anything."

She could, of course, do anything.

Was it the realization of imperfection, I wondered, that had cast this final doubtless pink?

She relit her Sherman. They kept going out because she didn't really smoke much. She was addicted to nothing. The smoke blew out of her soft mouth and she looked up at me from the floor and asked, "Can I spend the night?"

She froze your mind for lunch if you tried to think looking at her, so I looked at the typewriter and my work. "I'm supposed to be doing something later," I lied, and suddenly Karen's remark about denying Nellie scorched through my ears, the one about it being a crime against nature *not* to and my whole instinct fought against her complete assurance and power. I felt that not only was I committing a crime but a hairsplitting folly because how did I know anything, I'd never slept with a girl, and what could once matter and, besides, this was beyond lesbianism and into the Uffizi. Vanity is what stopped me. Who wants to lie in a bed of comparison against such odds? I apologized and lied, "So . . . I'm sorry. I wish I'd known you were coming over . . . maybe."

"Oh well," she said, glancing up again. She knew. She had met with resistance before, probably. I hope it was not vain resistance in more ways than one. "I'll call Grant if it's all right to use your phone."

"But he's all the way at the beach," I said.

"That's all right. I'll take a taxi. I have lots of cash."

"Do you owe Grant time?"

"I just sort of promised . . ." She dialed and let it ring. "Grant? . . . Yes, I'm back. . . . Is it O.K. if I come over and spend the night?"

All I could do was hate her.

The next day she was flying to London, and because I'd admired her earrings, she sent them to me from there.

"Well . . . the Suicide Girl's back," Karen said last week, hopelessly.

"What's the matter?"

"She's decided to stay in L.A., not London. Doing porno flicks."

"Oh."

"Those are nice earrings. I've never seen them before."

"They're from Guam."

"Oh."

EPILOGUE

"Guess what."

"What?"

"You know how I told you when Nellie came back to L.A. she started going with this darling guy, Stuart, who makes all those porno movies?"

"Yeah."

"Well, they're in love."

"What?"

"And you should see her now. She cut all her hair off, she got a job working in this dress shop for $2.50 an hour and she walks to work, a mile and a half, every day."

"God."

"And you know what else? She doesn't hit on Ted any more."

"God."

"Yeah, she comes down to the boat and she's real quiet."

"She's really changed?"

"See, the way I figure it," Karen concluded, "she just never had anything to lose before."

Thank heaven the privileges of beauty are not *that* enormous.

CARY GRANT

I once saw Cary Grant up close.
He was beautiful.
He looked exactly like Cary Grant.

XEROX MACHINES

There is no job more degrading or humiliating in all the world than making Xerox copies. The person who feeds the machine is so extraneous to the situation, so inferior to the machine and so bored.

Xerox machines break down at crucial and just ordinary moments, they are impartial. Xerox machine repairmen are Tragic Figures. They are young men who know how to repair Xerox machines. Secretaries, over the years, have spent so much time waiting for Xerox machine repairmen that they have learned to open Xerox machines themselves and fix them, and what a hollow life is the life of a Xerox machine repairman if that's all it takes, just freeing some paper that gets stuck.

XEROX MACHINES

Xerox copies are ugly, they are denatured eggs born without roosters.

Being put on hold and waiting for elevators are the only two pastimes that come anywhere near the humiliation, boredom and despair that accompanies the Xerox process. But Xerox machines are worse because they are always put into dark rooms with no windows and there's nobody to talk to and all that's there is this Xerox machine that creeps in its petty pace from page to page to light fools the way to immortality. If I ever get in the right place at the right time, I'm going to kill a Xerox machine.

★

THE LANDMARK

THIS STORY IS DEDICATED TO M.F.K. FISHER

When Janis Joplin O.D.'d one Sunday at the Landmark Motel, John Carpenter wrote a piece for the L.A. *Free Press* which clung pretty much to the theory, "What else is a Janis Joplin going to do on a Sunday afternoon alone in L.A.?"

At the time I liked the sound of it and thought, "Yeah, what *is* a Janis Joplin supposed to do alone in L.A on a Sunday afternoon?" because at the time I didn't question the notion that if you were from somewhere else and alone, you'd just naturally come to the conclusion that sitting around your motel room shooting up was pretty much it. On the other hand, she could have gone to Olvera Street and gotten taquitos.

In 1781 a Franciscan with 24 ex-cons and runaway

slaves decided to name something that didn't exist La Ciudad de Nuestra Signora La Riena de Los Angeles and proceeded to build a church and a street called Olvera Street. The church and the street are still there, preserved by this huge city called L.A. as a landmark from the days when one street was named the City of Our Lady, Queen of the Angels. The street is uneven and bricky and lined with terrific shops where you can get things you think you want, cheap. And taquito stands for in case you get hungry. Taquitos are much better than heroin, it's just that no one knows about them and heroin's so celebrated.

Taquitos are what forced my hand and made me leave Rome after six months when I was supposed to stay a proper year, though that's not what I told the man who sent me the $500 for the plane ticket back to him in L.A. Taquitos are what drove my father out of his hotel room one rainy Paris morning in 1932 to search the streets until he finally found a Spanish grocery store where, very dustily upon the bottom shelf, lay a can of bland tamales from California. He was suffering, as I did 30 years later, from chili madness in one of its more acute manifestations. He'd lived in L.A. while he was growing up and he had no idea when he set out on his scholarly pursuits that he would be in a continent devoid of chili and he also didn't know that without chili he'd die.

My friend Connie is a very sleek, dark, fashion girl who lends fastidious elegance to everything she touches so that no one would guess when looking at her that she is an L.A. Mexican who can't go a month without chili, and not just chile—chorizo—a Mexican sausage made out of pork and garlic and rough spices. You put it on scrambled eggs and go to heaven. "I have to have it," she told me, lifting her ladylike fork to her mouth in a subdued chic restaurant. "Things just don't look the same if I don't have it running through my blood. It changes my whole outlook, my dear, and I don't take any shit from anybody."

The kind of chili she meant and I'm talking about is L.A. chili.

I'm not talking about what comes in a can or from Denny's or even anything you get anywhere, say, for instance, in Mexico. Arizona maybe does it right, but farther East the food collapses. Once we ordered enchiladas in Albuquerque and they were made with BLUE corn. Can you imagine a black enchilada? Blue corn looks black to the naked eye. I am also not talking about anything called Mexican that comes from north of Santa Barbara or South of San Diego—well, maybe Tijuana if you've just come out of an abortion and are famished, but really the food in Tijuana is half-assed. I am only talking, really, about the food you get in downtown L.A. where a degree of perfection has survived and even improved upon itself, outdistancing the Rest of the World and certainly a landmark in the tides of man.

And Janis Joplin, all she had to do was get in her car and go down there. And she would especially have liked it on a Sunday, because on Sundays they have confetti and mariachi bands in the adjacent Plaza.

The mariachi bands are imported by L.A. Mexican promotors to play in the Montezuma and other nearby nightclubs, and mostly these bands come from Guadalajara, the best place for mariachis, as everyone knows. They often get stranded in L.A. by the promoters, and so you get to hear them for free on Sundays. Confetti seems to be inseparable from those afternoons and gets all over you, so you're still shaking it out of your clothes once you get home. A lot of Mexicans bring their children to the Plaza after attending Mass across the street in the historical monument church that survives and just keeps on going, christening babies, marrying couples whose cars await them out front decorated with paper flowers, saying Mass. The church acts like it doesn't even know it's the original site of the third biggest city in this country and a landmark, you have to wear a mantilla or something over your head when you go into that church, they don't think of themselves as a museum. Outside and across the street the mariachi bands are setting up as the people come into the sunlight from Mass.

The Mexican Catholic mothers dress their daughters to look like the pompoms they put on the cars of the just-married couples, like dyed carnations. The little girls could be floated camellias, angels. A Janis Joplin could have gone down to look at the camellia angels, eaten taquitos and drunk Dos Equis beer. She used to like Dos Equis. I saw her drinking it in Barney's Beanery more than once.

One Easter Sunday I went down to the Plaza with my parents just to bask in the gentle mob and wonder over those angelic little girls, four years old, dressed in lilac organdy with flowers in their braided hair, or mint green silk, or pink fluffy ruffles with white lace and their little black patent leather shoes with the straps and white socks. How beautiful they are, their faces like Fra Filippo Lippi's and their little gloved hands, how completely beautiful. . . .

★ 275 ★

But taquitos are still the main thing. You could be blind and deaf and that still leaves you the taquitos. The mariachi bands ahead of the beat and all out of tune together and the little girls like floating pompoms do not lodge in your heart with the flat assertion of a taquito.

The best place to get them, though they are also sold in other places throughout the mall, is the place on the Northeast part of Olvera Street. Here you can pull up and have a friend jump out, run over to the guys with money already out of the wallet and say, "Ocho taquitos!"

"Eight?" the guy says. Your accent isn't good enough for him to go along with it, he's not going to give you the satisfaction.

"Yeah, ocho, O.K.?"

"O.K., ocho." He changes his mind and gives you the satisfaction.

They don't make them as good in the other places. The other dishes they make at this place are better too. Even the orange pop.

Two guys stand behind the glass counter, or three, and they are interchangeable insofar as who's doing what is concerned. They wear Mexican shirts, the embroidered wedding shirts, but that's the end of it in looking touristy. They don't wear sombreros, they speak stacatto L.A./Mexican English and they play KRLA loud and KRLA plays only rock and roll. They move like master shell-game gents.

These adepts are involved in the highest form of gastronomical pulling off as anyone at Maxim's or on those French liners that cater to ancient millionaires with food the only thing left. These guys are the final link between you and a hot taquito with sauce.

Someone else has done all the stuff that had to be done before these guys could enter into it. Someone else has barbecued the carnitas—meat. Carnitas for taquitos are Mexican beef pieces of such loveliness and unimaginable perfection that I can't really tell you about it except to say that once in a time of blind dismissal of fitness, I bought two pounds in a Mexican butcher shop down past the railroad tracks. I took it like a man when they told me the price ($5.00), paid in silence as I watched them wrap and had eaten the whole thing out of the paper from the front seat of my car before I could get back to my apartment for a plate or fork. Someone, somewhere, made the carnitas, and I've never inquired too closely about it since certain phenomena cannot withstand plodding questioning.

Then, someone else somewhere rolled the carnitas up in real, hand-made corn tortillas and handed them over to the guys in the taquito shop for the final transformation. These raw taquitos await you. When you come, they will be cooked. Buying raw taquitos and taking them home and doing them yourself is a sacrilege against the nature of the universe, and you will have to account for the impropriety on judgment day with everyone watching. The guys must cook them for you then and there, otherwise you're a philistine.

When I first went to Olvera Street as a small child, taquitos cost 2 for 25 cents. Then, for a long time they were 2 for 30, then 35 and finally 40. Now they are two for 45 cents if you want them on a paper plate with extra sauce, which you do because it is an improvement. Two taquitos for 45 cents is much cheaper and vastly more reliable than smack. Even four taquitos are pretty cheap, and they don't vary. You can trust them.

They have black frying pans with long handles that

are about a foot and a half in diameter and have sides that flare out about 3 inches high so that oil won't hit the cook. With metal prongs, the guy lays the raw taquitos neatly in the oil over a fire of coal that produces a heat of such intensity that blast-furnace clouds encompass the buyer as he watches the taquitos cook and the guy turns them over when they're done on one side. You never see the same cook there twice; the heat is supernatural. Then, when the whole pan is done, he slips the entire thing to the guy on his left (your right) and is given an empty pan in exchange. The guy with the full pan is the one who listens to you say ocho and hands you eight. No one smiles and KRLA blasts away.

The pan of done taquitos awaits you while the pan of emptiness is rapidly filled neatly with raw ones, about 20 fit in a pan. Watching turns what has been only a stir in your frontal cortex into complete physical wanton craving. Like listening in whorehouses is supposed to do.

There are only two pans, I guess, but somehow there seems to be only one, and yet there also seems to be perhaps five, such is the pitch of excitement to which you are driven, especially if there's more than three people in front of you.

Last week I woke up at 8 a.m. thinking about taquitos. I knew that the place on the corner doesn't open until 11, which meant that I would be at time's mercy at least until 10:30 when I could get in my car and take a leisurely drive down Sunset. Most people would take the freeway, but that's a little too coldhearted. I mean, taking the freeway when you're on your way to get a taquito for 45 cents is like taking a jet to go visit your cat, the texture's wrong. If what you desire relies strongly on being all of a piece, you might as well face it or you won't get what you desire. It's like saying, "Oh, well, why even go all the way downtown at all? I'll just get these crummy Ralphs' tortillas and use hamburger and Kraft taco sauce . . ." You know?

So I ambled down Sunset, which was looking beautiful because it's been raining and everything is overcome with green and it's real L.A. with the freshly washed palm trees winning you over. The City of Our Lady, Queen of the Angels is not hard to take going 35 mph on Sunset with the hills and flowers and car part places where guys are transacting small business and ladies in jeans with their children are on the way to the laundromat and teenage girls practically sit on top of their boy friends in the car next to you at the light and steep inclines with staggered houses stand in the delicate lushness of morning glories. There is no one here in a Mercedes Benz looking fucked, and there's none of that emptyhearted shakiness that comes over you like when you go on the freeway. The convenient freeway. It's for if you don't want to know about anything, you just want to get there. Maybe you should stay in your motel and shoot up and get there once and for all.

Across the street from the best taquito place is a gas station/parking lot where I always park because I gave up even a pretense of trying to find a parking place down there. There isn't one. It costs 50 cents. The gas station is across the street from the beautiful pink post office and diagonally facing Union Station, the railroad station that is so magnificent and legendary that I'm waiting to be in love with the right person before I go hang around down there or take a train somewhere. The first orange was transported by rail out of L.A. in

1870. The city belongs to trains and oranges—that's how come the station's so beautiful. But I'm saving it.

By the time I got down there and parked, it was 11:05 and they were just starting. The new sign said 2 taquitos on a plate with extra sauce was 45 cents. Extra sauce! I'd never thought of it. Before they used to give you two taquitos wrapped together in paper, so only the top half was dunked in the sauce, while the bottom was simplicity, pure corn tortillas and carnitas, which was enough to pull me out of Rome, but now you could have sauce all the way through! And extra sauce was only 5 cents more!

The sauce, you see, is where heaven enters into it. It is better than anything. Maybe somewhere else in the world there is something to equal that sauce, but I myself have never tasted anything nearly as wonderful. "With a sauce like that, I could eat my own father" is an old quote my friend Diana Gould discovered and put on the front of her screenplay about food. That's the kind of sauce it is. You could eat your own father. In fact, it must have been that particular sauce.

I took the paper plate, but there was a red light, so I'd eaten the whole first taquito before I'd even gotten across the street. My fingers were dripping with extra sauce in which they put green chilis and I don't know what else, maybe there's cinnamon in it or something, it deserves the Nobel Prize for Science and Art. I did the thing with the guy about parking money, which took time, so I'd gotten halfway through the second and last taquito before I was there in my car ready to sit down and eat the taquitos, which was the original plan. It was a little sad, but I enjoyed what was left in comfort. I suppose I should have held my horses and waited

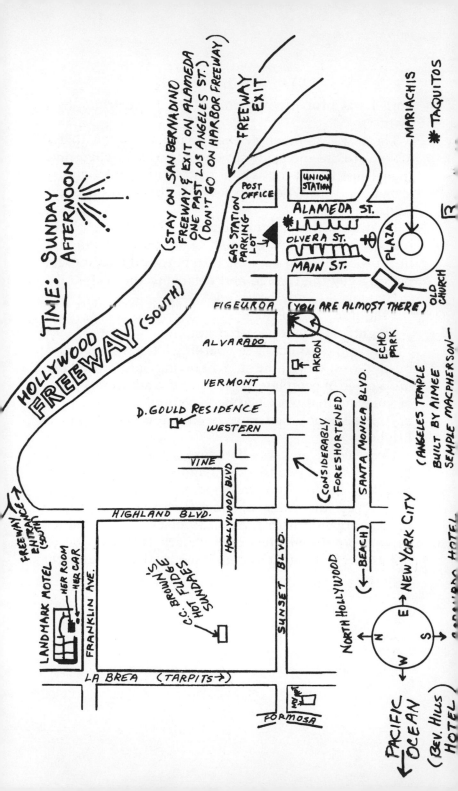

until I was properly ensconced, but I was triumphed over.

There was so much of that divine sauce left that I looked around and made sure no one was watching and then I just licked the whole plate with my tongue, a grown woman. When I looked up, there was this kid staring at me.

He'd been there, I realized, the whole time, a little black kid. He'd been standing behind a trash can and he'd probably even seen me torn between handing the parking guy the change and balancing the plate.

He looked faintly horrified.

"Taquitos," I explained.

"Right." He understood at last.

I drove the car out of the parking lot/gas station and headed west down Sunset, my craving defused and my life a place of complete grace with the additional prize of knowing that what had been ten miles ahead of everything already had now been improved. It shone brightly.

Even alone, as I was, I'm sure a Janis Joplin could have wandered into the joy of another people's way of handling lunch. And on Sundays in the afternoon, they've got the mariachi-confetti-four-year-old angels in lilac organdy with their little black patent leather shoes who attend Mass in a church that goes on as before even though it's been designated as a landmark.

THE WATTS TOWERS

The main thing about them is that I never understood why they were called Towers. They're not towers. And then the photographs have nothing to do with it. At least no photograph I've ever seen in the least reminded me of what it felt like to be surrounded by all that amazing grace. Plus all the stuff you see written about the place, even the stuff my mother's committee puts out, the Watts Towers Committee—it's all wrong; they keep saying things about "folk art." I felt like a child in the Emperor's New Clothes who sees all the adults going around exchanging words which can't do it and anyone with half an eye can see that. Words just can't do it.

The first thing no one mentions except in the title is

Watts. Our own slum, Watts. Of course, if you were living in Manhattan and had a house that had a front yard and a back yard with separate entrances, you'd be enjoying the envy of everyone you knew; they'd be having nightmares. But the slums of Watts are those houses.

To reach the towers you must take the freeway and get off on Century Blvd., traveling a mile or so into Watts. Watts is a dangerous place. Even in your car no matter what color you are, the people next to you may want you dead or they may have just made the last payment on their car and belong in what America aspires towards. But either way, if you're white, everyone knows everything the prophet Malcolm shoved into sight. Watts isn't Harlem, but it is ugly and smoggy and flat and plantless (unlike Mexican poverty, where all is abloom with whatever will live in color) and you have to pass a huge, monstrously grim power plant of some kind with utilitarian gray girding rising up, and it covers a giant block of land and is just really a major tribute to the God of Despair, immovable in the low dismal smog.

Car repair shops and girded liquor stores line the streets of business with iron guards weighing more than the stucco little buildings they guard. Hostile young women cross the street with each other or their children and rip through your tonnage of car with sneers of acetylene. Eleven-year-old boys look straight at your breasts if you're a woman and don't even make crude remarks to their friends, they are so solitary already. The map of instructions you have to the towers begins to misrepresent where you are now—whoever gave you directions didn't tell you about what the streets were like that you have to turn left and right on.

And you must have misunderstood anyway, because it is supposed to be only a block from 107th Street and those "towers" are supposed to be tall and here you are on 105th Street, where it says the place is near and it's dead end and those photographs you saw were all pink and blue and the only colors here are tempered by smog and heat and there are railroad tracks and utter Despair reigning everywhere.

Could . . . could *that* be it? *That?* Those spindly-looking gray things not a block away, rising not very high, really into the air, I mean, really, is that what it is? Well . . . as long as you've come all this way, you might as well park and go in, since you will never ever brave the streets of Watts again, nothing would ever persuade you to go once more through this desolation. Folk art my ass! Those people must be nuts!

So you park and lock your car carefully, looking suspiciously at some eight-year-old kids who stare at your car and your clothes with their dark faces and silent eyes and you try to decide whether to smile and say "hi" or if that would be patronizing, but they turn and run away, so your chance is gone. Thank heavens. The car is all locked, you leave nothing of value in it anyway, and with your friends you go to the towers.

From a block away the only difference between the Towers and the ugly Power Plant you passed just before is that the power plant is much more impressively big and sprawling as far as man-made creations go. This ahead could be a little power plant of the same genre.

As you approach the towers loom larger than you thought and the six-foot-high gray scalloped wall around them stops being gray and becomes a child's mosaic of shells and broken plates stuck into cement. And hearts and hammers are seen as though traced by a cookie cutter. The wall, when you are abreast of it, is too high to see over and you have to go around to the front entrance to enter.

I think you have to pay now, something like 50 cents, to step into Marco Polo's Eastern adventures of sparkling treasure and someone else's dream.

They say that for 33 years Rodia worked at a job for 8 hours a day, slept 8 hours and the other 8 he built the towers. He wanted to live inside a glass rainbow.

The prevailing color seems to be blue, turquoise seaside blue with dark green emeralds and pink enamel stones and pebbles, minty shiny greens, yellow lacquer, seashells, seashells everywhere, and you are only in someone else's dream, not in Watts or anywhere any more—you are completely and totally in a *fait accompli* of a dream.

The things they call "towers" are really rising baubles very lacy so the wind can go through them, and they grow wider at their base (they start from the top) until finally at the bottom, where you are, is a circular broken enamel bench to sit on so you can look at the other two "towers" and the flying buttress connections of emeralds and shells, scallops he used mainly and 7-Up bottles. Inside this boat, he shaped the inside like a boat with a helm because he thought a lot of Marco Polo, his fellow countryman, your friends change and defer to the sparkling and the sky, as your gaze turns upwards to follow up, up, up, far at the end of the beanstalk, the sky is bright blue like the floor beneath you and all your life is a matter of where you stand inside. Nothing is overlooked, there is not a space you could stumble upon where emeralds don't shine weeping forth or screwdrivers aren't etched on cement or more blue-water enamel doesn't prevail.

Children go crazy and begin to climb to heaven without a moment's hesitation, though after about five feet they look down and get scared. But Sam Rodia climbed and climbed, higher and higher with his broken jewels and shiny sparkling pieces of broken dreams and when he was finished, he left and never came back. Thirty-three years of dream building are left in Watts and called "towers."

★

THE RENDEZVOUS

She knew exactly, sort of, what she was going to do.

What she wanted to do was to end it, but she wanted the finish to be so gorgeous that the whole episode would stand away from ordinary life as an enameled example of something handled as though someone cared, for once, for the shape of the thing, the form.

Their affair had lasted all through the time she needed perfection and he had been utter perfection. If she had written out on a slip of paper and stuck into the suggestion box just exactly what she wanted, she would never have been able to imagine something as flawless as he turned out to be. What she would have said was that she wanted something elegant, unattainable and slightly tense, plus she didn't want to be interfered with because she had three months of thinking to do and she didn't want it all muddied up with slamming doors and waiting for telephone calls.

He, Michael, fell in love with her the moment they touched. He hadn't fallen in love with anyone for as long as he could remember, he wasn't expecting to fall in love and he was taken by surprise. The funny thing was that though she was expecting to fall in love, she was taken by surprise too. It's always a surprise, she figured, love. They were both so surprised that they could hardly speak to each other and certainly not about the fact that they loved each other. They told other people and it got back to them separately, so that as they sat eating dinner and talking about the West Indies, they could hardly meet each other's eyes because of the information they'd received that day, long distance, regarding what the others said about them. It was Junior-High wonderful.

They spent two nights together before he had to go back to the life that he was supposed to be living, which involved a wife, children, being an executive in a company where the work was fun and Thanksgiving. Those two nights were like old love songs that you used to believe. But of course, neither of them mentioned love except once when he told her he couldn't sing, that he had a terrible voice and she'd said she loved his voice. They were standing by her car, she was going to leave and he blurted, "I love you."

They were both embarrassed and pretended it hadn't happened.

When she dropped him at the airport, it was simple what she had to do, so she did it. "Thanks for the romance," she said.

("That just killed me," he told her later. "I couldn't get it out of my mind. I just kept thinking about it and thinking about it."

"But it *was* a nice romance," she said.)

She hadn't heard from him in almost two weeks when a friend telephoned from the East who knew them both.

"What's happening with Michael?" she asked. She had a feeling they loved each other and that something ought to happen about it.

"He's left his wife."

"He *what?*"

"That's just office gossip, you know . . ." Her friend instantly felt he shouldn't have said anything.

When she put down the phone she was reeling in ecstasy. She wondered if she was so happy because she loved him or if for once she'd been right about someone instead of ground underheel wrong. She was in her late twenties and he was somewhere in his forties. It happened every day.

The next morning she began what she had to do with fortified purpose. She didn't need to go out any more to find out if she were beautiful or charming, she could just stay home and gloat about Michael (who she wouldn't hear from) and work on what she had to finish in one month. She had all the pieces to the thing, she just had no idea how to put them together, none.

The next morning she began working and how to do it just kind of drifted in off the woodwork. How to wonderfully, fabulously, magnificently do it—the way! She could see exactly the process, exactly the distillation, she could see how it would end. All she had to do was do it. And she could do it, her usual dissipating was laid aside, Michael loved her and was fighting it out with his wife and she didn't even have to hear about it except second hand, she didn't have to hear Michael describing scenes and horrors. All she had to know was that he loved her, so she could stay home and work.

He telephoned her once because he was 500 miles away and felt that since they were in the "same state" he could call. He would be there in two weeks, he told her.

With that, she finished the first draft.

The second draft began when she learned through the local branch of his office that he wasn't coming for four weeks. By the middle of the third week she'd finished the second part and she was glowing in its unbelievable finish. She'd *done* it! It's shape was there, there was no doubt about it—it had form. It may have had a flawed form, but then *Tender Is the Night* is a flawed novel. All she was mainly interested in was having the thing have a form in the first place.

Then he telephoned.

He was there for a whole week, working, and for a whole week she celebrated the finish of her second draft in the luxury of his company among champagne and hollandaise sauce and a man that looked at her with eyes of couldn't believe it.

He couldn't believe it so much, in fact, that he began to get jumpy. She wondered if there was anything she was supposed to do about it, if she should tell him straight out that she loved him or what, but as the week went on they could say less and less to each other until finally when it was the day for him to go, they both read newspapers over breakfast instead of talking and, she thought, this certainly is a capsule version of the real thing. But what happened to the in-between part? He was afraid, even, to touch her skin because that made him jumpy, and she hated it but the affair was guilted, in a guilted cage, he couldn't help it.

As he left this time he said he'd be back, but nervously. So nervously as though she were work. Now he had three works, his wife, his job and her. She didn't want to be work, she wanted to be love. It was amazing to her that what had started out as love had turned into guilt hard labor, and yet she had written the whole draft under the divine misapprehension that there was a seesaw of understanding which had flown between them like opposite homing pigeons.

How come he wouldn't touch her, did he know how much he'd been used?

"I'm coming back in a week," he hurriedly said. They were saying goodbye.

She hadn't told him anything, all was empty.

So tonight she knew exactly, sort of, what she was going to do. She was going to tell him everything. Since they hadn't seen each other and since this was obviously to be the last time she'd lead him into the laborious situation of her company, she'd tie it up, make it beautiful and turn out a piece of human art so that she could go on cleanly broken.

"Listen, I have to catch a plane at 10," he said. "Where can we eat near the airport?"

She couldn't think of any place except a Japanese restaurant on La Cienega called the Benihana, and since they'd begun in a Japanese restaurant, she thought it circular that they end in one. She could imagine their rendezvous and what she was going to say.

First, she would tell him that she loved him. She might as well start there because you had to have a solid foundation for what she was going to build. Then she would explain how much he had given to her and how she had depended on the way he was to see her through and how perfectly he'd behaved and how grateful she was for his purity. She had decided that she didn't care if he, by this time, was straining at the bit to get away, she was going to tell him everything before the plane left at 10. Now, it was obvious that they were going nowhere and that she made him nervous, she would explain, so this dinner would be their last, but he was always to remember that he could count on her and she hoped that in the future if they crossed paths there would only be sweetness and good because that was all she felt about him, and sadness. She kind of anticipated the sadness with delicious tinglings.

She arrived at the restaurant in her best earrings and had brought him a book. For once, he wasn't too late and he looked, she felt surprised again, like someone she loved. He looked adorable.

"This way, please," the Japanese man said.

He sat them at the only kind of table they had there, a big table with a flat grill on the top, a table they shared with three strangers. She hadn't been there before, she'd just heard it was good. Three people she didn't know sat across from them.

God, she thought, now what am I supposed to do?

A chef arrived and began what she dimly remembered the chef in New York at the Benihana doing. He began this absolutely pizza matador bunch of circus tricks on the food that required the full attention of the diners. He arabesqued some shrimps on the grill and the three across from them watched, hypnotized.

How am I going to do this here? She began to panic slightly with this fucking Japanese chef throwing shrimps up three feet in the air. The whole damn dinner will be taken out of my hands, it will be over, he'll be gone forever and I won't have done a goddamn thing. Why, God, did I have to ferret out of all of L.A. this place when we could be having hamburgers at the airport in peace?

"Here, I brought you this book," she said.

He leaned away from her, afraid of her skin. It had been her skin in the first place which had seduced him out of his mind. He hadn't been in love with her until he'd accidentally brushed against her bare midriff one summer night in a friend's patio. He stayed as far away from her skin as possible.

"Listen," she said.

His face was covered with shadows of fear and intrigue.

"I want to tell you something," she insisted. This, her last chance, she was going to say the words no matter how insane the shrimp and the intruders opposite.

"What is it?" he said. He bent, a little, cautiously, closer.

"I wanted to say . . . I love you." She'd divested herself on the first part anyway.

His face, to her astonishment, filled with a radiant light and he looked as though he'd been immersed in sun. He said, "You'll kill me if you say things like that to me just like that . . ."

"But I want to say more . . ." she said the rest.

"No, no . . . don't say any more," he said. She noticed that her ears were becoming red and that she still loved him more than anyone she'd ever met, it was really surprising. "That's all I can . . . take . . ."

"Well," she filled in, "I thought you might know I loved you, but I thought I ought to say the words before you went anyway."

Slam! Onto her plate came 6 freshly cooked shrimps and that was it, she began to laugh. She'd never, she knew, be able to tell him the rest, it was simply too altogether hilarious trying to be Monte Carlo in this slapstick rendezvous and there was nothing she could do about it and keep a straight face, she'd be more ungraceful yet if she fought. Her cheeks glowed out of girlish and adult confusion, the whole thing was a manic act of God.

"Well, I was hoping you loved me . . . but I didn't *know* . . ." he said.

They ate in silence the crazy shrimp, but he seemed like he would float off the chair and sail upward and she wondered if she was wreaking havoc and in over her head and, God, what was she going to do? This wasn't the ending she'd so clearly polished earlier into a fine madeira glow, for Christ's almighty sake.

Outside they waited for their cars and she tried once again. "I wanted to tell you more . . ."

"I . . . this is enough. This is more than I can stand at all," he said, touching her.

"Well, listen," she said. "Don't *do* anything."

"Don't worry," he said, and she knew she didn't have to. He'd never given her more than immediate worries and fine romances.

She got into her car and turned on the lights and looked back at him standing there, waiting to get his car to drive to the airport. Then she turned right up La Cienega.

Two unannounced tears rolled down her unaccustomed cheeks. She felt like laughing. To herself she said, "Those goddamn, fucking *shrimps* . . . God!" Here she'd wanted this polished finish, and what it looked like she'd done was a jagged prologue.

THIS BOOK WAS SET IN

BROADWAY AND VIDEO GAEL TYPES.

IT WAS SET, PRINTED AND BOUND BY

THE HADDON CRAFTSMEN.

DESIGNED BY ANN SPINELLI